THE
SHALLOW
GRASS

THE
SHALLOW
GRASS

A Novel of Texas

TOM HORN

The Macmillan Company, New York
Collier-Macmillan Ltd., London

FIRST PRINTING

The Macmillan Company, New York
Collier-Macmillan Canada Ltd., Toronto, Ontario
Printed in the United States of America

FOR
Biggs, Edith, Madeline and Rachel
AND THOSE WHO BEFRIENDED THIS BOOK
IN ITS DOGIED YOUTH

THE EARTH is our mother and her body should not be disturbed by hoe or plow. The sovereignty of the earth cannot be sold or given away. The earth is also a part of my body and I shall never give it up.

TOO-HUL-HUL-SOTE
(*a Nez Perce Indian*)

THE
SHALLOW
GRASS

I

CELIBACY had never brought the consolation of lurid dreams to Roy Turner; or if it had they were so deeply disguised he had failed to recognize or benefit from them. He had passed the night as he did any of his bodily functions and now lay awake on his hard single bed in the corner room on the second floor of the Eddards Hotel.

His thoughts were night-lame. They limped with his skinny, sleep-bedraggled body across the room from his bed to the light switch like a pair of old men walking each other down a dim and empty street.

"That son of a bitch Buck, diggin up the dead," he said thickly and turned on the light.

Out to the east of White Dove, morning was sneaking around in blackface, fooling no one. An autumn moon waited for a cold morning sun. The dusty range grass was lightly crusted with frost as white and pale as the low moon, giving the open prairie the illusion of being carpeted with stiff grey hair.

As the great flatland still life came slowly alive, the silent frost sparkled, melted, and was absorbed by the dusty grass.

The distant whistle of a mile-long freight train drew the line between day and night, as it rattled a hundred empty box cars east into the rising sun.

As the train passed the deserted station house at Lea Switch, Roy Turner's old red pickup truck pulled up outside. Even with the noise of the passing train the abandoned building remained lonely as if it had fallen from a flatcar and remained to decay on the barren prairie. The windows were boarded up with warped, unpainted lumber and rusty tin roofing.

The rotting stock pens and loading chutes were a ghost town, the pens waist-deep in tangled tumble weeds. The tall corner posts leaned in all directions, sagging their rusty, strap hinges and warped gates into the dead weeds.

Roy slammed the glassless door of the pickup and started toward the station house. The gravel beneath the mat of goathead weeds made a soft crunching sound under his boot heels, like stepping on dry snow.

He paused before the rotten steps leading up to the heavy timber loading-dock. Mighty goddamned silly, he thought as he put his hands on the belt-high dock and vaulted up, driving a black splinter half as long as a toothpick under the heavy skin of his left palm. He stood erect on the dock with his back to the chipping yellow paint of the station house and looked east, out across the grassland of the giant Crows Foot Ranch known as the East pasture. Taking a deep breath, he drew his body up so he could get his hand in the pocket of his faded levis. He pulled out his knife, opened it and began digging at the splinter.

Although there was not enough morning wind to move the tall weeds, the yellow cat-hair on Roy's temples shifted like smoke around his ears. This fine yellow hair and his lean body gave him the supple appearance of youth. At fifty-one he did not look young; he looked unused. His hard flat stomach seemed to protrude a little against his

thin cotton shirt as if to balance his complete lack of back-
side. His body was shaped to, made for, and intended to be
a part of a saddle. It was thin and misshapen in favor of
youth. His skin was soft and wrinkled around his pale
eyes. His weathered cheeks and chin had that false plump-
ness and color of an over-ripe peach. He had no beard but
around his mouth and on his chin there was a scattering of
old woman's sprig hairs.

He was a throwback to that wild breed of perpetual
youths who followed the wind and rolling weeds, always
eating the dust from another man's cattle, saying "yes
mam" to all women and never finding time to marry or
own anything. A group now reduced to rented rooms and
day labor.

He dug out the last of the black splinter, clicked the
knife shut against his leg, dropped it in his pocket and
sucked at the palm. With his hand flat against his mouth
and covering one eye, he turned and looked past the depot
and down the tracks. Old times sake, my ass, he thought,
that goddamned Buck, sendin me out here to get ready for
a train to bring a body he ain't even kin to, home to a
ranch he'd get shot if he stepped foot on.

He tasted the blood and thought of the hay in the depot
loft, the hay and Elmira Gent. Taking his hand away from
his mouth he smiled thinking of her and the jokers at
the cafe. *Dammit Roy, she's so ugly she could look a
bulldog in the ass and give him heartburn.*

The sheepish smile slowly dried on his face as he moved
along the tracks toward the other end of the building. He
stopped before the rotted out waiting-room door and almost smiled again before pushing it open.

Inside, the somber pew-like seats were covered with dust,
marked with rat tracks and rabbit droppings. He walked
over to the potbellied stove, kicking aside a joint of rusted
stovepipe. The boarded windows leaked in tall thin slivers
of colorless morning light. He opened the stove door, then

3

slammed it shut. A sparrow fluttered around inside the room then out through a broken window in the door.

Roy left the dim room, returning to the pickup where he removed a nail bar, claw hammer and a pair of hawk-billed fencing-pliers. Using the rotten looking steps this time, he approached the station house. Starting at the bay window on the track side, he began removing the weather-grained boxing boards. *Clabber-headed fools, stoppin the train way-the-hell-and-gone out here, damn church ladies Buck has got all stirred up. Put the town on the map—shit.* He pulled away the board and a dried bird's nest fell to the ground; he kicked it aside. *I say when a man is dead and buried, by God he's dead and buried. And the same goes for Arron Parker if he wants to sit out here in his damned wilderness, I say let him, it's his goddamned wilderness.*

At noon Roy gathered up his tools, put them back in the pickup and drove across the tracks, heading northwest through the East pasture. The road was two parallel ruts winding over the grassed emptiness. As the loose-jointed pickup rattled its way along the ruts unguided, Roy tried to think just how he would tell the old Negro what the town was planning.

Old nasty mouth Buck, like a shit-eatin dog has finally nosed around the bank long enough to turn up Ronnie's last will wrote in his own hand, a hand that's been overseas in the ground now for seventeen years. Now me out here as likely as not about to get my ass shot off without benefit of war just to stir up a crazy old man and a nigger so old he's rotten. That fuckin Buck probably thinks cause Arron treated his own son like a stranger that he didn't want to get introduced to when he was livin, him being dead for seventeen years has helped. Well I say the whole damn town.... The pickup dropped off in a chug hole and bounced Roy up against the top of the cab. "God-damn," he said in midair, looking over his shoulder into

4

the back to see if the box of groceries had turned over. He turned his eyes back to the ruts and coughed from the dust that erupted from the floorboards.

As the dust settled in the cab and he stopped coughing, the windmill came into sight. Usually when he saw the windmills that were now useless and scattered over the empty pastures of the Crows Foot, sticking up like things lost or forgotten, he bid his respect in half memory to his father, a quick tip of his broad hat to Ott Turner. It was more a brief remembrance than anything else, of spinning windmills and fat cattle and Ott Turner, windmill man to the Crows Foot. It was no more than that even when he visited the one he now saw through the dirty windshield of his pickup, the one he came to every Saturday with the groceries, the one from which Ott Turner had fallen to his death.

As Roy stopped the pickup, a breeze set the snaggle-toothed fan in motion. He heard the thirsty sound of dry gears grinding without purpose at the top of the tower. The broken sucker rod nodded slowly in the air as it panto-mimed pumping water while the splintery old tower stood brave and fragile sentry over the rusted-out horse-tank and the tall grass.

He opened the door, got out and brushed at the dust from the floorboards that had settled on his shirt with two or three careless backhand strokes. Then leaning over into the back of the pickup, he slid the cardboard grocery box over to him. He had been bringing supplies out every Saturday for seventeen years, ever since Bobtail Smith quit coming to town. It made him feel like he was at least trying to earn the seventy-five dollars a month. That same seventy-five dollars a month, Ott Turner's salary as wind-mill foreman, which had gone first to his widow and now came to Roy, money given to mother and son in perpetuity by no legal paper or banker's note, given as a debt paid as soon as the words were spoken by Tom Parker.

Roy reached into the grocery box and picked out a little half-pint can of evaporated milk, then leaned back against the side of the pickup. After reading a few words of the fine print on the red and white label, he began tossing and catching it idly in one hand. *Four hundred sections of the best grass in Texas, and not even one damn milk cow. It may not be a sin like Buck keeps sayin it is, but I'll say its close enough to be called a goddamned shame.* He caught the can and dropped it back in the grocery box behind him without taking his eyes away from the stillness of the empty land, seeing miles of grass that lay around him, endless and arrogant under the sun.

Something like vertigo began to pull at the side of his head and he jerked his eyes to the dim road as if he had heard a sound. The wagon and team he saw coming over the rise may have been there when he turned to the road or they may have been some minutes coming. Time for him had also lost its point of reference under the oppression of that dead space. He strained to bring it into focus. It was hard for him to judge distance and he had quit calf roping, quitting early enough to still be known as the only man in the county sure-sighted and quick enough to ever put a rope on a jackrabbit.

He closed one eye and saw what he had thought to be a team was only one skinny mule hitched to the left side of a double rig. The other side was empty. *Well, he finally beat one of 'um to death.*

As the cock-eyed wagon came down the road, Roy heard the crack of the buggy whip. From the time the wagon came over the rise until it disappeared again, Bobtail Smith never stopped hitting the mule, except when the wagon was stopped beside the pickup. His blows were slow, deliberate, mechanically timed lashes.

Bobtail Smith was as black as the skinny, ancient animal he drove. His skin was loose with age, except around his face. His grey head looked as if it had been painted with

6

adhesive and then dusted with silver watch springs. The name Bobtail had come to the Negro in that part of the Crows Foot history which Roy knew only by hearing. Smith had been the top horse wrangler in those days and it was said that he had walked fifty miles leading ten thousand head of cattle in the great blizzard of 1912, walking for three days and nights cutting fences so the herd could drift south with the storm and keep from freezing to death. When the ranch shipped cattle that spring it was called the bobtailed herd because the storm had frozen off their tails. The Negro wrangler lost both ears, most of his eyelids and the left half of his upper lip to frostbite. He was not quite blind, his eyes were dark clots of fat.

Roy could smell the harelipped old Negro as he pulled the dilapidated mule up beside the pickup. As the old mule came to rest, his tormentor hit him once more, as though the blow had started back up the road and could not be stopped. Roy could smell the mentholated ointment. Smith turned his eyes at Roy, then reached in the grease-stained bib pocket of his faded and filthy overalls for a grimy little blue jar. Hunching over the reins on his lap, he screwed off the lid, holding his middle finger extended as though it already had something on it. Then he dipped the finger into the ointment jar, replaced the top and began rubbing it on the knotty grey-colored smear of scar tissue around the small black earhole in the left side of his head. When he talked he constantly ran his tongue over his shrunken, blue gums, but not once did it steal out to wet the drawn scars that clinched around his dark mouth.

"You bring the ointment?" This was always his first question and many times the only thing he said to Roy when they met. He never failed to ask the same question in the exact same manner every Saturday since Roy had been meeting him with the groceries. It was the same kind of unfailing regularity as his striking the mule. The ques-

7

tion seemed to keep time moving from week to week and year to year as his whip kept the mule walking from step to step.

"I brought it," Roy said, taking the regular-sized jar out of the grocery box that he had just carried to the wagon. He handed it to the Negro. Smith put it in his bib pocket without looking at it and picked up the whip. As he raised the whip the mule erected one of its ears, then let it fall back.

Roy walked around to the head of the mule and put his hand through the ring of the bit where the reins were connected. He held the mule still. "I got somethin to tell you, Bobtail Smith." The whip cracked down on the mule. "Listen to me," Roy said, "I got to tell you." The whip cracked again. The mule jerked its head slightly and blinked his eye at Roy as though only the sound affected it. There was a dim twinkle in the muddy eye of the mule as the lash landed on its scarred and numb rump.

"You get hands off that mule," screeched the toothless old man striking at Roy with the whip. "I don' want to hear, I don' want hear nothin." Roy held tight to the bit, the trembling old man stood in the wagon lashing at Roy and the mule, he burst into great sobs, water streamed from his clotty eyes down the gullies in his face. "You get on to town, I don' want nothin, we gettin on, we don' care, we gettin on. You tell it to the bank. We gettin on—you get off the place, get to town—we gettin on."

Roy jerked the mule forward, causing the wagon to lurch, throwing the old man down on the wagon seat. He quickly left the mule, climbed into the wagon and caught the old man by the shoulders. "Listen to me old man." He shook him, then stopped suddenly, for shaking this bony, loose-skinned old man felt like shaking a body stuffed with feathers and ivory dominoes. So he just hugged the sobbing old Negro to his side gently, yet with firmness; he held him still and began talking to him. "Listen old man."

Roy bent close to the ear hole. The mentholated ointment made his eyes smart. "Monday they're bringing Ronnie's body home. They're gonna have the train stop at Lea Switch, like the old days." The Negro stopped sobbing. He sat there shaking his head slowly from side to side, wiping his frost-shriveled nose on the loose-skinned back of his hand.

"You gotta do just like you done when Ronnie got killed, you gotta tell Arron. I ain't got a telegram from the government this time but all the same you got to do it." A death stillness came over the old man. Roy spoke as a child explaining something very serious to another child. "The army's sendin him home from overseas. Buck found it in the papers at the bank where Ronnie wanted it. He wrote the general of the army and they said they would send him home, he's gonna get a hero's burial. Buck says that seventeen years is long enough to be dead and away from home. He's a hero, he killed so many Red Koreans they give him a star." The two men sat huddled together on the wagon seat. The desolate silence of the surrounding grassland paused as if to listen, then returned its attention to the lonely wheeze made by the wind strumming the hundred mile perimeter barbed-wire fence that held out the world and contained the emptiness of the four hundred square mile Crows Foot Ranch.

The old man shuddered a little and reached in the bib of his overalls. Roy removed his arm from around his shoulders. "You understan me? They gonna meet the train at Lea Switch and have a funeral proccession clear into town to the cemetery. The whole county is gonna pay their last respects to him. They even got a chaplain from the air base down at Ruley to come and give a grave-side prayer." The words "grave-side prayer" seemed to startle the old man into speaking.

"Roy, you and them killed Ott Turner but I never tole on you."

Roy moved over away from the old man and turned to face him thinking, *I knew it, the old bastard is crazy, crazy as an inbred coyote.*

The old Negro was talking to his run-over boots and nodding his silver head in a dipping motion. "No, I never tole how you all killed Ott Turner or 'bout ridin up on you that time taking turns over that Gent gal—I seen him running off that night but I ain't said—I only tole Arron Parker one thing 'bout that boy and his eyes busted in his head. I tole 'bout Sarah—I tole him how that baby killed her, killed her afore he ever killed no Red. I done tole him enough on that boy when I tole him that. I ain't sayin no more. That old death telegram from the government, I used squattin behind a plum bush. I ain't sayin no more, that boy done enough———."

Roy grabbed the old man, lifting him off the seat, drawing his twisted face close, shouting into it, "You sayin you didn't tell him, he don't even know Ronnie's dead?"

"I done tole him enough, I done tole him enough," the old man repeated the mumbled words. Roy looked at the greasy scars on Smith's face, then dropped him back to the seat.

Smith, still mumbling, picked up the whip and with sharp, slow lashes began counting time for the mule to step. The wagon started to move. Roy hopped to the ground and stood there watching the wobbly old wagon jerk away until it disappeared over the rise.

Inside the pickup he sat numb, hunched over the steering wheel, staring through the scum-clouded windshield. The dry ruts of the road were shallow and thin, winding over the low-rolling grassland. He sat watching them quiver slightly in the noon heat and dead stillness. He made no effort to think or remember, yet his shoulders were tightly hunched and his arms, which were folded across the top of the steering wheel, pulled down against it. Behind his hunched shoulders the old windmill tower seemed ready again at any moment to drop Ott Turner's body. Roy sat waiting for the sound of it, playing one pull of his thoughts against the other.

He broke the tension and took off his broad hat. The slight breeze puffed his fine hair around his face like milkweed. As he brushed it away from his eyes, the tail of the broken mill made a long metallic screak. Roy turned and put his head out the window to look up at it. When he drew back inside, the memory was waiting for him.

"It's Arron's turn," shouted one of the small boys. "You got to do sixteen Arron or you're the pig's tail." Roy was seven then and thought Arron who was twice his age would make a funny pig's tail. Arron looked even thinner as he began climbing the wooden ladder up the side of the windmill tower. At the top he stood up on the square platform just below the tin fan blades and shouted, "You got the brake set tight?"

"Yeah, it's set, what's the matter you scared?"

"Count loud so I can hear you," Arron said loud.

"Go on get on the fan, I don't think you got it in you," the other boy yelled back.

Arron climbed up on the giant windmill fan. He locked his legs in the spokes, then stretched up as far as he could reach and tangled his thin arms in the opposite spokes, clutching the fan blades. He took a deep breath and screamed in a high voice, "Turn her loose!" As he yelled he looked out over the green pasture. An old cow with a sucking calf raised her head suddenly from her peaceful grazing to see a boy's body clinging tight to the windmill fan. The boy on the ground kicked loose the ratchet lock on the brake and the crank handle spun backward unwinding the brake chain. A fresh southwest breeze swung the tail of the mill out wide, slowly the fan began to turn. "One," screamed Arron as his head passed the tower platform and swung upward. "Two," as the horizon spun past his eyes. "Three," he felt the sickening effect of the centrifugal force, "Four," "Five," "Six," he felt the blood rushing to his eyes, "Seven," "Eight," the ground and tower were spinning crazily into the sky. "Nine," he vomited an orange circle of liquid in the air. The numbers stopped as the fan gained speed. He held on now only to save his life, the game was over. The boy on the ground saw the ring of vomit sling out from the fan and began winding the brake crank handle. The fresh wind was getting stronger. As the brake chain became taut and began pulling the tail around to stop the mill, the fan slowed its speed slightly. The boy pulled at the crank with frightened man strength. As he put his full weight against it, the chain snapped. The tail again swung wide and the fan picked up speed.

"It broke Arron, the chain broke." The boy on the ground looked up to the tower then at the dangling chain hanging from the crank. The frightened tears began rolling down his face, he turned the crank one more turn in a desperate hope that a miracle would put the chain back together. Then he burst from under the tower and to his horse and rode toward the headquarters house. On the speeding fan Arron vomited again and his vision blacked out. It was as though the world was rushing down a whirlpool drain and he was suspended over it. The tin fan blade was cutting into his slim finger, spattering drops of blood on the wooden tower platform. He retched again, then lost consciousness. His body, still tangled in the spokes of the fan, made a grotesque design as the galvanized wheel spun almost gaily like a toy pin wheel alone on a summer lawn.

A truck rattling with water well tools came speeding over the rise from the headquarters house. It slid up to the tower and two men and a crying boy jumped out. Ott Turner with a shovel handle in his hand climbed the tower two rungs at a time. He reached the loose end of the chain hanging just below the platform, tied it around

12

the shovel handle and levered the mill to a stop. When the wheel stopped Arron fell from it onto the square platform, one leg dangling off the edge. As his body hit the platform Ott Turner dropped the makeshift brake and quickly climbed the remaining rungs. As he stood over the boy, pulling his legs up on the platform, a great gust of wind caught the tail of the mill. It swung out violently, like the boom of a sailing ship, brushing Ott Turner off the tower like a bug. He fell forty feet, crashing into the horse-tank below, his head hitting the rim, crushing his brain. His body half floated in the bloody water as the other man, Bobtail Smith, climbed the tower and carried Arron to the ground. He laid him out on the wet grass next to Roy, the seven-year-old boy whose wild yellow hair was plastered to his small pink head like wet cat fur. He stood stunned and dripping from the great splash his father's body had made in the mossy horse tank.

The shock of that event had very little effect on Roy except that even now he seldom bathed and had never been swimming. As for Arron, Buck Harris and those who wanted the land spoke of it as something directly connected to his late-coming madness.

II

Roy drove the eight miles back to town without noticing the chug holes and washouts he had habitually cursed
for years. He passed the city limit sign which was riddled
with small caliber bullet holes. It was almost impossible
to read the sign: White Dove, Texas, Pop. 733.

He eased the pickup to a stop on the Santa Fe grade
crossing. Without looking down the tracks, he jerked the
shift stick into low gear and crossed over the levee-like fill
that supported the tracks. His failure to "look both ways
before crossing" was not an ordinary negligence. His mind,
out of some deep reservoir of prudence, had kept his eyes
from the glistening rails, somehow held them back, keeping them from dragging his reluctant thoughts down the
track to the west, back to the depot at Lea Switch and into
the dominion of Arron.

He let the pickup coast down the sloped crossing and
to the curb in front of the Eddards Hotel, a long, two-
story building which stood between the Santa Fe tracks
and U.S. Highway 60. It had been built during the oil

boom, the same year the two blocks of Main Street had been paved.

Except for Roy, who lived there, the hotel was empty most of the time. Some of the small rooms had not quartered a guest in ten years and the others only an occasional stranded traveler or cattle buyer. With each passing train the empty rooms trembled, rattling the glass in their narrow windows. At night, when the long freights came, the old building quivered in long rolling spasms like an enormous dying animal.

Roy tried the cafe door. It was locked. A note, hand printed with a dull lead pencil on the back of a waiter's check, was stuck to the glass with a postage stamp. "Closed till supper, if emergency we are out at the cemetery."

Well if that ain't a hell of a note, he thought, a man has to drive out to the graveyard in this town to get a cup of coffee.

As he turned from the door and looked down the empty street, he saw the postmaster in the middle of the next block standing at the foot of the post office flagpole. With one rope in each hand he began jerking them alternately up and down, causing the bright flag at the top of the pole to dip and bob.

Roy squinted against the glare down the street. Except for the postmaster it was completely empty. The only other hint of movement came from the blinking caution light hanging dead still over the highway intersection.

Back in the pickup, he slammed the tinny door and sat staring at the dying weeds on the lot between the hotel and tracks. *Squattin under a plum bush!*

Then with an abrupt urgent motion, he flipped the ignition switch, kicked the starter and backed out on the asphalt, letting the pickup coast to a stop. He shifted to a forward gear and drove slowly across the highway and into town.

The stores were all closed. Overhead, strings of colored

Christmas lights had been left strung across the street. The buildings along the street were unevenly punctuated with overgrown vacant lots, where thirty years earlier, after the oil boom had collapsed and died of a stroke, the shanty stores had been moved, leaving only their weather-crumbled foundations. The remaining buildings, some of them vacant, their glass fronts displaying emptiness and depression dust, bore signs completely unrelated to their present occupants. The faded and chipping word "Drugs" echoed the past on the high false front of the barber shop and beauty parlor. The bank and post office were the only ones that had not been caught out of place in what looked like a store game of musical chairs.

As Roy drove toward the post office the postmaster waved him over, first putting an oil can down on the outside mail box. With two fingers, he pulled a dingy handkerchief from his hip pocket and began wiping his civil-servant soft hands. Roy stopped, leaned over and opened the door even though there was no glass in it. "Howdy Wendell, you already through readin the mail?" he asked by way of greeting.

"Roy, Mrs. Phillips stopped by at the cemetery as she came in a while ago on her way to the doctor. She says the ladies out there need the iced-tea crock from the Baptist Church, wanted me to tell anybody coming out." The tall, gaunt postmaster stuffed the handkerchief back into his hip pocket with an excess of motion as if it were the size of a pillow case. "I guess you're about the only one in town that's not out there, except maybe Elmira over at the phone office and me. I'd like to go myself but you can't just close up the post office everytime you feel like goin somewheres," he said looking up at the flag.

"Did she say where the crock was at?"

"Brother Morris told her it was downstairs," the postmaster said, taking the draw ropes from the cleat and holding one in each hand, "not in the kitchen but in that storeroom to the left of it as you walk in. It's the room where the heaters under the baptizin tank are, up on top of one of the cabinets next to the burners. He said to be careful when you took it down, it probably has got water in it, the baptizin tank has got a slow leak. Says its alright to take the crock out now though since the tank's empty."

"You reckon I ought to save the water?" Roy asked innocently. "Can't never tell about you Baptists, it may be a sin just to throw baptizin water out on the ground."

The postmaster looked up quickly at the top of the flagpole, in order to avoid commenting either way on Roy's disrespectful remark.

"What you doin with the oil can?" Roy asked.

"I'd like to oil the top pully," he said indicating it with a jerk of his large head. "It sticks ever now and then. It would be embarrassing as hell if the United States Post Office was the only one without a flag up when they get here with Ronnie's body."

"Well I don't know about you Baptists," Roy said, "but by me it's already embarrassing as hell. If I had got my ass shot off I'll be damn if I'd want to come home to a circus."

"My thinkin is that you're right, Roy. I voted against it at the deacons' meetin, but you can guess how much good it done against Buck and the preacher. Especially when Buck showed that photostat of Ronnie's will around, talking on the one hand like it was wrote yesterday and on the other like we were sinners and communists for letting it lay there unnoticed at the bank for almost twenty years.

"Now you take my own wife," he continued, "she didn't give two hoots about that boy all the time he was around here lookin half starved 'cause Arron Parker thought more of that damn nigger he keeps out there than he did his own son, but just let him get killed and win a star and she's all tears and patriotism. I went home for

1 7

dinner yesterday and there she was, with one of the post office flags in the washing machine. I worked for the post office long enough for her to know you never *wash* a flag, if it gets dirty you *burn* it. Now I don't know what to do; if I burn it I'll be burnin a clean flag, destroyin government property, damn if I know," he said squinting into the noon sun at the top of the flagpole.

Roy started the pickup motor. "Well it beats me," he said, "I guess I'll pick up the crock and get on out there, even if I'm not runnin for office."

As he drove away toward the Baptist church he looked down at his outside rear-view mirror and saw the flag bob up and down two or three times, then sink out of sight.

Roy held the bouncing crock with his right hand to keep it from falling to the floorboards as the pickup rattled its way along the road to the graveyard. It was about two miles out of town, a plot of native grass the size of one and a half city blocks.

The small graveyard and the giant sprawling Crows Foot Ranch were the only remaining evidence in Gentry County of what fifty years before had been named by the map makers "The Great American Desert." The plow and the windmill, with the passing of those few years, had transformed a grass country that was as vast as complete silence into a busy, noisy, grower of wheat. The tiny graveyard with its granite chunks had stopped the plows, as had the Crows Foot; halting the rude and vulgar destruction of grass with barbed wire and cocked rifle.

Today was the annual day when the townspeople gathered to tend the graves. They left the town empty, the stores and homes silent as gravemarkers, and spent the day chopping weeds, mowing grass, filling in the sunken graves and reminding themselves that life is short.

The women brought food for dinner on the ground,

and spent the morning preparing the noon meal. The tent used by the Baptist Church for their summer revival was erected to keep the sun off the food. At noon everyone gathered at the tent where one of the town ministers, depending on whose turn it was this year, would deliver a sermon-length prayer. The prayer dramatically utilized the abundance of evidence confirming the fact that "sure death awaits us all."

As Roy approached the cemetery he saw the cars, pick-ups, and trucks parked end to end along both sides of the road, each sprouting its assortment of garden tools.

He drove past the gate and parked. Carrying the crock back, he noticed in passing that as usual the car of every elected official in the county was dutifully present.

Inside the gate Roy stood for a minute trying to locate Buck Harris in the crowd of weed choppers and water carriers. A mixture of noises churned the air. The gathering looked like a county fair or camp meeting. Women in deep sun bonnets were puttering around the graves, arranging bright new coffee cans which were to hold flowers on the day of the funeral.

Under the tent other women were busy fanning at flies and setting out gaudy bowls, each design different from the other, on the newspaper tablecloth which covered a rough table made of long one-by-twelve planks laid on evenly spaced sawhorses. The hot thick oily smell of the sun-heated, waterproofing of the tent, met and mixed with the rising aroma of fried chicken, green beans, red beans, black-eyed peas, navy beans and cornbread. There were gallons of gravy, biscuits the size of fruit jar lids, a new washtub full of potato salad, creamed corn, a cord of corn on the cob, a square yard of pickles, olives, sliced tomatoes and celery, a dish pan heaped with pickled peaches, more fried chicken, two baked hams and jello salads of all colors containing infinite and varied combinations of agglomerate fruit. The dessert table might well have been the county baking contest, with entries in either the pie or cake field, and sometimes both, by almost every woman present.

The mention of Arron's name stopped Roy just outside the tent. He stood holding the crock listening.

"I can't help myself, everytime I pass by here and see her headstone and I think the way Arron acted, I have to shed a tear. Not so much for her, Sarah's got her reward, but him—Lord knows about Arron Parker. I just hope and pray that the years he's been sitting out there on that ranch eatin his heart out has helped him. It'll be a fine kettle of fish if he acts about Ronnie the way he done when they tried to bury poor Sarah."

"You know I was just thinking last Sunday sitting in church that even after all these years I can still see Arron, proud as proud, sitting up there in the choir bellowing out that off-key bass and smiling down at Sarah as she played the piano. She was such a pretty thing, no wonder he can't make his self believe in death do us part."

"Well if you ask me there's a good deal he don't believe in, and if he don't straighten up it's gonna send him to eternal hell, to think how he treated that boy, a body would think that it was Sarah that he took as his Savior and not the Lord."

"If I know anything about him, I say he won't even show up at the train. He never cared if the boy lived or died, even when he was under his own roof. So why should he care now?"

"Where do you want the crock," Roy asked as he ducked under the edge of the tent.

"Oh Roy," Raytha Ellins, the barber's wife, brushed her forearm against her wet brow, "just put it there next to the coffee urn." She motioned with a flour-covered hand toward the urn sitting on the bed of a county truck that had been backed up to the open side of the tent.

"You wash it out?"

Roy turned from the truck, holding the crock in front of him. "It come from the church."

Raytha laughed and looked around at the other women whose heads had lifted abruptly like hens when Roy said church.

"Roy, we're gonna have to get you married."

He turned his eyes away from her, knowing she was about to mention Elmira, to give him some indelicate female prod toward her. His eyes fell on the tall, slim-necked wine bottles and his face flushed red as if he had, by looking at them, drunk their original contents.

"Sorry Roy," she said, following his line of vision to the bottles and beaming at the irony of it. "Elmira's grape juice has gone to vinegar. Now don't you tell her, bless her lonesome soul, don't you say a word."

She took the crock from him and set it down. "You better get yourself in hand Roy Turner, grape juice ain't the only thing that can turn to vinegar on down the road." She picked up a fat wishbone, broke it, and handed him half. "Now git," she said, "and don't let my kids see you with that chicken."

Roy ducked out of the tent into the cooler air and stood a moment eating the hot, greasy chicken, thinking about what the women had said. *If I know Arron Parker, he's liable not to even show up at the train.*

He finished the chicken, dropped the bone in the grass and walked toward his own family lot. Two young boys dashed by and chased a cottontail rabbit over to the far corner of the graveyard. It was the poor section of the cemetery where some of the graves were marked with the tin all-purpose markers from the funeral home. Many of them were unmarked, remembered only on the plot map kept by the City Water Office.

The rabbit squeezed through the fence and was gone. As the boys turned back they noticed a grave in the corner. Instead of a metal marker, it was marked with a simple uninscribed wooden cross made of fence posts. It was weathered and rotten and the ends had not been sawed to length but were rounded, as though an axe had been used to cut them. It was joined in the middle with crude wooden pegs and it leaned backward as if it were being drawn into the grave.

Roy watched the boys trying to straighten the cross and thought of the halfbreed whose grave it marked. Well, he thought, it's been a long time since anybody got killed on purpose at the Crows Foot, but I'll be goddamned if that's much comfort.

By four o'clock Roy had finished chopping the weeds from the graves of Ott and Mary Turner and also cleaning the narrow plot in which Elmira's mother was buried.

The activity in the graveyard had dwindled away. Roy walked past the new flagpole which stood gleaming, complete with a new cotton rope that stretched tightly from the top to the cleat at the bottom. The Baptist men were loading the tent and poles on a truck. Near it Roy saw Buck and an air force man that he figured to be the chaplain, standing with a small group of men. They were gathered around Deafy Jon, the gravedigger, at the Parker lot.

Well, Roy thought, I'll give Buck one clear shot at askin about Arron and if he don't by God he don't.

He remembered that the women in the tent had said, "If I know Arron Parker...." *By God maybe he won't show up, if he don't they won't think nothin but what they been thinking all along anyways.* He started toward the truck carrying the hoe by its gooseneck.

At the Parker lot the old gravedigger wanted to finish digging out the soft dirt that filled the grave marked Sarah Parker. He was getting slower with age, and knew the digging would be much easier and faster if he were allowed to remove the looser dirt from the unused grave that he had dug thirty-five years ago for Sarah Parker.

22

Few people in the town knew Deafy Jon's last name. He had come to White Dove after the First World War, a shell-shock victim. He lived in a shack at the rear of the cemetery and received a monthly check from the county. The check was a combination pension and retainer. He also did yard work in town and other odd jobs. His work mostly consisted of digging. He dug cesspools in town and the graves at the cemetery.

Buck Harris shouted in his ear, "You just dig the hole where I tell you and let me worry about how hard the ground is," then in a normal voice to the chaplain, "the old son of a bitch is stone deaf—Oh I'm sorry, chaplain," Buck said putting his finger in the groove on his head.

"That's all right, Mr. Harris, I understand about these things," the chaplain said in over-serious tones through a shallow smile he had developed from being forced to seem interested in every thought of his military superiors, and especially the problem-burdened flock, both underling and overlord. He had done this for so many years that his face carried a perpetual expression of arid interest, almost siphoning words or thoughts from the one it was turned to.

Although the chaplain felt some pity for Deafy Jon, he did not show it in front of Buck Harris. He had been in the military long enough to know that compassion for a man of lower status is a direct affront to his immediate superior.

Buck squatted on his haunches shouting to the gravedigger, who was smiling and bending his dirty ear over into Buck's face. He had already dug down waist deep into the old grave.

"We'll put it right *next* to Sarah. There's no use calling it to everybody's attention that she ain't buried there. What kind of town do you want people to think this is? We're gonna have all kinds of newspaper reporters out here Monday. You just dig it right here and don't pile the dirt on Sarah's grave. I don't care if she's not in there, it won't look respectful." The chaplain had been absorbing the reference to Sarah Parker with such interest that he had forgotten the polite look of indifference he usually wore when not being addressed directly.

When Roy walked up behind the gravedigger the chaplain nodded and gave him the uneasy smile he gave all strangers.

Roy squatted, slapped his hand down on the old digger's shoulder and said directly up at Buck, "Well Jon, you takin old Buck's measurement for a hole?"

The gravedigger felt the hand and turned to look at Roy. He had not heard what Roy had said but he smiled and dipped his head as if to stretch a muscle in his thick neck.

Roy spoke low enough not to stir up old Jon but in a way that looked like he was trying to make the old man hear. "That's the thing about burying the Parkers ain't it Jon, a man don't ever know if he's got enough holes dug, or when he's gonna have one left over."

The chaplain sensed an inside joke and turned to Buck who looked as if he had the same feeling.

"Roy, stand up here and meet Chaplain Sutton."

"I'm pleased to meet you," Roy said as he stood up.

The Major came to a slight attention, "Thank you," he said, shoving his small hard hand into Roy's.

The size of it startled Roy—he had the silly feeling of having accidentally touched a woman's corseted rump.

"I was about to show the new flagpole to the Major, Roy. You want to come along?"

"Naw, Buck, I already had a pretty busy day."

"Well we're gonna be gettin in pretty soon too. You got your pickup?"

"Yeah, Buck, I got it."

As they walked away from Roy and the half-buried grave-digger Buck said, "Did I tell you that I got a call yesterday? *Life* magazine may be sending a photographer to cover the funeral story?"

"No, no you didn't Mr. Harris. Well, that should be quite an honor in itself, having White Dove in a national magazine."

The two men walked past the new flagpole and then to the new red station wagon that Buck had strategically parked inside the cemetery, where all the people who had been there could read the white lettering on both front doors: Ford Motor Co., Buck Harris, White Dove, Texas, "It's Good Luck to Trade with Buck."

The chaplain was silent as they got in and slowly drove out of the cemetery. He was aware of his status as a guest and also of his duty to generate and maintain the best possible military-civilian relations. Yet, many questions were rousing his curiosity. An unanswered question is especially bothersome for a man to whom the most sordid details of human existence are usually willingly exposed in hope of relief or forgiveness.

The chaplain's absorbent face was turned to Buck, he nodded gravely, yet serenely at every pause in Buck's summation of the days activities. But his thoughts lingered in the graveyard. He felt himself becoming involved in something more than his orders had stated. He was beginning to feel oppressed as he always did in civilian circumstances; alone in a foreign land. The spiritual and material life of those outside the military seemed to him anarchistic and on the brink of riot. He had noticed that November 4, 1932 had been given as the death date on two different headmarkers. And from the conversation with the gravedigger, one of them, Sarah Parker's, was empty. Where is she, he thought, who is she? Why has no one even mentioned the boy's family, he must have *some* family.

As the late afternoon wind blasted through the window of the speeding station wagon, the chaplain decided, against his better judgment, to ask at least some of the questions that evening after dinner at the Harris home.

III

Buck Harris brought a special reverence and evangelistic energy to the Ford Motor Company, as if the company and Detroit were Mother Church and his Ford Agency at White Dove an outlying mission from which accounts and tithes were regularly collected. He in fact thought that God in modern dress would look a good deal like Henry Ford.

However it was not Henry Ford or God or Buck's attitude toward them alone that had set him standing once again before the opportunity to trigger an avalanche of events which could bring him nothing except bitter recognition as "the son of a bitch that started all this."

Having left the chaplain to his unpacking, Buck sat alone at the dead-end of a rough pasture road seven miles north of White Dove. He had switched off the air-conditioner in his station wagon. The noise seemed irreverent.

Before him, towering above the car, the huge, black pump-jack of an oil well churned and rocked, plunging its brass polish-rod into the oil-soaked earth. The turning counter-weights under the walking beam rose and fell slowly.

Buck closed his eyes and listened to the powerful, sluggish motion. He could feel the power of it moving inside him like prayer. Without opening his eyes, he rolled down the window and the pungence of fresh crude oil filled the car.

He had come many times to this old well. The ponderous rocking of the pump and the isolation calmed him as if he were alone on a long crescent of empty beach watching the slow rolling surf run aground and fall away. But in the last few years his visits had become more an exercise of bitterness than anything else. That he did not own this well or any other galled him. That he must drive onto another man's land even to see it working was malicious and insulting to him. The envy he felt was in some aspects sexual. He felt robbed of a carnal pleasure.

This moving iron mistress was with him always. Even as he lowered himself onto the body of his wife Mildred. His entrance into her was unrelenting and mechanical. He plunged and withdrew himself deliberately, slowly, oblivious to her pain or pleasure. Even in the heat of that private act the black mechanism was in his mind, as a memory of another woman might spice the bland act of a man too long married to the same woman.

Buck opened his eyes. Running the middle finger of his right hand over the top of his bald head, from one ear to the other, he felt the sweat that had popped up like small water blisters on that tightly drawn skin. He slid his finger across and back, feeling the sweat and taking some pleasure in it. To him there was not a more interesting or gratifying act than the running of this finger over the top of his head, pressed firmly into the small groove it so perfectly fit.

He clamped his hand across his sweating head, tilting it slightly to rest his elbow on the back of the seat, and watched the black monster moving before him.

His mind began to pick up the rhythm of the pump as

the plunging sucker-rod thrust into the earth's history and pulled from it, like memory, oil and the aroma of ten million years. Buck inhaled the earthen musk and thought of the look that had come to the lawyer's face in Austin when he also had begun to smell the oil. Five hundred miles away, no closer to the spot where Buck was now parked than the county abstractor's map of ownership which Buck had unrolled on his desk, the old lawyer had smelled oil.

Sneaking out of town to drive the five hundred miles, Buck had carried with him nothing but the map of Gentry County and a word plucked from a *Saturday Evening Post* article about vacancy hunters.

He stood in front of the huge desk behind which the lawyer sat and pulled the rolled map open before him on the glass top, holding it open like a scroll. Gentry County was square. The blue lines of the map crossed it like a grid, marking off small blocks, each a square mile of land. On every section was printed the name of its owner.

The north half of the county was pocked with black dots, each dot an oil well. The field of dots splayed across the map like spilled peppercorns. As Buck leaned over the desk with his arms spread wide holding the map open, his wide black tie hung like a dead pendulum over a long block of sections, the north half of which lay within the peppercorn field but unmarked by the dots. It was ten miles wide east to west and forty miles long, lying high on the granite-wash oil trap, unmarked except by the name of its owner printed across each of its four hundred sections. And under that name the words CROWS FOOT also appeared four hundred times.

Buck looked down his tie at the empty land and said the *Saturday Evening Post* word, "Vacancy."

"Buck"—from the moment the lawyer had scented the oil he had called him Buck—"I'm sorry," he said, leaning back against his great black chair, "there can be no vacancy." He hunched forward over the map, moved Buck's tie aside to read the name printed on the sections. "Tom Parker et al., according to this map, hold title to the land."

"But he don't," Buck said struggling for words. He felt oppressed by the plush office, cornered by the surrounding walls of books. "He's dead and the et al. part is only his crazy old son and his grandson who was killed in the war." Buck stammered, "It's—it's gonna be vacant."

The small bent lawyer who looked like a sixty year old child prodigy leaned against the huge back of his leather chair. "Buck, you been badly mislead. The legal term 'vacancy' applies only to that land to which the state of Texas holds original title, land which was available for homestead and due to oversight or incorrect survey has never been filed upon." He put the statement before Buck as if it were a set of scales that he had just balanced, and waited for them to come to rest.

Buck was silent as if he too were watching the swinging scales find their balance, thinking: *Dammit—it is vacant— and the oil is there. One old man who is dying right now as I stand here, dying on that empty land. It is empty now and will be vacant—vacant of them all—I won't even bury him in it.*

Buck sat down in a chair near the desk. The map, when his hands were lifted from it, rolled itself into a long tube and dropped off the end of the desk.

The shrunken lawyer leaned forward suddenly like a small owl pouncing on a mouse. "What could, and in fact will, happen to the land you describe, is disposal under the escheat statutes."

Buck stirred in his chair, he felt accused by the word escheat.

The lawyer having caught the word, began tearing at its meaning. "Escheat is the actual reverting of title to the state. Land becomes subject to escheat upon satisfactory proof that there are no living persons entitled to it by right of heirship, and that it had not been conveyed prior to the owner's death intestate. Which would be the case here, if as you say this Tom Parker died leaving no will, having survived his wife who also left no will, and his son———"

"Arron," Buck said.

"Arron is mentally incompetent to make a will, and the grandson———"

"Ronnie," Buck supplied.

"—Ronnie died in the war also without leaving a will."

"There was a letter from Ronnie," Buck said, "but it never said anything about the land. It come to the bank. They was appointed by the county over the Crows Foot money when Arron went off his head."

The lawyer blinked, "It could be a hand written will. What did it say?"

"Nothing but that he wanted his body sent home if he got killed. But it didn't ever come and no one sent for it. With Arron being like he is they didn't want to stir him up."

"Buck, the first thing for you to do is get that letter probated if it *is* a will. Send me an exact copy."

The small hands of the lawyer were pressed flat against the glass top of his desk. He began to talk faster, a voraciousness had begun to work into the tone of his voice. He owl-hopped back to the word escheat. He was no longer tearing at the word, he had begun to consume it. "Of course, after the land escheats the surface can be sold, but the mineral estate, the oil that is obviously under it cannot be sold. It cannot ever again be owned by any person other than the state of Texas, it will remain a part of the public school lands. The income from the oil will be the property of the school children of this state," he said removing his large round glasses. "But," he leaned over the desk, "it can be leased," he said through a sly old smile. "It can be leased."

Buck had sat across from him, rubbing the groove across his head slowly for a long time before a smile something like that of the lawyer's began a sluggish rise to his face. The polished desk and the print in the books around him filled the room with a faint odor he remembered later as being very close to the smell of oil.

Now, almost a full year later, sitting alone in the darkness of his car parked before the giant moving shrine, he could no longer see; he listened:

Vacancy it whispered. *No, old owl says we got to let it escheat. It will be vacant, Ronnie's body will not go into it nor will the bones of Arron, and Sarah will be ripped from it, dig her out myself. I will make it vacant and we will lease the oil, get it from the children paying them something, a book or some band uniforms for it, but we will get it.*

Thinking of the owlish Austin lawyer had made Buck aware of the darkness. He straightened up behind the wheel and jerked on the car lights. The beam of light on the moving pump made it look bizarre and unreal. Buck started the station wagon, circled the well and drove back down the one-way pasture road toward White Dove and the small cluster of lights seven miles away.

IV

The events since morning, though mostly unknown to the Negro, had given the night a lopsided shape. Time and the night hung around the headquarters house of the Crows Foot for long moments, then jerked dizzily on at the least sound or movement. The great house, open and ragged, was filled now with a thick darkness. Smith moved through the ground floor rooms without light.

Arron too, awake and alone in the great master room upstairs, could feel some new current in the liquid black. He could feel the Negro moving below, like someone scratching words on the sole of his shoe. Then it was gone with the gentle slam of an old screen door.

The Negro, by lantern light, went to the roofless barn and bridled the mule. The flickering light was reflected dimly in its milky dark eyes. The leaning, plank-board sides of the unroofed barn walled off a garden of stars.

"I'se fixin to ride you mule," Smith mumbled into the unblinking eye. "We gonna find thet paper, mule, we gonna find thet yeller paper telegram."

He rode out of the walled star garden holding the lantern to the side of the mule's head. "We gonna get to dat plum bush—you knows dat bush 'cause you wouldn't do nothin but watch me squattin under it—so now we's gonna find it." Riding the mule with the easy gentleness of a horseman, he became a part of its motion and of the night's darkness as he passed away from the house.

Arron slept now in the house, suspended somewhere in the bowels of that decaying prairie mastodon. And Smith leading the mule around a plum bush out in the East pasture looking for a scrap of the government telegram could not really hunt it. Seventeen years had hidden it from him and he could not watch the lantern and the mule and hunt it at the same time.

"Don't you look mule, you jest work on not dyin, I'll scratch up thet paper. We gonna rake up dat paper, an if thet rain done unstuck the little strips of words on it, we gonna spit on 'um an stick 'um back."

He was no longer feeling around the bush. He stood at the head of the mule, holding the flickering lantern in its face, running the boney fingers of his free hand through its mane. Slowly he raked them through the shaggy coarse hair feeling it gratify an itch between his fingers and looking out into the night. The darkness comforted him. Without light the haunting dimness of age did not close in around his vision. The awkwardness of unfocus did not occupy his attention. He could think a little beyond himself. As silence cures deafness the night restored his vision, released a part of the sorrow he felt each time his old body humiliated him and itself in failure. Failure to withstand time, failure to keep step with the ageless soul, failure that is a soul sorrow as much as a body sorrow. He stood by the mule enjoying the itch between his fingers; an itch that reassured him that the flesh cocoon around his soul had not yet rotted completely.

33

Standing like this, leaning a little now on the mule, his thoughts came to him as weightless things and people suspended in the air, floating through his mind.

We gonna tell Arron, he thought, like we done before, like we tole him 'bout Sarah. I tole 'bout her then I quit tellin him, I seen it bust him in the eyes and I quit tellin him. I tole him, I tole and his eyes jest exploded like somethin blowed up deep under water or so far off you can see it but don't hear nothin.

The Negro stopped running his fingers through the hair. His arm was getting tired from holding the lantern. He took hold of one of the mule's ears and tried to push its head down so he could set the lantern on the ground, thinking the gleam of the lantern would hold the mule's attention.

"Bow yo head mule, I'se gonna set down this light, this ole man can't be holding up yo life light all night. Now bow yo head! Now, be yo own judge mule, this ole man kin still walk and he knows the way home better'n you, so jest stick yo head up out'en the light if it was to please you, won't no tears come to these eyes to leave yo carcus here to rot, 'sides I may need to find this bush again and yo bones might jest make a good marker."

He turned away from the mule and looked out across the miles of darkness, which filled the Crows Foot. To the east he could see the light-speckled oil field. The lights were dimmed to orange by distance. They spattered the land as far north and south as he could see, but not one shone on the Crows Foot. It was as dark on the surface as the black pool of oil which lay untapped thousands of feet beneath it.

The uniform derricks stood covering the land beyond the Crows Foot boundary like a division of troops standing row on row in the perfectly aligned offset pattern of a military cemetery.

The old mule, addled with age, stood head down, its

eyes fixed on the yellow tongue of light that flapped lazily
inside the cozy snugness of the smoke-blackened chimney
of the lantern. Its rump was high and it seemed to be
pulling back from the light. The Negro rested one arm on
its neck which sloped down.

"Mule you do look funny with yo boney ole rump stuck
up like thet in the air. Looks like you gonna try to make
yo water agin the wind. Is thet it mule, you gonna try
thet? Well let dis ole mule myself tell you thet it takes
way-gone-and-yonder lots more'n two ole black bags of
bones the likes of us to get it done. But you jest point yo
old boney rump up wind 'cause thet shows you belongs to
dis place, an you and me is 'bout all thet's left—but we
gonna keep it pointed. An we gonna start by tellin Arron.
I'se gonna scratch that yeller death paper up outen this
grass or outen this ole head, cause it done come agin,
they is tryin to swarm us agin. And thet paper's gonna tell
us what with and we gonna be ready mule, we gonna be
waitin on 'um this time."

He stepped back to the plum bush and got down on his
hands and knees. His movement was stiff and abrupt. As
he put his face close to the ground, he felt the coarse dry
grass against his face. He closed his eyes and rested the full
weight of his head against the hairy earth, feeling the stiff
curly mat of dry grass against the welts of hard scar tissue
around his earhole and on his slaggy face. It made him
think of Jesus, the beard of Jesus Christ and the colored
Bible pictures of Him. Jesus an the good Lord theys a
stompede prayer fixin to be scared outen this ole man an
he ain't gonna cut it off at the root with some sinful act
like he done most times before, like with Miss Edith
Harvest, some sin that chopped it off 'fore it could ever
get growed up there to heaven. I feel it comin, somethin
I can't see is fixin to scare some important prayer outen
me like squeezin a ripe skin boil. And Lordy Jesus you
jest got to disremember all them sins, an hear dis ole man's

prayer. You got to disremember, you got to help us hold on. I know that if you was wantin for this land to get plowed and for that oil to come up outen it you got plenty ways— I knows 'bout thet flood and I has myself felt the ground shake and I has seen yo wrath in the lightenin. Lord you jest has to loan us some of thet wrath. We got to have somethin.

They is comin in here one tomorrow or the next, carrin thet boy's body, they sayin they wants to give him honor— like yo own Son, Lord. But you knows it like this ole man, all they truthful wants is to show off thet he's dead, thet he's dead and this earth is free for grabbin. Disremember our sin Lord an know like you done on the third day. Let this ole man rise up Arron. We ain't much with outen him, jest me an this mule but we's fixin to try. Disremember our sin and we gonna try.

The old man raised his head. Some of the dry grass stuck to the ointment on his greasy face. As he looked along the flat ground he saw the late rising midnight moon. Its pale light pulled the mule's eyes away from the lantern and set shimmers loose among the silver watch springs that covered the old Negro's head.

He straightened up and looked back at the mule now also erect. "You O.K. now mule, thet ole man on the moon gonna take care o' you now."

He picked up the lantern and without looking at the bush or the ground, walked around it three times. Then feeling an urge and recognizing a thought that had kicked alive at the same moment, and came from as deep in the thick almost dry mud of his mind as had the urge from his bowels, he set the lantern down. It's yellow light was now absorbed in the milk-wash moonlight. It was so dim that had he not heard its flickering tongue, he would have left it burning as he dropped his overalls and squatted in the moon shadow of the plum bush listening to the strips of Western Union words being drawn slowly through his mind by the palsied and senile fingers of memory. "We regrets to deform you thet yo son, Ronald A. Parker. . . ."

The moon was now bright enough to illuminate a black column of smoke that was rising like a clotty funnel tilted at an angle against the bleached sky. Twenty miles away, out across the perimeter wire of the Crows Foot and into the heart of the derrick cemetery of oil wells row on row, a slush pit was burning. The waste oil burned alone in the night like a final pyre of the slain.

And the land beyond the perimeter wire, now in this light, appeared as ghostly and ravaged as that land which men have destroyed with the great turning plows of combat; land defiled, its dignity gouged from it. It is exactly this light which exposes the scars. The tangle of pipes and half-buried cable spools that are forgotten and rotting like wrecked caissons. The land was embedded with the wasted remains of heavy machinery, hulking wheels and ruptured boilers which rose in this light out of the crushed landscape and clotted the horizon.

And even in this poor light the sagging, barbed perimeter fence of the Crows Foot holds out the drillers. While inside its slender wire, two old men and a mule move slowly around in two hundred and fifty thousand acres of darkness.

Arron, in the bowels of the great house no longer asleep, but rather filled with darkness, could also feel the drillers waiting, their jack-knife rigs leveled at the gut of the Crows Foot.

In the early part of night he felt it most in the trees. It was also in the dead trees which bore only the weeping strings and dead grass of abandoned birds' nests, that Arron felt the Crows Foot sovereignty which had since the death of Tom Parker been under siege.

His mother once had said the trees would give something for the wind to blow through and Tom Parker the morning after she said it, told his men, "If Mae wants to hear the wind flap somethin besides her skirts then by God we'll have trees—if it harelips every puncher that rides my brand."

So later in that year the sapling trees were hauled from that very spot in Louisiana where he had found her fifteen years earlier, right after the war. Finding her at the end of a wild horse trail his own father had worn from Texas driving large herds of Texas horses. "Horses for Jeff Davis to sit his raggedy ass on," Sam Parker had said.

But Tom found her after the raggedy-ass-days of Jeff Davis, after Sam had been drowned in the Sabine trying to beat the Yankee blockade with a thousand wild horses.

Across the Sabine, with the bones of Sam Parker and most of the horses not many years yet in the mud, Tom found Mae Batten, driving an old stud through the morass of twisted sugar cane that covered the land. Only the black chimneys remained erect in the wild growth; dumb cold totems punching up through the neglected mat of rotting cane.

He brought her from the sugar cane swamp. One stud, one girl, and one Negro boy, said to hell with Sam Parker and Jeff Davis and a thousand horses and brought them to Texas, saying fifteen years later to his men, "If she needs trees I'll get trees, I'll bring her anything they got down there that'll haul—anything but black tombstone chimneys, sugar cane, or that damn sickness they caught from the war."

Some of the men about to return for the saplings had come to Texas with him and remembered him talking the same way fifteen years before on the banks of the Sabine, when they that first followed him were still freshly orphaned by war, and the girl unmarried. Talking as much to her as to them he had said, "I'll be damn if there'll be a man on my place who'll look like you jest broke an egg

in his drawers when you mention Jeff Davis. This is Texas
and it's just tough enough to look you right square in the
eye. It can stand most things, this land, you can spit, bleed,
shit or die on it but we don't get near enough rain to wash
out the salt from one tear dropped on the grass by a
quitter or a coward—if you feel like lookin back across the
Sabine and start feelin lonesome for what it was like before
you kicked the dung pile all over the lot and got your nose
rubbed in it, jest head your horse in that direction. But
be sure it's your horse 'cause this is Texas and where we're
goin is a hell of a lot more Texas and she'll kill you—if
she can beat me to it. And I swear by the bones of a thousand horses and one fool that's fattening the catfish in this
river that it'll be a close race."

Some of the men now going back for Mae's saplings had
heard and remembered young Tom Parker, who appeared
with a string of forty horses. Looking for buyers and finding only the gutted land and men ragged and beaten sitting
on great steps of burned out houses or wandering lost in
the cane brake morass of neglected fields.

And as they tell it, he didn't sell horses, he bought men.
He loaded every horse. Loaded them with gutted men and
the woman with the Negro boy.

Some of these same men going back for the trees remembered and told the others of first crossing the Sabine. One
of them even remembered the cameo. The boy Tom
Parker pulling his mother's cameo out of his hat band and
dropping it in Sam's river grave. "Thought you might
want it, you worthless wandering son of a bitch!" and
plowing his big stallion up out of the muddy water saying,
"This is Texas."

Tom Parker, twenty years old, plunged up out of the
thick muddy water of the Sabine with a sucking, thrashing
crash as if God himself had exploded the river, jerking
man and stallion as one out of his own spit and clay, and
sent them shimmering in bronze mud and sunlight on the

Texas bank. A dripping statue, caught, stilled for a split moment of infinity in youth's violent perfection.

And the forty began to catch it, even the woman seeing that splendid glimpse of natural glory, felt a genetic twinge. Without knowing that she was now and for all time seeing man at his absolute full stride, felt that this sight would somehow stiffen her blood line, jerk true some of the kinks of inbreeding.

The forty beaten horsemen felt it as if a sack had been lifted from their heads. The guilt of self abuse lifted from them as they came up out of the waters of the Sabine. They put aside self-destruction and began erecting themselves again as men.

Fifteen years after Tom Parker had dropped the cameo and baptized them in the Sabine some of them rode back for trees. They crossed the river and cut back into the country of their blood and youth and saw the sickness he had warned them to leave. It hung still in the land, like nets of heavy moss on the black chimneys, stifling and starving the spirit. It was sick with the lethargic sorrow of blood defeat.

They dug the saplings and left the sickness behind, yet when they returned with most of the trees alive and she asked one of the older ones about it, he looked quickly around to see if he could be heard. Then he removed his hat and said, "Miss Mae," even though she was now Tom Parker's wife, "it's eatin 'um up, they are just sittin there listenin to the marsh crickets in the evenin and the taxes are eatin 'um up."

He did not say more, nor did he need to for he had smuggled to her in that wisp of news a packet of fresh infective sorrow. Though he did not know it, and she also kept it hidden from her husband, the sorrow spread to the trees. Tom Parker's attempt to make the wild prairie wind her plaything had, though unknown to him, orchestrated her loneliness and sorrow.

He had killed the sickness in the men. It had melted

out of them in the solvent of sweat. With this troop of dedicated cowboy-cavalry he slugged back the grass frontier and rolled great rivers of cattle north to Abilene. And chose the Crows Foot, paying gold for the patent as easily as he would have paid leaves from some tree he had mounted. He knew those who issued the seal could not own the land it conveyed for they had not even seen it nor buried a friend in it, not even this much claim did they have. Yet for their government quitclaim he paid in gold. Gold from the rivers of cattle.

And with the papers in his saddle bag he rode to the Indian Territory and sat seven days with the Kiowa Chief who had hunted that land and buried many warriors there. He told of the payment in gold and the old Chief spat on the ground. And on the seventh day late in the evening he sat with the old Chief close to a small Indian fire. They smoked slowly and thought of the land. Then in the silence Tom Parker burned the papers with the great seal in the campfire and the trusteeship to four hundred square miles of Texas was passed.

This was in the years before he sent for the trees or built the great house. And in the following years when the trees were big enough to sing their wild wind-strummed song like mournful hounds howling thin at the moon, the Kiowas would come.

In the late fall the old rheumatic Chief and a few men would leave the Indian Territory and come to the Crows Foot, making camp in the North pasture, near a treeless dry gully where the black petroleum oozed from the ground. And when they came each fall, Tom Parker left the headquarters house and made camp with them there where they said the Great Mother bled. Anointing himself as they did against the great white bear that in winter hugged the warriors to him, stopping their breath and causing their life to run like clear water out of their noses until they died.

Then he would return to the house and, in the years

after Mae had died, he did not bathe until spring. And the smell of the Indian land of the bleeding earth would fill the house.

Arron lying now in that same bed which death had emptied first of Mae and then of Tom, though in the last years Tom never used it, could not remember its smell and if he had he would have thought only of the mentholated Negro.

Outside, the wind made no sound in gnarled and broken limbs of the dead trees that grasp up at the night sky around the dark and hollow house.

Arron heard only the sounds of the Negro locking the mule in the roofless barn and later felt him moving in the darkness below like words being written on the bottom of his shoe.

V

In town the lights were blinking out. Roy Turner was the last supper customer in the hotel cafe. He had eaten a large meal. As he stood waiting at the cash register for the Mexican waitress he stuck a toothpick between his front teeth and picked up a twenty-five cent Baby Ruth candy bar.

"You want to get paid tonight?" he asked loudly, dropping the candy in his levi pocket.

"You jest wait a minute Roy," she called from the kitchen.

"Money's here on the counter and that extra quarter ain't a tip, I got a candy bar," he said, back over his shoulder as he went out the door.

The main street was empty; barren and artificial under the arbor of ravaged colored lights that hung across it from the evenly spaced street lamps.

Roy stepped off the curb and saw across the street that Mason Holton, the night watchman, had parked his car at the highway intersection. Be funny as hell, he thought, if the highway patrol was to pick him up for sleeping parked too close to the right-of-way.

43

He opened his pickup door and took from the seat the four long-necked wine bottles that belonged to Elmira. Closing the door easy, he looked over to see the night-watchman open his lunch sack and look down into it.

Mason did not see Roy slip quietly away from the pickup and across the highway carrying the bottles. If he had, he would have just chuckled a half-chuckle, coughed up from some warm youthful memory. He and everyone else in town knew about Roy and Elmira Gent. Most of them, at least the men, knew about his nighttime journeys from the hotel down the alley behind the Ford garage to the small unpainted house that was the town's central telephone office.

The loneliness Elmira knew as telephone operator was a paradoxical loneliness, as if she were dying of thirst while drowning. It was through her that the townspeople communicated their feeble descriptions of living. The black earphones she wore brought her the sounds of life, the rigors and ecstasies of existence. She had taken the job from her mother who was widowed by a ranch accident. It passed naturally to Elmira as if she too had been widowed by her ugliness.

Roy had called on Elmira and her mother on Sunday afternoons. When Mrs. Gent died, he stopped calling in the afternoon.

Roy stood outside the backdoor of the small low roofed house that would have been called a shanty if it had been in another part of town and not owned by the telephone company. A slight hunger pang crossed his mind as he stood there holding the empty bottles in one arm. He dropped his other hand to his pocket feeling the hard lumpy candy bar as a man feels for his billfold before going to pay a check. Satisfied, he opened the screen door and knocked quickly before the screeching noise made by the rusty spring frightened Elmira.

"Somebody at my door?" she called from inside, not to him but more to herself.

44

"Yeah, it's me, Roy," he said, leaning his face close to the unpainted wood.

He heard her get up quickly as though half startled and come the few steps to the door. She opened it a crack, paused, then let him in.

He handed her the four wine bottles that he had carried from the hotel. As she took them she backed away from the doorway and he stepped into the room.

"The women out at the graveyard said to tell you that the grape juice was better this year than it ever was," he said, taking off his broad hat. His damp yellow hair clung to his scalp. He looked over-neat and unnatural like a small boy fresh from the bath.

She gave him an abrupt smile which closed like a trap over her small rodent-like teeth.

"I didn't make it out in time to get any, but that's what they said. It was the first thing they run out of."

"Roy, do you want coffee?" she asked, turning from him toward the kitchen.

He did not answer; they always had coffee. He crossed the crowded room and sat down in the overstuffed chair next to the swayback double bed. She had bought the chair second hand to avoid the embarrassment of Roy having to sit on the bed when he came. The room was hot. He leaned over the arm of the chair and turned down the gas stove that was next to the wall. As he pulled himself straight, Elmira came back into the room carrying two mugs of coffee with a small box of grocery store cookies balanced on top of one.

"Well, does the cemetery look nice?" she asked with a high thin voice.

"As far as I can tell it does, 'course I can't speak for them that's in it, they may think it looks like hell," he said taking a loud gurgling sip of the coffee.

She waited until the sound of it died away and asked, "Did you take some new coffee cans out to hold the flowers?"

45

"Yeah, the cook at the cafe gave me two of the big ones. But if you're wantin to put red flowers in 'um they're gonna have to be pretty red to outshine the cans," he said, taking another long pull at the coffee.

She did not answer and he did not expect her to. Their conversation was more of silence than anything else. They were together to avoid being alone. They came to each other out of that same deserted loneliness which causes old people, forgotten by everyone, to take pleasure in the mail they get addressed to "Local Box Holder."

The hunger Roy had felt when he bought the candy was gone now as he drank the hot coffee. The large Baby Ruth melted and became soft against the hot skin of his leg.

"Vera put the post office flag in the washing machine yesterday," Elmira said, looking down into her cup.

"I know, Wendell told me."

"Roy?"

"What."

"Does it really look nice, I mean really nice?" she asked raising her bewildered eyes from the cup. "Does the place where they're gonna put him really look nice?" A look of pleading stirred the bewilderment as she looked at him, turning her pinched face up to him, speaking with a whining tone from behind her small caved-in teeth.

"Well, goddamn, Elmira, what do you want me to say? Yes, it looks *nice!*"

Her eyes pinched out the soft bewilderment and became brittle. "Now you watch your dirty mouth Roy Turner. You don't have to take the Lord's name in vain. All I wanted to know is how it looked. Everybody's outdoing themselves trying to do proud by Ronnie. Look at Buck Harris, look how he's working, he's proud of Ronnie and of White Dove. We may even be in *Life* magazine." She said it with a haughty contemptuous look that Roy had seen before but without the wildness that there was now in it.

46

"Yeah Buck's proud alright, he's proud that old Arron don't have to pay county or school taxes on all that oil they say is just waitin under his grass. He's so proud of Ronnie that he's havin his body dug up and brought home to Arron, ole Buck thinks Arron has sat out there so long huggin that rotten ole nigger that he's forgot to die; that diggin up some of his own flesh and blood and paradin it around under his nose might remind him. For my money, Buck's jest liable to remind that tough old coot of more'n he bargained for. Crazy or not you wouldn't get six bits out of me for all that talk of Buck's about oil boom or new school, even if you throw in Buck's tail feathers." Roy leaned back against the chair, a little winded, and ran his fingers slowly through his hair.

"Well I still say Buck's trying to do him proud," she said crossing her ill-shaped legs tightly under her house-coat. "Ronnie is a hero, a boy that the U.S. government has pinned a silver star on. And that is something you don't get for breaking wild horses or selling new Fords." As she spoke an ugly bitterness came into her tone and she began swinging her crossed leg, a rapid unrhythmic motion almost like kicking.

Roy was silent. He knew Ronnie Parker was a subject about which they could not talk. He knew this and he knew the reason as did she; and they both knew they would never speak of that reason. He put a cigarette in his mouth and shoved his hand down into his levi pocket. The wrapper around the melted candy bar burst, filling his hand and the inside of his pocket with a warm chocolate nastiness. He was shocked and disgusted when he felt it on his hand and angrily began squeezing it between his fingers, mixing the small change he carried into the peanut and paper ooze.

She looked at his red face. "There's lots of things you don't see. You don't know how people think, if you knew half as much about people as you do about that horse of

47

yours you'd be a lot smarter. You don't even curse when a spooked steer tramples you half to death but you just can't understand it when something spooks a man and he shies away like Ronnie done from Arron."

Roy began breaking matches that his hand came across in the chocolate. "All I know is there ain't been a Parker yet since ole Tom fenced that damn county out there that he called a ranch who wasn't spooked on something or another." The cigarette in his plump, weathered mouth flopped up and down as he spoke. "I say they are all spooked, spooked in the head. You got a match?" he asked, breaking another one in his nasty pocket.

She uncrossed her legs slowly, rubbing them apart niggardly rather than lifting one from the other, got up and went to the kitchen. Roy sat forward in the chair and after she had been gone a few seconds, put his clean hand on the warm spot Elmira's buttocks had created and left cooling on the edge of the mattress. Again he felt the dull hunger but the mess in his pocket cured it.

When she came back Roy was standing by the door, one hand still in his pocket; he took the match and lighted the cigarette. They went through the long established routine of careful parting. It was tenderly guarded against any show of regret or loneliness and especially submerged in their impersonal good-byes were any tell tales of memory.

He said good-bye and closed the door. As the screen door slammed, the knotted spring struck a lonely sound as its vibrations died in the outside night.

Roy walked a few steps away and jerked his hand from his pocket. He stood in the darkness outside the shanty slinging the warm chocolate from his hand as if it were something filthy and outrageous.

VI

In preparing for bed, Elmira had applied nothing to her thin, drained face nor had she rubbed anything from it. She lay naked in the bed, which even without a body in it curled up at the edges like a slice of bread toasted on one side. She had now for the past week gone to bed without her musty gown. Tonight again she lay alone and trembling at her thoughts of Ronnie Parker.

After she had listened to the dull ticking of her clock until she no longer heard it, the trembling slowed and finally stopped as if it had been alive in itself and was now exhausted, resting. She passed into that time between sleep and unsleep when reality is blotted out, yet the nerve relay to physical reaction has not been disengaged; that twilight in which one half dreams, half thinks of things that can startle the body.

Her mind, floating in a limbo of thought and memory, saw a red fog rolling in over town, then she heard the sharp solid sound of a car door being slammed. At the sound her body jerked and she drew her thin thighs up against her neglected breast. She saw red mist fall from the sky like something brittle and be sucked to the metal skin of the bright new pickup truck, leaving the sky clotted with gray cotton. A small bottle of mustard smashed against the red metal then disappeared as Roy got out and covered his yellow hair with a black hat.

It was 1950 then and Roy was driving the first new thing he had ever owned, the violation of which he enjoyed fully as much as he had that of Elmira who now rode beside him again returning to that point of frustration to which she had willingly come for over a year.

"It looks like rain Roy, you better put the grocery box up here with us," Elmira said, drawing her legs under her on the new leather seat.

"Don't worry, they'll be alright, that crazy old nigger can't tell dry from wet anyhow." Roy said as he reached out the window and adjusted the rear-view mirror.

"Your new pickup sure rides good," she said squeezing her arms close to her sides and raising her shoulders as if she were trying on a soft coat that made her feel rich and beautiful.

"Yeah, I think I finally got one over on Buck Harris; he sold it pretty cheap considering all his talk about a war comin."

"Roy, why don't you take me by Lea Switch first?" she asked. "I brought some things to make sandwiches. I can make 'um up while you take the groceries."

They drove on in silence, Roy thinking about the sandwiches, and Elmira feeling the urge to remember bawdy songs and sexy jokes. Ugliness had compounded her desires. Now that she had opened herself to Roy, there always seemed to be a vivid dirty joke just beyond her memory.

"You bring mustard?" Roy asked as he turned the pickup along the gravel siding of the isolated depot.

"No Roy, you don't put mustard on tuna fish," she said.

"Well I do," he said, "I put mustard on ice cream—ask Harry Eddens; he's got a bottle he keeps for me right on

50

the soda fountain counter." He stopped the pickup next to the loading dock of the station house and got out. As she was gathering up her things, he reached over into the back and took a small bottle of mustard from the grocery box. She got out and looked at him across the red metal bed of the truck. "Here," he said, tossing the mustard to her. She jumped to catch it and missed. The glass jar broke against the metal side and the bright yellow paste ran jaggedly down the red paint. "Well goddamn, Elmira!" he shouted. She looked at him helplessly, shocked more by the fact that he had thrown it than by its smashing. Before she could say anything he got into the cab of the pickup and slammed the door. Without looking at her he started the motor and backed up to turn around. He stopped backing abruptly and reached out to straighten the outside mirror that had been jarred out of line by his slamming the door.

"I'll be back as soon as I can," he said looking up from the mirror. He then roughly jerked the gearshift down into low gear and spun the new tires on the loose gravel. As he shoved the shift stick up into second gear he thought of the other jar, the big family-sized jar of mentholated ointment in the grocery box. "Wait 'til the old bastard sees that," he said half aloud, jerking the shift down into high gear. "He can stick his whole head in it if he wants to."

Elmira slowly turned her back as Roy's pickup dropped out of sight over a rise. She went inside the station house carrying the clean lard bucket of food. She put the tip of her white blouse collar in her mouth and sucked at the speck of yellow mustard on it. It had begun to rain.

Inside, up in the loft on the musty hay, sitting on the old army blanket, she sucked at the collar and listened to the timid rain as it speckled the dry worn shingles.

They had been there many times and she well knew the frightening, unfinished experience for which she so impatiently now waited. It was as though she were carefully

5 1

blowing up a paper bag, planning to explode it between her hands behind a friend to frighten and delight them both. She knew that the bag would not explode and the person whom she expected to startle was deaf, yet she could not help trying.

Roy had seduced her in the legal sense, in that penetration, no matter how slight, constitutes seduction. Yet, even though unknown to her, she in every other sense remained virginal. It was her cheated maidenhead itching for destruction which fanned her passion.

The sound of the rain's tender progression to power and authority on the roof mixed with the perfume of rotting timbers and cured hay. As she lay listening in the warmth of the nest-like place she had burrowed out in the hay, she closed her eyes, taking deep, perfumed breaths of the dusky air and without shame or any thought of it, explored her body with hands she imagined to belong to any man that would not leave her gasping, crying, biting her own palm until the taste of blood confirmed her despair.

A noise, almost drowned in the downpour, came to her from outside. Her hands slowed their soothing deep massage and she sat up in the hay and waited for the warm itching astonishment to clear from her head. It must be Roy, she thought, when the swirling wildness had settled back to that place inside her from which it had been teasingly coaxed. She did not rebutton her blouse, she did not even remember unbuttoning it. She crawled quickly through the hay dragging a part of herself as if she had been wounded or lamed. At the edge of the loft she crouched looking down. Her hair was already wild with straw and she was now again sucking on the collar of the loose blouse. It pulled her mouth down at one corner into a grotesque slash. With one hand she stuffed the waist of the open blouse into the top of her skirt carelessly covering her breasts which hung under her crouched body like large tear drops.

5 2

As she watched the door unable to see through the sheet of rain falling from the gutterless edge of the roof, a dark figure burst through the skin of falling water dragging a saddle. It was not Roy. Elmira's black eyes glistened and she was still, even the wild breath left her. She watched as he dropped the wet saddle and blanket and took off his hat, pouring the water from its wide brim. His clothes, soaked black, clung to his body. He looked gaunt and shrunken in the half light. He walked to the door and faced the sheet of rain. Elmira dropped the chewed lapel from her mouth as she recognized him. Her body relaxed from the crouch and she sat at the edge of the shadowed loft looking down at him. Then after awhile when the pounding rain had given her courage she spoke.

"Ronnie," she said lowly in perfect harmony with the rain, "is that you down there?"

At the sound of her voice he spun around and grabbed his stomach as if he had been kicked. "Oh God," he grunted, shooting his eyes up at her.

"It's me, Elmira," she whispered secretly.

"Gosh, Elmira," he said without moving, his lean body was still humped over, his hands on his stomach, "what are you doin out here, who's with you?"

"Nobody, I just rode out with Roy Turner. He's gone to take the groceries to Bobtail Smith," she said, pulling at the blouse. "We were gonna have a picnic." She spoke softly just over the noise of the rain, following an instinct that he would come to her voice. "I was gonna go with him to take the groceries, I wanted to see Bobtail Smith, but I got scared at the last minute so Roy left me here."

"Well, you're better off never seeing him," Ronnie said speaking low and into the steady rain sounds. "If you saw him as much as I do you'd get enough pretty quick."

"Roy says he's crazy, the way he never says anything and uses all that mentholated ointment."

"Naw, he ain't crazy," Ronnie said walking toward the

ladder, "jest old and mean and useless like everything else around here."

Elmira looked down at him where he stood directly below her at the foot of the ladder. "I've got the picnic pail up here with me, come on up and I'll make you a sandwich, it won't hurt to eat one while we wait for Roy," she said crawling away from the edge of the loft.

Ronnie took off his wet hat and tossed it across the room where it landed on the dark saddle. He shook himself and climbed the splintery ladder up into the hay. As he came into sight in the semidarkness of the loft the light from below gave sharp relief to his knotty muscles, they moved like the slow bulging surface of boiling lead under the clinging wet cotton shirt. His wet hair lay flat and brown against his scalp. His thick jaw accented the solemn, almost sorrowful expression that the blue of his Parker eyes had given him at birth. Gaunt in the wet clothes that covered his small but delicately defined body he looked at her with the blue Parker eyes in which despair had been planted even before his birth. She could not think of age; she could no more think that he was not yet eighteen than she could have looked into those same Parker eyes in the craggy head of Arron, his father, and thought of him as old and dying.

She crawled back to him and took his hand, "Come on over here," she said, "there's a blanket, I'll make that sandwich if you want it."

She led him over the hay to the blanket. It was darker now and the rain hammered the roof. They raised their voices.

"You're soaking wet," she said, "you better take off that shirt and wring it out. I've got a cup towel in the lunch pail that you can dry off on." She knelt before him on the blanket.

"I'll be alright," he said looking back at the bright spot in the loft floor where the ladder came up. "If old

Roy don't get back pretty soon, he'll probably be stuck. If he drives on the grass he'll be O.K., but jest let him slip off in them ruts and it'll take two weeks dry weather and a team of good mules to get him out."

"Don't you worry about Roy," she said squeezing his hand, "if he's dumb enough to get stuck, then let him stay stuck."

"Yeah, but what about you, Elmira? How you gonna get back to town?"

"Mama's not expecting me till late," she said dropping her hand from his, rising up in front of him closer than she could have ever walked, closer than any woman had ever been to him. Her breast almost kissed his belt as she rose up before him. "Anyways, I don't think its gonna rain long," she said as her face came straight up from the hay, inches from the blue Parker eyes.

She could feel the steamy heat from his body and put her hand on his shirt. It was soaked with rain water now hot from his skin. "Here, let me get you out of that shirt," she said low and exactly loud enough to rise tenderly above that shredded sound the rain made against the cedar shingles. She started to put her fingers to the top button of his shirt and he raised his hands between their bodies, as he pulled them up they rubbed against hers and his own. She felt them rising until they were blocked by her breast. The back of his flat hands, the palms of which were pressed against his wet shirt, nudged against them, she fumbled with the button and leaned slightly against him feeling the dampness of him against her stomach, trapping his trembling hands. The button at his neck gave way and as if it were a signal to him she felt his hands clinch into hard fists against her.

She leaned away from him slowly to make room for the fists and dropped her fingers to the second button. Looking down at his hands she saw white knuckles, luminous in the pale darkness.

55

Elmira knew what she meant when she told him to get out of the wet shirt. But to Ronnie, who had never heard it, in this sense or any other, it represented something else.

To Ronnie, who had never known the warmth of even the slightest concern whether he was wet or dry, alive or dead, it was something he did not understand. The clothes would dry, just as his skinned knees and bloody noses had healed, they would dry unattended. Yet he let her remove the shirt, as he would have let Sarah, now buried on cotton-wood knoll, wipe his nose or kiss the skinned knee.

Elmira pulled the too small shirt from him, her warm cheek brushed his arm and a softness swirled through him.

Standing dumb before Elmira with his clinched fist pulled tight to his chest, the glowing white knuckles show-ing dimly against his pink chilled skin, his confused and trembling mind could only bring him the memory, later whispered to Elmira, of wandering from the rotting house where the old men cursed and screeched at each other over the table to be near the knoll and Sarah, sitting waiting for the mother he knew only as Sarah never as mother to whisper him something. Sitting alone by her grave in the shadows until the rattling whispers of the cottonwood leaves washed around him hiding his loneliness in their moonlit susurrant murmurs.

It was this whisper that Ronnie felt in Elmira's atten-tion, even in a matter so slight as a wet shirt. As she touched him he felt the fuzzy lint that the late summer wind eddied down from Sarah's tree tenderly strike his face like warm dry snow flakes.

Elmira was again standing in front of him, drying him with the cup towel she had taken from the lunch pail. His hands were no longer clinched into fists against his chest. They hung loosely at his sides. As she vigorously rubbed his head, her blouse which she had failed to button parted and Ronnie's eyes, protected from her face and detection by the draping towel, fell on her wobbling jerking breasts, held loosely like small white ballons of water in the cheap black lace "Quickie Brassier" she had secretly ordered with a coupon clipped from the back page of a movie magazine. As they wobbled and shook before him, his eyes began to swallow them. His eyes that had never, even at birth, seen the form of a living breast (for Sarah's death quiver had birthed him, death's reflexes had thrust him into the world), began drawing his head down to them. And the same force that had urged him as a death born, to crawl in his own birth filth toward Sarah's cold pap crushed him down upon her. As hands fumbled, each helping, cheap cloth was ripped with Elmira's husky urgent consent.

Outside in the rain Roy Turner, who had slammed the door of his mud-buried pickup with a curse and had walked the remaining quarter of a mile back to the station house, slugged along on the muddy grass.

As he came close enough to see the rain-drenched horse waiting outside the station house, with its head bowed low in a mournful beaten stance of lonesome dignity, he heard a shrill scream of ecstatic agony pierce the rain like a glass sliver of lightening.

Elmira, at that moment was impaled on the cruel fact of manhood, her enraged, unplumbed maidenhead shredded, ruptured into history.

Roy ran nine paces, then stopped, the tight throated sounds smashing him to a standstill. It was as though her vocal cords had been stretched taut in her throat and their sound came through teeth clenched tight by her locked jaw. The pulsating *Oh* . . . God, *Oh* . . . God, *Oh* . . . God sawed the rain silence with a rusty coarse-toothed saw. Then as if it had come out of the slicing rain around him, he heard the other voice, crying in oscillating despair, "Aaah . . . *ah* . . . maaa, aaah . . . *ah* . . . maaa," a sound of punishment as if he were being slugged across the small

57

of the back with something dull and heavy. The wild, ugly exchange of cries increased in frequency and intensity.

The horse jerked his head erect. Roy stood pile driven in his muddy tracks, the animal cries from the station house tearing his brain. He felt the voices in his stomach and spine. He was stunned by the ugly butchered sound of her final orgastic outcry to God. He heard no other sound.

The crack of the whip falling on the team of black mules that were pulling Bobtail Smith's wagon up behind him was lost in a shroud of numbness. The Negro waited. Before them the wet iron rails lay on the grass empty from east to west, thus locating Roy, Smith, and the quiet station house across the track at the dead center of isolation.

"Roy, I want dat 'ere big jar of ointment."

At that moment Elmira appeared in the doorway of the station house, her hair matted with straw, and wearing Ronnie's still damp shirt. Her torn cotton blouse had been used to wipe up and in an attempt to stop the bleeding, not hers, for that blood belonged rightfully and with simple tragic dignity to that eternal river of waste to which each hymen is destined to become a tributary. It was not this blood, it was the blood let by the flesh-tear her teeth, in passionate outrage at the injustice of the curse that bleeding should be left to woman alone, had slashed into Ronnie's shoulder. Ronnie, naked to the waist and holding the faded print blouse to his wound, followed her.

The rain had stopped, a humid chilled silence filled the late afternoon, broken only by reluctant drops from the eaves of the station house and occasionally by a drowning noise from isolated insects. The black mules moved nervously in their harness sensing they were also in the eye of the storm. They were all caught, stilled as though it were a scene done in grey-blue water color, smothered in isolation and silence on the raw canvas of endless, oblivious grassland.

Even now as Elmira lay dangling over the edge of consciousness in the stuffy back room of the telephone office, the musty slightly rotten smell of that moment and the chill of the rain made her shiver and with that shallow spasm she crumbled over the edge into the dark chasm of sleep. A fitful sleep, where she wallowed her naked body against the hot sheets, from time to time sucking loudly at the wet corner of the one she held clenched tightly in her drawn mouth.

VII

WHITE DOVE was house-dark and sleeping under a high moon, surrounded by a black sky blasted with jagged points of shrapnel stars.

On the farm-to-market road south, that might have been unrolled across the flat land like a roll of grey gauze, Harry Eddens, the druggist, sat patiently behind the wheel of his old bullet-nosed Studebaker. He drove as if waiting for his destination to come to him. He could feel the time and distance moving under him until his destination appeared. Finally arriving he would step from the car, never having felt a sense of his own movement.

Harry was now sixty-seven and about to catch up to the age that had shown on his face most of his life. His skin had rushed ahead of him into old age. The wrinkles were thin as cracks in a tea cup. The lines splintered straight down from his hair across his forehead and spilled out under his eyes to hang like plumblines across his cheeks. Others came from under his thin nose, falling across his lips, marking his hard natural chin with a net of perfectly set fractures.

His eyes were grey like a bottle of smoke. An imprisoned glint of mirth dashed itself against their surface when he smiled.

He was thin except for his small distended stomach which pooched out his pants below his belt. Standing, it was the body of a tall and frail child-bride six months pregnant; her low, hard, green-mellon belly the only hint of form.

Ahead he saw the old Harvest mansion. He could not call it anything else even though Buck Harris had owned it for almost twenty years, having bought it cheaply from the estate after Miss Edith Harvest died. It loomed ponderous and medieval under the moon.

"Barbed wire Harry, barbed wire, that's what built it," Gilbert Harvest had said in 1903. "Why, if I had all the wire that's been shipped in here to me in the last two years and tied it all together—why, it'd make a three wire hatband for the man in the moon—yessir a hatband for the man in the moon."

Harry smiled in the darkness thinking of Gilbert Harvest, the hardware man: *selling wire and windmills, with garters on his sleeves, a sweating roaring grounded drummer with that black mustache an inch thick hanging over his mouth like a cow catcher on the front of a Santa Fe freight engine. Hatband for the man in the moon.*

The old mansion was near enough now for Harry to see the small gleaming sign which hung from one of the large brick gate posts that flanked the drive like guard houses. As he turned slowly into the drive, he read it: Harris House. *That damn Buck, I'd like to see him own just one thing that he can't write his name on.*

As he stopped the car under the dark, moon-shadowed carriage porch, the yellow bug-proof porch lights came on and Buck appeared at the door. Harry killed the car and shoved off the lights. As he picked up the tube of patent medicine from the seat beside him he heard Buck say,

6 1

"It's Harry . . . Harry Eddens, go put on the coffee." Inside, Mildred, his wife, got up and went to the kitchen leaving the chaplain alone before the large color television which cast a pale green light on his face, leaving it bloodless.

"Get out Harry," Buck called, "it's about time you gave me a chance to build up a little coffee credit."

Buck enjoyed the Christian sadism of giving. He knew the exact number of coffees he had served Harry and always reminded him when the merchants gathered for a morning cup at the drugstore. "Well that's about fourteen cups of credit I got comin," he would say dropping a dime on the counter, "but I guess I can wait to collect." He had never accepted a free cup. "Hospitality is one thing Harry, but business is another," he would say, poking whoever happened to be sitting next to him.

Harry followed Buck into the dim living room. Buck crossed to the television set and turned off the sound, leaving the silent colored pictures.

"Here," Harry said as Buck turned from the set, "you forgot to pick it up this afternoon."

"Yeah," Buck said, taking the small tube and quickly laying it aside on the top of the TV, "we was late getting away from the graveyard." Buck nodded at the seated chaplain who looked as if he also had been turned down along with the television set.

"Major Sutton," Buck said, calling him to attention, "I want you to meet the one man who has done more and still does more for the good people of White Dove than all. . . ."

"Buck," Harry interrupted, "that pile ointment melts at body temperature, you better get it off the TV."

Buck, caught with his mouth open, looked blankly at Harry a moment, closed his mouth and turned to the television. Harry stepped across the room to the Major.

"Harry Eddens is my name Major, I am pleased to make your acquaintance," he said offering his hand.

6 2

The chaplain shook hands as if he were offering some private and tender part of himself for Harry to squeeze.

"Very glad to meet you sir," he replied, meeting Harry's eyes briefly.

Buck stood holding the tube, then as if to escape, turned quickly and left the room. The chaplain's eyes were drawn back to the jerking green sickness of the TV.

Harry called to the kitchen, "Mildred, don't fix coffee for me, but if the chaplain or Buck want one, I'll buy it."

"No, no, none for me sir," said the Major.

Buck came back into the room, "Go ahead and drink one Harry, do you good to sample the competition."

"You bought a Chevrolet lately Buck?"

"What?"

"I said . . ."

"Oh . . . O.K. Harry," Buck said, laughing uneasily. He turned to the kitchen. "No sale on the coffee Noodles," he called without asking the chaplain who was in the act of declining.

"Sit down, sit down Harry," Buck said waving him toward an armchair.

"The chaplain here is about to retire he tells me," Buck said as they sat down into the blue-green dimness of the overstuffed room. To Harry everything in it seemed to be inflated; the chairs, the pillows, even the lamp shades were fat and clumsy.

"I didn't know you could retire from God's Army," Harry said sitting down.

"Who said anything about God's Army? I mean the U.S. Air Force. He's served his God and country for almost twenty years."

"Well that's good," Harry replied as if he had been told a stranger had died without pain.

Buck turned his eyes to the TV and put his hand across his slick head. The lime shadows flickered on his face. He knew Harry was about to say something he did not want to deal with, something frustrating or embarrassing. The chaplain felt only the social discomfort of loaded silence. As Harry watched them, the revulsion he felt for petty greediness was soothed a little by the gangrene of Buck's complexion.

"Buck," he said into the dead silence, "when you gonna tell Arron?"

"Tell him what?" Buck answered too quickly.

"You know damn well what," Harry said reaching up under the shade of the floor lamp beside him. He's gonna lie, Harry thought as he grasped the string of shot that would switch on the light.

"If you mean the funeral, Harry, he already knows. I sent Roy out there this morning. You can say what you want to but this town is trying to let bygones be bygones. They don't care anymore that it's the Parkers that killed the boom and caused White Dove to die on the vine. You know yourself Harry that what they done ain't natural. And Arron went on with it, failing the town and even his own son. Well there's some things that he can't deny that boy and a Christian funeral is one of them. Christian decency is one thing that the Parkers didn't get all fenced in before the rest of us got here."

Harry jerked on the light so hard that the metal chain tangled itself in the spokes of the shade. Buck's face contracted into a squint then relaxed. The Major's eyes betrayed his effort to appear disinterested.

"Well Buck, I didn't come out here to judge, I'll do that later. You do your Christian duty as you see fit, but my advice is, don't go getting the idea that jest because God give you Baptist open season on other people's souls that it covers their private property. As I understand it the soul is something a man is free to keep to himself, something you don't get away from him with an electric can opener."

"Harry, the people of White Dove don't want nothin like that; this don't concern nobody's soul, least of all Arron's. For my money a crazy man ain't got one. All we want is to claim our own, Ronnie is one of us. He fought and died for us, gave his life so we can do the very thing we plan to do; hold a Christian funeral for him."

Buck's face was getting red, and he ran his hand across his head. The chaplain's dilated eyes darted from Buck to Harry.

"The way it looks to me," Harry said leaning back into the obese chair, "you are about twenty years late, I didn't hear much about him being one of us when the word came that he was killed. All you done then was to try to get Arron committed because he didn't do then the exact same thing you are trying to do now. Nope, Buck, it seems to me that ever since you started visiting that Austin lawyer, Ronnie has been gettin to be more and more one of us."

"Now wait a minute Harry," Buck exploded.

"Naw Buck I can't," Harry interrupted as he got up out of the fat chair. "I just came out to clear my mind, your business is your business; I can't do to you what it is that I cuss you for doin to Arron."

Buck struggled out of his chair as if he were holding something heavy in his lap. The chaplain was confused; to stay seated he felt would be impolite but to get up, he felt, would be insinuating himself into their conversation.

"But you don't get it Harry, it is your business, we all got to pull together."

"Against what, Buck? A feebleminded old man and a wore-out nigger?"

"Not *against* anybody Harry, we just got to pull together."

Harry reached under the shade of the floor lamp and pulled off the light. The room fell back into the blue-green TV dimness.

"Buck, Arron's an old man, like me, you don't have to pull or push him, all you got to do is wait—stand back and wait. All I know is this: no matter how old and rotten a

6 5

tree is, how near it is to fallin, the one who waits for it is a hell of a lot less likely to have it fall on him than all them that wants to pull, together or otherwise."

Before Buck could answer Mildred came into the room. She was a tall round-shouldered woman whose face was always flushed, her eyes perpetually bloodshot. The pressure of her blood seemed about to burst her face as if she had been hanging upside down for a long time.

"Harry you don't have to go," she said, standing in the doorway rubbing cream into her hands. "I just got the kitchen cleaned up. Now sit down and talk to me a little bit."

"Sorry Mildred, I just dropped out to bring Buck his medicine." He turned to Buck. "Man don't want to have his picture in *Life* magazine with a pain naggin him."

The chaplain felt free to get up when Mildred entered the room. As he did so Harry turned to him.

"Well Major it was nice to meet you. I'm sorry I didn't get to talk more with you, I've always wanted to hear a soldier-preacher's views on the Sixth Commandment." The wrinkles in Harry's face hung straight as thin blades; his dead grey eyes were fixed from behind them on the confused Major.

"Thank you sir," the chaplain answered bringing his hand up from habit of saluting, then stopping it halfway where it hung superfluous and limp.

"Mildred honey, you make him use his medicine." She flushed crimson in the dim light.

Buck stood by the door rubbing his head. As Harry passed him going out, he said, "You better doctor up good Buck, 'cause by my notion you got a hell of a lot more than tight nerves ahead of you the next few days."

Later, alone in his dark room, the chaplain watched a thin oar of moonlight that had been dipped through his

66

half-shaded window move slowly across the deep oak sheen of the floor. He could not sleep. The giant oak bed was too tightly made. It was too large, it bowed up in the middle. His weight had depressed it, yet at any moment he expected it to pop back up like a metal spring leaf, rolling him off onto the floor. His weight alone did not seem to be enough, he felt himself straining downward.

Finally he pushed back the tight covers and sat up on the edge of the bed, his body hunched over, his hands hanging down between his legs. *God's Army—God's Army —you don't retire from God's Army.*

The chaplain was frightened by the strange civilian world. Men like Harry Eddens to him were wild and unpredictable. They were savage because neither will of God nor opinion of man exercised authority over them. He felt civil order to be insecure outside the military chain of command; a feeling consistent with his inability to contemplate the soul free of the necessities of heaven and hell. Isolated in a civilian environment, he felt a real threat of civil and spiritual anarchy.

Now he was being thrust out into a society of terrorists like Harry Eddens. For the past year, ever since he had known of his certain retirement, the fear of it had been growing. He had not, until ordered to come to White Dove, been outside the gates of Rulley Air Base in eleven months.

His life, like the deepwater sea creatures', had always been confined by external pressure. He, like the ocean bottom fish and the rest of life to its own degree, did not contain himself. It was as if he had been born body and soul tightly wrapped in a winding sheet of circumstance. As a fat baby he had warped his mother's womb. His orphaned youth was spent in the closeness of New England hills and trees, where he walked narrow winding roads to small boarding school rooms. Then after that came Christ and overweight; sexually unattractive flesh and the Church;

and finally, the added girdle of ubiquitous loneliness which led him into the vise-grip of military procedure.

Sitting now on the edge of the uncomfortable bed in the strange house, he could feel the winding sheet beginning to unravel. Tiny bubbles of fright were forming in his blood, slowly building toward something like the spiritual bends. It was not a new feeling to him. Although the causes of its coming were different, the form of panic in his blood was no stranger.

To him, God was missing in action; not dead to be remembered; not alive to be felt; but missing out there somewhere at the apex of hope and prayer. His prayers had for a long time now been prayers for prayer; a calling of the repairman on the dead phone he was to repair.

Oh God hear this old soldier of the Cross, help me Lord to honor Thy name even ... even in retirement.

He raised his damp hands to his face, pressing it into the tight corner they formed and began his desolate monologue: *Oh God what is it about this place, these people, what is this thing that I am now to become a part of— lead me, oh God lead me. ... Now that my military ministry is ending, Lord is this a sign, this belated burial of a soldier, shall I too bury that part of my life ... oh hear my prayer lead me, lead me, oh God of my soul lead me. ...* With his fleshy face pressed into the heel of his hands, he sat rocking slightly on the edge of the bed. Thoughts and words dropped away from his petition until his mind held only: *lead me, lead me.* For a long time in the darkness he rocked and spun the repetition like a prayer wheel in his mind. *Lead me, lead me, lead. ...*

Then after a while he was still. He sat numb and empty waiting an acknowledgment that he knew was not to come.

He did not wait long. He had learned to avoid that kind of confrontation of faith. He turned instead to duty, the idolatry of faithless believers. I will give some thought to the funeral, he thought as he switched on the bed lamp

68

and stood up at the edge of the bed. The old wooden floor cracked loudly and he tensed his muscles, trying to hold some of the weight off his feet to stop the sound. Then he walked tenderly, as a man with sore feet walks, across the screaking floor and sat in an overstuffed chair. Even after he had been in the chair some minutes, occasional screaks grumbled from the floor.

He listened until the last indignant screak was absorbed by the approving stillness in the great house.

He felt the loneliness of the room sift down on him like dust from the ancient rafters. In this room Edith Harvest had lived and died in loneliness—a loneliness that imbued the very materials from which the room was made. As a smoke house, after years of disuse, hanging only spider webs and dust on its meat hooks, holds the scent of hickory smoke and sugar cure, so this room was pungent with loneliness.

He knew only so much, so many stingy, naked facts, facts given to him in isolation by Buck Harris. Now in this room at this moment he felt more. He felt the presence of a hidden, mystic, almost religious, undertow that could give those facts and left-handed hints meaning and order. It was there, just as it had been in Sarah Parker's empty but marked grave at the cemetery that afternoon. He had felt it as Buck and the gravedigger talked, a mystery self-consciously ignored by all except Harry Eddens, who also had revealed nothing.

In town, Harry, still sitting in the bullet-nosed Studebaker though it was now parked in front of his small dark house, could not pull his mind away from the Harvest mansion. He thought of the chaplain sitting upstairs in Edith Harvest's convent cell (now a guest room). Where she had lived and practiced with saint-like intensity her religious dedication to a man—Tom Parker, father of Ar-

6 9

ron, grandfather of the bones that were at this moment under military escort from the other side of the world, to be placed on Monday in the earth beside him.

Were she alive, Edith Harvest would see those bones placed next to his with the same humility born of a crippled dignity, that she had called upon to bury and mourn, first Mae Batton Parker, then Tom Parker.

Her faith was born on a July afternoon in 1903. This was the year Tom Parker began putting the Crows Foot under wire. In those years he lived on the thrill of new wire; with each mile of taut, gleaming barbed wire he felt more the absolute victor over his land. Land he had overrun all before him to possess, not own, but possess like a woman or the life of a man at his gunpoint. She knew this man and his legend but she was not yet converted. And why should she be? She worshiped still at the naive shrine of her father who had prospered in this new land. Had built a large country house, fully as large as the headquarters house on the Crows Foot, a house in which her coughing East Texas mother had lived one year and died leaving it and Edith with a comfortable aura of profound and dignifying sorrow.

Yet she was converted.

"Edith honey, bring Papa's wagon around to the back of the store," Gilbert Harvest shouted from the back room of the hardware store where he held a man at gunpoint. She went out front where the team was hitched and climbed up to the seat. She was thirteen and enjoyed "helping" at the store. Gilbert Harvest didn't want her to be at the store so much but realized how lonely the large house was for her.

She pulled the team up at the back door. She could hear her father's voice inside.

"And mister, when I hire a man to work I expect him to do the job he's hired for—and when I pay him in advance, by God I'll see to it that he does."

7 0

"Mister Harvest, you done the wrong thing turning that gun on me."

"Mister *you* done the wrong thing when you took my money then walked off the job."

They walked through the high back door into the hot July sun. The man at gunpoint was a tall hollow-chested half-breed with big widely spaced yellow teeth. His straight Mongolian hair hung over his forehead, covering one eye. He was sweating a greasy sweat.

"I ain't gonna get cut up by that wire, I'll do anything else, but I ain't standing by that wire. They're crazy out there, puttin a mule on the stretchers."

"Mister, you'll do what Tom Parker tells you to. I contracted to furnish wire and labor and I mean to do just that, if I have to keep this Winchester in your ear from now till Tom Parker runs you off. Get in the wagon."

They got in and Edith headed the team out of town the back way in the direction of the Crows Foot. They rode in rough jolting silence, the half-breed slipping a long dirty thumbnail slowly in and out of the wide gap between his front teeth.

When they saw the fencing gang working in the distance he began mumbling.

"You done the wrong thing—it was wrong to turn that gun on me."

Harvest did not listen. He was watching the work. A straight line of cedar posts, standing like dominoes on end extended out of sight to the north. They looked, without their wire, more like an endless single file of identical, evenly spaced soldiers, standing at rigid attention, isolated on an unexplored and otherwise uninhabited continent.

As the wagon pulled up near the crew someone a quarter of a mile up the fence shouted, "Stretch 'er up. Number one wire ready to stretch." The bright new barbed wire lay on the ground along the post. It still retained some of the curl from being rolled. As the men attached the

7 1

stretchers and gave the wire a preliminary pull to take out the loose slack it snaked through the grass, its sharp galvanized barbs ripping little tufts of grass with a sound of slowly tearing cloth. Tom Parker was at the other end where the wire had been tied to a center post stretch point.

Tom Parker handled the treacherous wire as he did all other things, with a savage, physically arrogant, brutal aggressiveness. This beyond maximum, frontal attack had no conception of physical limitation or impossibility. Patience was never with him, for to him it smelled of death and defeat. He was sickened by the sight, by the very existence of defeat, humiliated as a man even when he, by his own hand, administered it. Thus he was never the victor, for as he subdued man, he humiliated and defeated himself. It was this drive, this unyielding, relentless, absolute faith in the potency of man that had crushed the boundaries of the Crows Foot Ranch into the face of the earth. In this wilderness he found an adversary with ultimate courage and dignity and the gall of absolute confidence. And he loved it as a fighter loves that first taste of blood brought to his mouth by his opponent's fist.

Gilbert Harvest prodded the trembling half-breed out of the wagon.

"Now mister, you walk right up that fence to Mr. Parker and tell him you are here to work. And remember this," he prodded the air with the rifle, "you break and run and I'll waste the lead it takes to kill you."

The half-breed looked down at the wire slowly ripping through the grass, sawing a groove at the base of the post as it was drawn by. His eyes turned back to the rifle point and the pupils, colored like cloudy tea, looked smaller as the whites that held them enlarged. He made a final plea.

"Mister Harvest—they killed a horse out here this morning—the wire broke and it sawed off his front leg—don't make me do it." His eyes were drawn again to the ever-tightening saw-toothed wire.

7 2

"You just walk." He tossed the half-breed a new pair of hawk-billed fencing pliers. As he caught them it seemed to break the spell that the moving wire held over him. He turned and began walking toward the other man at the far end.

Gilbert Harvest followed him for about thirty steps and then stopped still holding the rifle on the other man. Edith relaxed and the spring seat of the wagon screaked a little as she saw her father silently put the rifle on safety, still pointing it at the back of the half-breed.

The wire was tight enough now to support its weight and it slipped reluctantly by the post about twelve inches off the ground, each barb snatched into the stringy cedar bark like passing fishhooks.

The men at the stretchers had taken up all the slack they could. They locked the block and tackle stretchers. One man tapped the ratchet lock into place tightly with the pointed hawk-beak side of his hammer-like fencing pliers, another hooked a large black mule to the pull line. As the mule leaned against the harness, the wire moved slowly.

The man with the rifle looked at the wire and saw that there was no more slack, that they were actually now stretching the metal. A man at the stretchers cracked a double strand of smooth tie-up wire across the mule's rump and inches more were gained.

Then as in sudden conversion, Gilbert Harvest, having witnessed the vision in wire, believed. *They're crazy out there it was wrong—you done wrong turnin that gun on me.* He tried to scream for them to stop but he could not, for he, like the half-breed, was caught in the spell, his attention snagged, like the bark and the grass on the barbs. He stood charmed by the dramatic intensity of the tightening wire.

At that moment the half-breed shattered. He ran to the wire and struck it with his fencing pliers. It snapped with a sharp metallic snap. A backlash recoil of tangling saw-

73

teeth and fishhooks whipped through the air whistling toward the still mesmerized Harvest with the sound of a thousand snake whip ends.

The first wire slashed his face, sawing into his skull, recoiling on through like an endless band-saw blade carrying with it in its teeth chunks of flesh and bone mixed with the now bloody cedar bark and range grass. Then the tangling spring-like mass hit him. He was in the same instant shredded to pieces, then bound together by the now still and bloody galvanized wire, the impotent rifle still cocked in the air at the exact angle as before.

Then in the tilting pause after death and before he fell to the grass, Tom Parker walked to the half-breed and buried the steel hawk-billed side of his fencing pliers in his skull, killing him instantly with a blow like that of a butcher to the head of a slaughter calf. Again like a butcher he had done it without passion, as he would reflexively kill a rattlesnake or a stinging mosquito.

It was in this instant that Edith Harvest was converted. She saw on that afternoon with only a flicker of time between, her father's murder and the vengeance for it— vengeance is mine saith the Lord. Her sorrow was displaced by a passion of dedication. To her it was a debt.

The bodies were taken to town, both victims of a fencing accident. Gilbert Harvest was buried beside his tubercular East Texas wife. The half-breed in the far corner of the graveyard, his grave marked with a thin cedar gate post cross—a cross later accidentally broken off at its rotted base by small and frightened boys.

Edith Harvest lived alone in the Harvest House and never left it except to bury Tom Parker and Arron's wife Sarah. She was away four years attending the funeral. She attended it at the church, at the graveyard—and finally four years at the headquarters house of the Crows Foot, where she mourned Tom and slept in the bed of Arron, who thought she was Sarah, for she was there with him

74

under his cloak of madness, a cloak which made her Sarah to him and him to her, his father.

These things floated in the lonely air of Edith Harvest's death room, as microscopic lint particles swim the air of dim rooms and are seen only as they pass through golden sun rays that sometimes in the late afternoon punch through leaky shingles or torn window shades.

VIII

Downstairs, though the chaplain did not know it, neither Buck nor his wife Mildred were asleep.

Buck sat in the large high-ceiling kitchen at a round wrought-iron, glass-topped table. He had taken a hot soaking bath and now sat in flannel pajamas and wool bathrobe before a dusty half-filled bottle of whiskey. He was staring down through the glass tabletop at his hairy white feet and thick horny toenails.

He had not poured any of the whiskey into the tall yellow water glass. He did not drink. This fact had made it almost impossible years ago to follow the medical advice which Harry Eddens had given him. But tonight his "troubles" as he and Mildred called them were especially bad.

Mildred had noticed at dinner. She felt mixed emotion when she saw the tension drawing his mouth into a tight-lipped pucker between coffee sips. Her flushed face had taken on a deeper shade as she had tried to soften the short almost rude way that Buck had answered the always polite questions of the chaplain. She was not trying to protect the chaplain, her interest was an unconscious, selfish one: a desire to conserve Buck's fury, to protect it from dissipation until she alone could open herself sexually to its discharge. At best, she knew it would be a wilting violence.

His "troubles" to her were a windfall. They generated in him a wrath she alone could not provoke. She goaded him always toward a point of rebellion, a rebellion whose outraged violence would burst open, briefly terrorizing her, until it was put down, smothered in her body.

She quietly hummed a wisp of some tune as she drew her bath, and later in the tub, she smiled a secret smile known only to women deluded by the belief that their existence is justified, secured in a man's need. She did not worry or even give a thought to the flaccid breasts that hung over her gutty and creased stomach. She washed under them just as she would other parts of her body she had never seen.

In the kitchen Buck poured about two inches of the whiskey into the glass. He stopped pouring, looked up, moving his eyes around the room quickly, then poured again, down the side of the tilted glass, letting air in the neck of the bottle as he poured, making no sound.

He sat holding the glass, doing lip service to his conscience. A conscience that had been silent now many years, yet the silence somehow pained him more than had the original discomfort. He thought again of Harry Eddens. The thought was a part of the ritual by which Buck convinced himself that the drink he was about to take, in direct opposition to his beliefs, could be rationalized on medical grounds. He even used the same ministerial illustration that had affirmed those beliefs in absolute temperance. "The body is the castle of the soul." Therefore, a healthy body is good and whatever it takes to maintain or especially restore a body to health must also be blessed, or at least not soul-condemning.

It was Harry Eddens who had suggested the theory to

77

Buck. It was not that Harry believed either particular part of it but he did believe a good shot of strong whiskey would help Buck when he suffered the "troubles."

Harry Eddens was probably the only example of a genuine humanitarian the town could produce. He was neither a doctor nor a pharmacist, yet he was called Doctor Harry by the Mexican section hands who worked on the railroad and lived in the small junky houses across and near the track. He had delivered many of the slippery dark-eyed babies who had been born in the brownish-yellow, black-trimmed railroad houses of the Santa Fe.

The State Pharmacy Board had visited him many times on suspicion of administering drugs without a license yet not once could they produce a witness even among the many shiftless part-time cowboys headquartered around the Eddards Hotel coffee shop. And for good reason. Many if not all of them at one time or another had been let in the drugstore after it closed and led to the back where Harry opened the small refrigerator in which he kept cattle vaccine, removed a vial of penicillin from way in the back, loaded a dull needle and with excessive and unwarranted brutality (born not of malice or sadism but rather of an almost comic fatherly chastisement), shot a large dose into their calloused but tender backsides. It was to cure the "Johnson Street cough" or "sportin house flu" as he called it. He expected and treated it in almost epidemic proportions each year during and right after the annual Amarillo rodeo and fat stock show. His "victims" were not always farmers' sons or cowboys, a fact that made several leading members of the town's civic and religious organizations uncomfortable when he chose to attend their various meetings. His proposals either at the Lions Club or City Council meetings received courteous attention and long and serious consideration. A certain wry sparkle in his eye had dampened as many collars as the lack of air conditioning in any of the public gathering places.

Buck felt the glass now warm in his hand. He had decided not to add any water to the whiskey so he would not have to get up later in the night and though he would never admit it, he liked the taste and the flooding fumes in his head and the invading warmth in his stomach. Though Buck could not, without doing what he considered damage to Baptist doctrine, he would have liked to thank Harry for that day he had called the druggist to the back of the store and after some talking about the new school plan, got around to saying:

"You know Harry, I haven't been feeling up to snuff myself for about two weeks."

"What's wrong, Buck? The Ford Motor Company sold out to Chevrolet?" Harry drove a Studebaker. He put down the coffee cup he had carried from the soda fountain where he had been having morning coffee with Harvy Ellins the barber. "Harvy tells me that Ford is using up all the old jeep springs they had left over from the war in their new model this year, and that's the reason they ride so rough."

"Well maybe so, mine seemed a little rough on me this morning," Buck said.

"Buck, you must be sick, I never thought I'd see the day when you took the name of the Ford Motor Company in vain."

"Well, I don't know Harry, but either I'm about to give birth or I've got the piles. I don't hurt so much but it makes me edgy as hell."

They were standing at the back of the store before a white swinging door that led back to the prescription room. Harry walked through the door holding it open for Buck without looking back. He was reining in a runaway smile that had gotten away when he thought of Buck Harris giving birth. As they entered the small room lined with shelves of multicolored and various-sized bottles, Harry said, "Drop your pants Buck and I'll take a look." The acrid smell of the drugs topping the base antiseptic odor

79

frightened Buck a little, but he did as Harry asked, bending over as if looking for something small on the clean floor.

"Yep, you got 'um." Buck straightened up, tucked in his shirt and turned to Harry.

"Well, have you got anything for it, I mean some patent medicine or something? I don't want to go into the doctor with something like this," he said from under a deathmask face.

Harry had gone to a small sink and was washing his hands even though he had not touched Buck.

"It's nothing to be ashamed of Buck, happens all the time, I used to have 'um myself years ago from standing on my feet so much. You'd be surprised how many cases there are right here in town."

"What do you mean be surprised? How many?" Buck asked greedily.

"Well, I'm not saying—just like I'm not saying to anybody about you, most people think it's kinda personal." He dried his hands and picked up his cigarette. "Now I am gonna explain what it is and how to cure 'um.

"I'd call what you got a case of chronic hemorrhoids, that means that ever once in a while you get the piles—but sounds better in case you feel like explainin it to Mildred. Now," he took a last drag off the inch-long cigarette, blew the smoke up into the air diagonally to his face from the lowered corner of his mouth, "the main thing that causes 'um is tight nerves—and then they turn right around and cause tight nerves. It's like a flea biting a dog's tail. The dog snaps at the flea and gets part of his own tail and he thinks it's the flea biting again so he bites harder and round and round he goes." Harry lit another cigarette, offered one to Buck, who was already smoking, then looked over the swinging door out into the front of the store to see if any customers were waiting and if they were, if they were within hearing distance.

8 0

"Now," he turned back to Buck, "what we got to do is break the circle, in other words, relax your nerves." Buck had begun to sweat and the galling stinging itch he felt was getting worse.

"Now, you're not gonna like one part of this prescription and probably think you're too old for another part, but I'll tell you right now, its way-yonder-and-gone better than having an operation. Because when they get through cutting on you, you'll sure enough think you're giving birth, only not to something simple like a baby or a watermelon, it'll be more like a roll of barb wire with broken beer bottles and rusty tin cans."

Harry was laying it on pretty heavy but he felt he had to because of the fact that Buck was a deacon in the Baptist Church and didn't believe in drink. Another reason he was being a little hard on him was in gentle, wry, harassment innocent of any personal vindictiveness for Buck's having bid against him when the old man from whom Harry had bought the drugstore building had sold it. He knew Buck and knew that had Buck succeeded in buying he would have been a good landlord, probably better than the old man. It was just that Buck *wanted* to be landlord. Harry recognized this desire in Buck for what it was and understood it. Buck himself did not understand it or even realize it existed.

Harry walked to a back shelf and took down a brown medicine bottle with a red skull and crossbones on the label.

"Now, Buck, I am not going to lie to you, this is whiskey, straight bourbon whiskey. The Bible says, 'take a little wine for the stomach's sake,' well this is a little whiskey for the sake of something else."

"Harry you know I don't drink."

"Hell, Buck, you arn't a dope eater either, why don't you tell the dentist that the next time you get a tooth pulled—tell him you arn't a dope head and to pull the

8 1

tooth without giving you a pain killer." This stopped Buck long enough for Harry to finish giving him the proposed cure.

"Now, when you get home tonight I want you to do three things. I want you to take a hot sitz bath, just as hot and long as you can stand it, then pour about an inch and a half of this 'medicine' in an ice tea glass—you can put some water in it if you want to—drink it down then go to bed." Harry paused and looked at Buck.

"I thought you said three things."

"I'm coming to that. Now when I said to go to bed I didn't mean exactly to bed, I mean go to your wife. Go to her like it was your wedding night. In other words I don't mean once, I mean as many times as you are man enough and then one more. You do as I tell you and you'll be surprised how the world looks to you in the morning." He looked over the swinging door again, saw a customer waiting at the patent medicine counter and walked out, leaving Buck sweating, holding the brown bottle, feeling the cool breeze created by the swinging door as it fanned his hot face.

Now as Buck sat at the kitchen table in the old Harvest mansion, to him the new Harris place, his face was flushed from the hot bath, his bald head glowed like a fresh bruise. He no longer felt under the town. He was on top of it, the finest house, Mayor, President of the School Board, even though he had no children, and landlord to a dozen city and farm tenants. He rolled the glass between the flat of his hands. He thought, dear God I hope Tom Parker can see me from wherever he is, how I would rub his nose in it. I'd housebreak him to my house, my town: *heel Tom Parker. You've done it again in my town Tom Parker and I'd rub his nose in it.* Now he could think of Tom Parker and hate him without the pain of remembering why. *The last of the Parkers—with their nose rubbed in it—lead them to the grave I'll lead them to the grave—Ronnie on Mon-*

*day and some Monday or Saturday Arron will dry up and
I will pull him off that land like a leech off a sow's belly.*

He drank down the warm whiskey. As he sat there
feeling it run distant brush fire through him he heard the
upstairs floor creak out the chaplain's careful footsteps.
He got up, took the glass to the deep sink where he rinsed
the whiskey out of it and ran enough water down the drain
to wash away any possible odor.

He then turned from the kitchen, and without desire,
excitement or any harbinger of anticipation, he went to
his bathed and powdered wife, who lay in her passionate,
expectant lubrication; going as mechanically as he had
turned off the kitchen light.

IX

Light from the high moon lay on the Crows Foot grass like flour dust. Inside its splintered old mansion the darkness had jelled as if some chemical agent had been added to the atmosphere. Loneliness and fear had become a black gelatin filling the house and oozing out onto the land.

Arron lay in the thickened night of his room, wounded by the memory of the thing he had done this morning to Smith. He was very still, listening to the Negro moving through the rooms below, waiting to remember morning and what he had done.

I was a child, he thought. I will not lose Smith, he will grumble around down there but I will not lose him. He can't be mad now, *I was a child.* When he laughed *I was a child.* Only Papa can piss off the porch. Papa dead in the fire and him the one who told about the drovers and the trail boss gettin all the new hands up in the middle of the first night out, "Wake up and piss, the world's on fire." *I was a child* standing there lookin at the sun coming up waiting to eat takin a thin high-arching leak off the front porch, and Smith laughed—he tried to hide it but when Papa came out the door and jerked me up like a sack of

84

feathers and turned me upside down like he was pouring something out of a joint of pipe and rubbed my nose in it while the mud was still hot and the foam was on it— Smith laughed *when I was a child.*

Arron had not laughed this morning, fifty years later, standing at the edge of the rotting front porch, as he had almost without exception every morning since the death of Tom Parker, relieving himself at sunrise. Watching the dark stream he would sometimes think of all that happens to a man between the time he had to hold it down to keep from hitting himself in the eyes and the time he has to hold it up to keep from wetting his feet.

He was not thinking of Smith, who had this morning, as every morning since the only laying hen made her nest under the front porch, crawled under it after the egg for Arron's breakfast. But this morning when Smith's grey head nudged out from under the rotten porch, Arron with the sun in his eyes thought, "Wake up and piss, the world's on fire," and aimed the brown stream at that black silver head that was to him gold in the light of sunrise.

Smith ducked back under the porch.

"Arron—Arron!—now you done it, you showed yo true self Arron you done a mean thing—I'se gettin this egg for yo breakfass—me and dis hen been workin all night so's you can eat—workin all night while you up dere savin yo water—you done a mean thing Arron." *But it wasn't a mean thing because I didn't laugh, he laughed. If Papa had seen him laugh he would know what it feels like with the foam still on it—he knows now even without Papa, and I didn't laugh—he won't be mad tomorrow and I'll miss him, I won't even think about the fire. I'll ask him about Mother only I'll call her Mae so we can talk man to nigger —in fact in the morning I'll just call her black Mae so we can talk nigger to nigger. Then he can't be mad because he knows I didn't laugh—how could I laugh when the world was on fire?*

Arron jerked his feet up quickly and rammed his narrow

old rump out into the rancid darkness of the quilts. The bad times came at night. In the daylight he could hold the fear, he could contain it within the limits of what he could see and touch. He did not look at the things which hurt nor did he touch them. He learned quickly never to walk up or down the stairs with his eyes open.

Do not see the stairs, do not see the landing halfway or the tall wide window there that looks out to the open North pasture. Hold the rail and step over the landing to the second flight of steps. Do this and you will not see her lying there in the blood of death and birth. Do not touch or look at the dust-covered Mexican saddle in the saddle shed and the charred body of Papa will not rise up out of the blackened grass.

But in the night the skinny yellow-eyed coyote of fear was loose to prowl all space. Free to hang limp behind the ragged and rotting drapes or lie stiff and cold in the bed beside him.

He had done that to Smith this morning and now the punishment was coming. He lay wounded by the act, yet painless, waiting for the shock to melt away leaving only the pain of that punishment.

Tonight it will be the fire. Maybe it will be the fire, it is the bad one maybe the bad one will happen tonight. He lay sweating now waiting for the vision to begin.

Then he thought, to hell with Smith, I can't wait, I will commit this act upon myself. And he forced his mind out like a running plunge over a high cliff, a plunging out to meet an echo.

First I was a child when Smith laughed. Before the fire, I will think before the fire, before it enough that maybe the sun will come before it does. There is Mother Mae dead now with the softness gone with her all before Papa and the fire. It was about the softness, Papa said, "It's that damn dry rot southern sloppiness, Mae. We live in a house that would sink out of sight anywhere you can think of

86

'back home.' I sent for the trees, I've done everything but transplant the county graveyard from 'back home.' Do you want me to do that, to fence off a patch out back and haul 'um in?"

He said it in the fall of that year before she took her bed out to the bunk house to be with Smith.

"Mae, when you come to Texas you come to a new land and I've hammered it out like a silver dollar on an anvil, flattenin it and rubbin it jest tryin to make you a hand mirror and all you do is hold it up and look straight through it like it was clear glass, right back at that damn county graveyard. And if that's what you want well then I'll do my best to see that you have a clear sight but leave the boy alone, don't get that dry rot started in him. Arron's gonna stand on this land with his legs set proud and wide enough apart to let this wind whip around his man parts. I'll cut him myself before I'll let him set cross-legged around the house with the smell of mildew on him. I seen very few bulls that's worth a damn stand around chewing a cud and as long as I can still handle him he's not gonna stand around chewing some dry, worthless raggedy ass notion of what he missed by not being sired by some gentleman planter. You yourself know as well as I do if he had, he'd probably be so inbred he couldn't find his butt with both hands and three nigger guides."

Arron was seven that fall sitting at the dinner table in a tall heavy chair from which his short legs and boy feet were suspended inches from the broad waxed oak floorboards, feet that never swung relaxed and idle under the table. Sitting there with the tension manifesting itself in his rigid legs, he saw that flicker of sadness make her eyes cloudy like tea sometimes does, then it would clear and they would finish dinner and talk of other things. And Arron not knowing what it was could feel a pull in his stomach, a pull of disappointment, a boy sadness like fear. It was the mother side of the same feeling he got when disappointment and benevolent exasperation showed in Tom Parker's eyes when Arron hurt himself and lost the battle of tears. Even now Arron because he was twisting with fear in the bed that had been Tom's felt in his old stomach the shame and final defeat that his father had seen and fought in him as a boy.

Tom had been afraid that a congenital rot was in him and watched for its signs, sometimes striking at shadows as he had done at branding time in that year Arron was eight. It was the same year in the winter of which Smith, forever after to be called Bobtail Smith, drove himself down to raw and fundamental courage in the snow. That same snow which killed all but the Crows Foot herd leaving the others where they had drifted against fences and stopped to freeze, packed so tightly together that the blowing snow drifted over them smothering those who would defeat the cold by self-generated mutual body heat, leaving them there swollen and stiffly entangled, stiff now in death. They unfroze to emerge like dead and rotting stumps and roots as the white swamp of melting snow drained from around them. It was in the spring of that year, the spring that seemed like fall because cow death and stillness filled the land. That spring when you could walk a hundred and seventy miles along the railroad right-of-way fence without stepping off the matted hair of bloated, death-stretched, rotting cowhide. Only the Crows Foot was left uncobbled by cowflesh, an unnatural gap in the highways of death that crossed the land from east to west along the fences.

When the Santa Fe passenger trains crossed the Crows Foot that spring the Negro porters would pass down the aisles saying, "You can lower yo windows for the next twenty miles, you can lower yo windows," and the news butcher would pass with sandwiches and candy, "Better get it now, there's sixty more miles of it jest ahead, better get it now," and he was also selling oil of clove and pine

88

for the handkerchiefs which all of the ladies and some of the men held to their noses.

It was a silent spring, silent as growing grass or the echo of falling snow and Tom Parker felt some sacrilege in the noise and wild bellowing that spring.

Dust clouds rising from the noisy, crowded corrals of the Crows Foot could be seen for miles in the empty and solemn spring sky as they worked the calves and shipped the bobtailed herd.

Arron was eight and he saw the search for defeat for the first time in the eyes of Tom Parker during the spring roundup of the herd. He was eight and tended the branding fire. He dodged the running men in the thick dusty air that hung like smoke over the milling pens of cattle, air hot and heavy with the acrid white fumes, smoke from the thick winter hair burning between the glowing branding irons and the seared flesh imprint of a crow's foot they left on the bawling fighting calves. The smell of Lysol, blood and pine tar was sharp against the full heavy pungence of dust and fresh manure.

He carried the scrap wood to the slit-trench fire. Twenty branding irons heated side by side in a row lying half-buried in a long shallow grave of coals. He was to keep a wet gunny sack over the handles, so that when Tom came running to the fire in that half run, half walk of absolute urgency, the handle of the iron he took would not be too hot to hold.

And he forgot, forgot the handles and the wet sack. The sack had dried and was now smoldering to white ashes as it lay draped across the handles. Arron was at the dehorning chute collecting the bloody horns, watching the spurting fine sprays of blood and collecting the best horns to make a fox horn. A hunting horn like the one Mae had told him about, the one his grandfather had used when he rode behind his hounds, the one he had as an old man carried into the war, the one he was drawing a short old

89

man's breath to blow at Atlanta when the bullet from a shoemaker's apprentice from Boston killed him.

Arron remembered the fire and returned just as Tom grabbed up a hot iron handle. He dropped it and jerked Arron up off his feet in the same motion almost without breaking the harried half walk, half run.

"Arron-boy can't a man count on you!" he shouted holding the boy up by the shoulders close to his face. He held him like that for a long moment. Arron could see the pinpoints of sweat soaking up through the dust on his father's face and the thin line of slimy dust mud on his teeth. Then he dropped him. "Get to the house, get on to the house, get to your mother."

And that was all, but for Arron now twisting in the bed, an old man himself, it was more. He jerked his head from side to side like a man whose arms were bound to his sides trying to sling a spider off his forehead. With helpless jerks he tried to sling off the darkness, the stifling, frightening night. But he failed, his anguished thrashing was lost in the gelatin blackness.

Now I will see it, this is not the happy time. The visions would not allow even a contrast and now relentlessly, they gained control, depriving him of the satisfaction he had sought in self-inflicted agony.

Plunged back into the dusty corrals he heard, "Maybe you can help her with Smith, surely, undoubtably you can do that much." In a space of time no longer than that space between the dates of birth and death on a simple tombstone, Arron saw it in Tom's eyes. Saw there, though he would not understand it until later and even then only in part, the beginning of defeat. To Arron who then looked up into those eyes that crouched deep back under the ledges of craggy brows thick and wild with long hairs that were as black and strong as hog bristles, it was only anger. From these cliff-side caves, blue flames pointed out, two identical piercing blue cones. Yet at the moment he grabbed Arron up off his feet they flickered as if some of the corral dust had gotten in and passed through the flames causing a momentary orange sparkling fuzziness.

It was anger and pride and the harassed wounded fear that comes to the eyes of fathers when they see in sons not yet men the gaping possibility that they may never be. It is an instant of hatred for an enemy of their pride, against which they find themselves impotent.

But to Arron, who was eight, it was only disgust, a painful disappointed look of betrayal.

Even later, when he knew that the look had come to Tom Parker's eyes only partially because of his failure at the irons, he still felt in his gut projections of defeat.

Tom had that spring felt the grassland trembling in the empty silence. The blizzard-stricken ranchers, even some of the forty who had come with him and pushed the rivers of cattle north, who now owned surrounding land, were listening to the drummers; listening in the stillness and despair of empty ranges, listening to the plow salesman and watching the quotations of wheat prices.

Tom offered them seed bulls but they avoided his eyes, listening more and more to the plow salesmen. And the actions of Smith in the snow had its effect. The Negro had saved the Crows Foot.

"Let ole Tom Parker say what he wants to about Jeff Davis and his raggedy ass but that nigger sure as hell saved the shootin match for him. You'll notice it wasn't him out walking three days cuttin fences ahead of his herd. There wasn't no hide froze off his nose when the sun come out."

The old blood stirred in the southern refugees, a haunting nostalgia for the old days and country. For the time and land where black hands built a perpetual stack of fists, a column of fists which formed the black spine of their remembered South. They were lonely for the past, and for the perpetual boyhood of that prewar South where father slavery protected and provided. Where they roamed the hills in adolescent innocence riding and hunting and playing house to full scale on fairyland plantations that were briefly real. The sacrifice that Smith had made turned their heads back and they looked and longed for something out of their youth, something before youth. A loneliness felt by troubled and defeated men who stand alone in a long hall which is hung with tall dark portraits of their blooded ancestors.

In that spring they stood around outside the bank and listened to the plow salesmen who came to the Harris hardware, looking at pictures of the giant steam tractors and bright red turning plows.

Arron even then, carrying the burden of hollowness which Tom's eyes had cast upon him, could also feel the difference in his mother. And this too reflected in Tom's eyes, this drawing away, not from him or Arron or even from Texas, but a shrinking of herself inside. Tom knew it was the sickness yet he forced himself to fail to notice it. He would not notice the long walks among the trees, the long slow walks when she would closely examine each trunk as though she looked for some carved initial, and how without a hint of realization she would at times refer to the bunkhouse, where Smith and the other cowhands slept, as "the quarters."

Yet when Smith was frozen, and during that spring and summer when she nursed him, her life seemed to expand within her again. She abandoned the trees and tended the Negro. She moved a cot to a small room in the bunkhouse and bathed his rotten flesh.

He lay dying all spring. She allowed no one else to tend him. Though she had not been past the garden out to the corrals six times in the ten years they had lived in the headquarters house she now went four times a day with a freshly scrubbed lard bucket and a pancake spatula.

Arron, sent away from the branding, met her as he walked from the pens toward the house. She did not notice the tear marks which ran down his face like first rain on dusty windows.

She went directly to the barn where the three range cows which were brought in daily from the grass were penned. Each day three different cows were brought to the dark barn and five times each day she went with the lard pail and spatula to kneel in the damp dust of the barn floor to scoop up the fresh green manure. Arron followed her, watching as she carefully filled the pail avoiding any dirt from the floor and meticulously picking a foreign straw off of it like a hair from warm butter. Long yellow poles of sunlight slanted through the dusky dark from cracks in the wall like magnified wheat straws. The air was warm and damp and sweet with cow breath and evaporating urine and heavy with humid dust.

She rose as if from picking jamberries, turned to the door and saw Arron in the bright frame of the doorway.

"Papa sent me to help with Smith," he said into the dimness, "he thought you could use me."

"Why sweetie pie, how nice, but a man like you shouldn't be around the women and the house in the workin day—why your father must be foolin you. Now you just run on back to the menfolk, and when I get finished in the quarters we'll have a wonderful supper. I'm makin hush puppies, you love hush puppies and if you whisper to them just right 'hush, puppie' they'll wag their tail." She stepped outside through the frame of light. "Won't that be fun? Now close the door for your mother."

Outside she wagged the green-smeared spatula at him, "Remember, Hush! You hush-puppie!" She turned and was gone. Arron waited by the door until she was past the garden and then followed, wiping his nose and streaked crusty cheeks on his small and boney hands.

He followed her to the bunkhouse and stood just outside the screen door watching her work over the mummified Negro. She washed him carefully with warm soapy water,

93

removing first the wrappings, then the green manure that had accomplished its six hours of analgesic action. It colored the water like split pea soup, the blood and bits of black skin floating on the surface. Arron could see the raw flesh around the Negro's mouth and eyes and saw also that one of his ears had sloughed off and the scab around the dark little hole was knotty and rough like dried prune skins.

Now he was clean and the low, constant, sunken moan seemed to quiet a little. She reached into the deep pocket of her apron and mined out a blue jar of mentholated ointment. She removed the lid, laid it aside on the bed and with her forefinger, gently smeared some of the cold grease under the Negro's nose, then she changed hands with the jar and with the same finger of the other hand she smeared some of it under her own nose with two motions of the finger like a man smoothing a ruffled mustache. She replaced the top, wiped both fingers on the apron and dropped the jar back into the deep pocket.

The Negro started to moan again as she dipped up a handful of the green manure, holding it like clay on an artist's palette, and began softly applying it to his swollen and raw wounds. As she gently plastered a thick layer of the mulch over his face and ears she did not listen to the sunken, hollow, open-throated moan. The smarting coolness of the ointment reddened her eyes and the tears came freely now. And though they were artificial and born not of grief or pain, their hot wetness performed as a solvent, melting away the present, dissolving the hardness of what she was doing and where she was, diluting it into the warm liquid past, until she sat again as a late-born doll on the gaunt knee of her father.

"Papa, where do niggers come from?" and the old man, for he was old in those days even before the war and the cobbler's minnie ball, shifted her on his knee where he sat in a great leather chair before an empty fireplace that had been scrubbed pale grey.

He sat before that summer fireplace and she asked him, "Where do you get new niggers when you need 'um?"

The old man pulled her deeper into his lap and smoothed the ruffles of her dress and looked at her long yellow curls thinking that they must look like the wide shavings Jesus made as he pulled a wood plane over a long straight piece of clean yellow pine when he worked in the carpenter shop.

"Well sugar pie, when we need new darkies we go way down in the black swamp and when the weather is just right there's a black mud down there that we make 'um out of."

"Do you make baby ones too?"

"Yes sugar, most times we make baby ones."

"Will you make me a baby one, will you the next time you go make me a baby one for my own? A high yeller like Mammie Wide's Spitney has?"

"Well now honey I can't promise, we never know when the weather is gonna be just right and it takes a special kind of weather for that high yeller, like they have in the North. But we'll see, when the weather gets just right, we'll see."

Arron watched her finish the half-inch layer of poltice, smoothing it here and there with gentle swirls like icing a cake. Then the green manure deathmask was finished and he turned from the door as she began wrapping the Negro in long white strips of cheese cloth.

Later, after the corrals were quiet and empty and the branding irons had been taken from the shallow grave of embers and lay cold beside it on the hoof-powdered ground, night came to help time absorb the aura of noise and frantic animal action and excitement that hung like warmth in the silence, a silence broken now only by the sluggish buzzing of flies over the pile of horns which lay on the ground around the blood spattered dehorning chute. Arron sat with Tom alone, the two of them at the long table of slab oak which, had it been strapped with heavy black iron hinges could have doored some thick walled cathedral. Sitting alone without Mae as they had done each meal since she had moved a pallet to the bunkhouse, with the table bare between them except for the little clutter of dishes and utensils by each of them and by the place set for her, a starving loneliness grew like distance between them.

Arron could smell the faint odor of Lysol and pine tar that lingered on Tom from the corrals; a reminder of his own treachery. He could not meet those eyes, and his father, knowing now that he had struck at a shadow, realized that his outrage was at youth.

Looking across the bare oak now at this frail unsexed doggie a new sadness came to Tom Parker. And Arron, the food sickening him and the sweat of guilt on him, could not look at the eyes; eyes which could convey no other meaning to him than dull endured pain, that pain of endurance, not of the wound, the event which caused the disappointment but the reflection of its control, that secondary pain of the long suffering, dogged endurance of defeat.

Yet later deep in that same night Arron tried. Compelled by a pressure in his chest as if he had half thrown up a hot pocket of air and it was lodged between his lungs, he left his bed and ran from the house; away from the inverted snarling of Tom's pendulous snoring.

He ran barefoot and frail past the bunkhouse where he heard the sunken moan of the Negro grow softer like dying wind through the glassless windows of an empty house. Past the garden and to the branding pens and the shallow grave of coals which glowed still under their cracked grey frosting of ash. The corrals were chill and silent, even the the flies roosted, cooled to stiffness and grounded for the night.

Arron was sick and scared as if he were waiting for a punishment. He stirred the coals and the heat chilled him as they responded to the rough fondling. He buried fourteen of the cold Crows Foot irons in the deep embers and waited, in desperate faith, not knowing until later that he had heated a glowing red iron for each of the trees.

Those same trees which now in the after years claw at the moon-washed sky around the dark house of shadows, trees bearing still the scar of a seared Crows Foot. Though they are dead now, it grew then, scabbing over first with a knotty rope of bark covering the brands then in the following years upward, from the waist-high to an eight year old boy, preceding him in the wet years, to belt-high to a tall man. That man who flounders awash now in a stormy night-sea of visions in that same house of shadows, surrounded by fourteen dead trees that would grasp the moon.

X

Aʀʀᴏɴ waited for morning. His gnarled body no longer fit the matted lumpy mattress. The rancid quilts were heavy with body smells and accumulated night moistures.

He lay still and unblinking as if he had been slammed down hard against the earth and waited in that long instant of numbness for feeling to return; to warm up like an old radio clicked on to receive the pain that was already in the air.

He blinked and listened to the tacky night mucus in the corner of his eyes make a faint elastic snapping sound in the darkness. *It was mornin, and wasn't too long till light when I woke up. The visions was mostly about Papa and Mae and that was good; must not be much sin to piss on a nigger. I always thought about Sarah when mornin come, when it come around before the sun did.*

Though he was speaking to himself of *was* and *yesterday* he was actually backing into today, walking backward with his rump stuck out a little. He began remembering, setting the time and place. From his memory he pulled the furnishings and set them out on the grass like stagecraft, then waited for his dreams to take place among them.

When he could wait no longer, he began telling it, telling himself a story of Sarah to prime the dream. When he said "used to" think of Sarah, it was the actual beginnings of today's thinking of her. With his foresight gone in the fire, each repeated remembering came first like a vivid memory of a dream, then melted into the dream itself.

It was the revival meeting, he thought. The outdoor meetin, the one where Papa started gettin God and the grass mixed up. And after the meetin, with Sarah alone in the grass, not far from where the wooden benches that they hauled out from the church basement sat facin the leaning pulpit under that cottonwood tree, where she still is; then I knew he was right. I walked her out in the darkness and the lights were all out around the meetin place except one, those tall lights on poles I had soaked all day in oil and stuck up around it so we could have flare-light for the meetin, flare-light that smoked and shook shadows over the hymn books and everybody holding them up at different angles tryin to get the light on his own book, and then a gust of wind would come along and blow the yellow light off the flares leaving only a little blue around the wicks and nobody could see his words and the hymns died down low like the wind blew them off too; then the wind would quiet and you could feel everybody relax their eyes and the singin would get louder.

And even when they was almost blowed out and we was almost in the dark, you could always hear her like light, not some flickering light but some strong thin silver light like a star. You could tell that her Papa was a preacher, that she was a seminary girl and could sing in the dark, book or no book, she knew all the third verses even when old Mr. Adkins our song leader didn't.

Arron felt a scrap of something stuck in the back of his throat. As he waited, he began to cough, slowly at first,

99

then harder. Finally after a spasm of dry hacking coughs he relaxed and put his crooked old finger down his throat to scrape out what might have been a hair from a pony's mane or a piece of dry grass, but in fact was a coarse strand of his coming dream.

It was fall revival time when Sarah came to White Dove. The roundups had been made and those who now planted wheat, on what Tom later called their naked and obscene earth, had combed shallow seed furrows into thousands of acres of brown land, marks that covered the county like those left by a garden rake pulled through shallow dust. "I'll give it back to the Kiowas before I'll scratch around on the bare ass of the earth," he had said to the visiting preacher and without a pause in conversation the old revivalist translated it to "naked and obscene earth." Tom Parker liked it. It sounded his contempt more fully and he used it until his death. In exchange for the oath, he gave the revival preacher the use of the cottonwood knoll for night camp meetings. During the week of meetings, and at the hands of the old preacher who he said had a good hard saddle ass because he had been a circuit rider, Tom gave his soul over to God.

This was after Smith was well and Mae had moved back to the house and had found the church.

Her new work at sinlessness and the Crows Foot money built the White Dove First Baptist Church, in which Arron was baptized and repented his inheritance of a dirty mouth. Arron had found that good hard cursing when he worked with Tom seemed to calm the fear that sometimes made jagged edges bristle around his father's eyes.

Arron also knew the hymns, even without the sheaf of yellowed and brittle pages that had lain forty years in the dust at his bedside. Had the dream demanded, as it sometimes did, he would have, from the bed, bellowed out in song, coughing and singing until Smith came and prayed him quiet.

At revival time that fall, winter was hanging back in the

north. The hot Texas winds had blown themselves out, making room for a winter that had not yet come.

The Baptists gathered by torch light on a knoll in the center of the Crows Foot Ranch to hear an old circuit rider turned evangelist preach about love. To sing hymns in a dark vastness that dwarfed their singing and to sit listening with their feet on thick grass saved for winter pasture, under a single cottonwood tree. And in the night when a wind took away the torch light and swept the hymns away like smoke, two voices rang strong in the darkness among the muffled applause of the leaves. When the breeze died, only one old man started to sing again and was silenced by a sharp poke from his wife.

It was the night Tom got God mixed up with the grass and gave his heart to Jesus. With the smell of burning kerosene in the air, and the intimate feeling of smallness, even helplessness, he felt while sitting in the group listening to their frail hymns retreat before the wind, a compassion worked in him. He somehow felt God to be outmatched, that apart from justice, apart from good and evil, the fight was unfairly matched. He did not associate the dark sky or the wind or the vast openness with God but with some evil created for the express purpose of humiliating them.

During the invitation on the final night of the week of meetings, a week poorly attended and unfruitful to the Cause, Tom Parker came to the aid of God. The wind stilled before him and he walked like a man into a brawl down the grass aisle to the old preacher who hobbled round the leaning pulpit and met him halfway.

It was during his testimony that the grass became God. With the preacher beside him he faced the small crowd of people and confessed his sins.

"This grass you're standin on is my God and as you all know I have done hard things to get it and keep it, well like the reverend says, his God made it—your God made my God and I been worshipin second hand. Well I'm here tonight willin to admit His proper ownership of it and all the rest, I'll take Him as owner if He'll take me as tenant. No man has taken it from me and no man will, but if God wants it, all He has to do is kill me and I'll be ready to settle the books. Until then I'll try to run things accordin to His likin."

The old preacher said, "Amen, amen, Brother Tom, amen," and they all went to their knees in the grass to pray. The preacher and many of the congregation bowed their heads and looked at the grass for a long moment as the yellow flickering light gave it movement, before they closed their eyes tightly and prayed, feeling even then the cushion of it under their knees.

Mae wept as she knelt and Arron beside her felt a strange disillusionment. He felt for a moment Tom Parker's loss of sovereignty. Yet he did not feel it strongly, it was only Sarah he felt strongly. Even now he did not hear the words of the prayer over his father; he was fighting the desire to open his eyes and look at her.

She was kneeling in the front, close to the old circuit preacher who had fathered her late, after his saddle days, her long thick hair hanging over her shoulders and around her face catching and holding the yellow light around her face like a veil.

After the prayer they stood up and sang the closing hymn, and again the wind took it away. All the voices except Arron's and Sarah's were swept out into the night.

During these times (and they had been happening for a week now) Arron felt a deep sensual harmony as if her voice were folding him into it and lifting him up. He felt himself get lighter as if the grass under his feet was pushing him up into the night sky, as if the song were singing him. And since Mr. Adkins, the song leader, had told everybody to face into the center during the singing, "So the wind can't discord us," Arron had watched her face, and she his, and he sang the word "love" with a new and frightening meaning, a meaning unknown even to him.

At the end of the service he left Mae and went for his horse as he had done each night of the meeting, to ride alongside the preacher's buggy and show him the way back to the main gate. To do that and try to talk to her, which he could not, and watch her silhouette against the soft light from the buggy lamps.

Smith was sitting in the Parker buggy waiting for Mae and Tom, saying good night to people as they passed. Tom's horse was tied to the back of the buggy and Arron shoved it over a little to untie his own.

"Yo daddy's callin," Smith said. "Says to bring the hosses." Arron had not heard, he was still hearing Sarah's voice and feeling it on him like a warm breeze.

"You sounded tolerable tonight in the singin, I tho't fo awhile you never wuz gonna get yo man, the way you talked like a bucket of rusty hinges fo so long. He wants bof horses." Arron did not answer.

"He's comin," the Negro yelled toward the benches. Arron, thinking still of her, led the horses down the grass aisle between the benches to the front.

"Arron," Mae said as he arrived at the front, "don't bring them that way, where is your reverence?"

"What do you mean, where's your reverence," Tom said, not yet thinking of himself as a part of the church, "if that horse does somethin he shouldn't in your church, remember that last week it was his dinner table and you're walking all over it."

The old preacher laughed a little but Mae turned her head and looked at Arron. Sarah blushed and Arron saw her before she turned away to gather the hymn books.

Tom turned to Mae, "The preacher and me are takin the horses, Smith'll take you, and Arron can bring the girl in their rig. We're goin to the house for coffee." He turned to the preacher who was looking at Arron's horse. "You can't tell, a good night ride might jest jolt your old butt enough to rattle some scriptures loose in your head. I got a few good questions for you when we get there."

103

The old minister took the reins from Arron. He was now holding once again a good horse and his thoughts were of horses and men, of men like Tom Parker. Of the days and nights with them, reading from a Bible that smelled like horse sweat and saddle bags. A book that had been many times dropped in the dust and forgotten for a horse like the one he was now holding, which had carried him and the rest out flying against the night, riding wild, guided only by the sound of pounding hooves. He held this young bay stallion, and thought of the men like Tom Parker. Men that cursed the Lord in the night silence and then at the moment of action without change of tone prayed to Him their stampede prayers during the thunder of that wild event.

With his hands on the animal's neck, savoring for a moment the anticipation of seating himself down hard in the saddle on a good horse, he did not think of Sarah.

Forgetting his daughter, and any responsibility for her on this first trip out with him, he moved his hand along the horse's hard, bulging neck and grasped the horn of Arron's saddle. He felt the hard rawhide of the dried calf's scrotum which Arron had cut from a Crows Foot bull calf and slipped over the battered horn where it had shrunk and hardened. Feeling the wild old thrill of reality, he tightened his grip and swung up astride the saddle, landing hard feeling a lonesome sadness rise into his stomach with the pleasant ache from his jarred testicles.

Tom wheeled his big sorrel and led the way back up the grass aisle between the empty benches and shouted to Arron who was helping her gather the hymn books.

"Arron, you bring the Missey to the house in the reverend's rig when you get done. But don't get in a fool's rush to do it. I want them torches cold to the hand before you leave, and you bring me the last one you put out so I can feel it and get some sleep tonight." He turned back to the preacher. "I lost more sleep this week worrin if these fires was out than I ever did over the fires of hell. You can see how dry the grass is." He turned back in the saddle and headed the horse north and homeward into the star-pocked night.

The preacher turned back in Arron's saddle before he rode out of the patch of flare light. "Sarah Lee honey, bring Papa's Bible off the pulpit when you come and hurry along now, when Arron gets the torches out cold you all hurry along now, you hear?" The horse tossed his head and the old man turned back straight in the saddle. As he turned he noticed and relaxed the clenched grip he had still on the horn of Arron's saddle.

Alone with her, Arron felt the futile desperation of knowing that a ground swell was building under him. He dumped his thoughts out in his mind looking for some way, some ordered way to speak to her. Being now finally alone with her confounded him.

He moved faster, bending his hard body over the wobbly benches, gathering song books. Working down the row toward her, then meeting at the center aisle only long enough for her to smile a flushed pink smile and turn quickly back up the next row. He felt heat rush to his face.

Halfway down the next row he stopped and straightened tall, looking toward the front of the meeting place. Standing tall enough, as he had done now for four years, to look directly and on an absolute level line into the eyes of Tom. He was now a man in the image of his father.

And yet when he thought of his father, a thought almost like a prayer for guidance, the same throb of disillusionment came to him that had come earlier tonight as he watched Tom walk down the grass aisle and take the preacher's hand.

Arron had not said her name, even alone he had not said it, yet Tom knew. At noon they had been in the cake house poisoning rats. Standing in the narrow walkway between the high stacks of cottonseed cake sacks. Tom held the poison. The odor of cottonseed oil was heavy in the air. Arron had climbed up to put the poison on top of the stacks near the ceiling when Tom said:

"You didn't sound half bad singing with that preacher's daughter out there last night." It was then that Arron almost said her name. "An I got a pretty fair look at you when you was doing it, since I wasn't trying to read the song book. And though it ain't as easy to tell as bloat or screw worms, I'd say you was comin down with a worse'n mild case of the taffy ass."

Arron did not say anything but when he climbed down and started to slap the back of his levis to dust off the yellow cottonseed meal, Tom laughed. Arron stopped, looked at him defensively from under his broad hat brim, then laughed too, slapping harder at the yellow dust, acting as if it were stuck to him with molasses.

As they walked toward the door, Tom said it back over his shoulder without turning to look at Arron, knowing it would be wrong to watch his face, to see the smile crumble from it.

"Jest remember when you're standin out there singing about God and love and when we all get to heaven, that you're standin on the earth, on Crows Foot earth and me and it's got first lien on you. And if you can't think about that when you look at her, well jest remember, like the feller said, 'A good girl is like a good mare, and they don't either one shit cream puffs.' "

Arron stood looking out into the darkness, past the flare light toward the sound of the dark leaves of the cotton-wood tree, listening to that sound and the flapping ragged flames of the torches that fluttered softly, making rippling hollow noises.

Sarah had collected all the books on the benches across the aisle, and Arron knew it though he did not look at her. Now she will speak to me, he thought, she will say something and I will shout it, she will say and I will hit every high and low note they got in the song book, God let me have 'um, all the notes and all the lines and words and rhymes and tunes and even the page numbers, and I'll say her name, say it out straight like a grown man. His chest squeezed around his heart. I will say *Sarah,* and it will take my breath from me like a cat in the crib. *Sarah,* I will squeeze it out of my chest like pouring blood in a swift stream. It will flow out and away in the cold water and I will forget to live, I will speak *Sarah* and empty my vessels into swift Jordan passing by.

Arron, thinking wild and hollow thoughts, afraid to look at her, though he knew she was restacking the books waiting for him, felt a tingling itch inside his nose, and only after he raised his hand to it realized he was humming, that the tickling was the bull resonance in his head. Then the words passed through his mind stilling the wild thoughts. "On Jordan's stormy banks I stand and cast a wistful eye, to Canaan's fair and happy land where my possessions lie." Then he heard her voice. An alto, complex with huskiness, a smoky moistness that rose softly through and surrounded his melody like night mist in an empty forest.

He turned to her, knowing now that he would not shout or even sing her name, that he would not forget to live. The cat could not take the baby's breath. Humming still, she looked at him across the aisle of grass and hymn books and he at her from the knee-high patch of benches.

The hymn left them as it had come.

"Arron," she said the exact moment when the silence had thickened enough to frame and support it, "save one torch." She did not blink, yet as she spoke, a bright ripple ruffled the surface of her eyes. "I want to see it from the rise, from up by the tree." Then she turned, picked up a stack of hymnals and took them to the wagon. Arron began putting out the flares.

After snuffing all except one, he stood waiting at the front of the benches by the warped pulpit, watching its shadow billow and jerk on the grass; waiting for her to come to him out of the darkness where the horse slept hitched to the preacher's surrey. Seeing the Bible lying closed on the lectern, he stuck his finger into the middle of the limp pages and flopped it open to the center.

Then before he could lift his hand from the Book she came out of the night and stood at the back of the grass aisle; standing in the dim, fluttering yellow light of the single torch which exposed her fully in short squibs as if he were seeing her by the light from sluggish yellow lightning flashes. Her long falling hair was parted like thatched wheat around her thin face.

Arron lowered his eyes to her body. It was beautiful to him, like rain in August. In the dim light, he felt her beauty as if it were a cool breeze and he a becalmed tree having its crisp leaves set trembling.

When the moment began to die, his mind reached out to grab the feeling. Her full body pressing against the soft thin cotton dress brought a rush of acid guilt as his clumsy thoughts fumbled with a memory of melons and Bobtail Smith. Before her in the silence he felt naked and humiliated as he had seven years ago when Smith had caught him in his pubic debut standing on a milk stool behind the milk cow with his pants down.

"Well mister bull," he said, "what you gonna do wid dat big ole cigarette butt you got down dere, yes suh, wid somethin like that this ole cow'll be following you up the stairs at night." He doubled up, slapping his leg and laughing, stopping only long enough to say, "I ain't really laughin at you Arron, you at a bad age. Too old to lope you own mule but too young to go gal'n." He shook his marred head which had almost healed. "When I come to that age down home, we didn't have no cow for milk much less such sportin as dat, but we did have a world of watermelons. Now a big old red-meated watermelon that the sun has hotted all day and you cut a little plug out just about right size is somethin a man don't forget. I had me lots of women since, and I'll still say its a purdy close match. Now you get up your pants and do what yo's suppose to to thet cow. Yo mama's waiting on the milk."

Sarah stood now at the back of rows of empty benches, knowing the sin of ripeness, feeling the burden of it, watching Arron close to the torch and the Book. She felt drawn to love, to Arron, to God, drawn, and sucked down that grass aisle to God, to love that is God. I will come to Arron, she thought, thoughts sung not spoken. I will come—come to Arron and by the last torch and on that rise, we will sing the wondrous story of the Christ who died for me. With the refrain leading her, she walked slowly down the aisle toward Arron, committed now and feeling the frightening ballooning of her spirit as the burden of entity and sin fell away from her. She smiled at him and almost spoke, for the singing thoughts were dying down, but instead she smiled and listened to their fading away.

Arron could not smile at her immediately. He could not think to do it nor did he do it instinctively. Then he felt it on his face like reflected heat, he was smiling because he could physically feel the radiation of her. I will tell her the torches are out, he thought.

"Arron," she said, "you put out all the other torches."

"Yes," he said.

"Will we walk to the rise now?"

"Yes," he said.

"Will you remind me to take Papa's Bible when we go?"

"Yes."

"He loves that ole Book more than me."

"We'll take it," Arron said.

And they walked past the lectern, out of the light toward the rise; they could not hear the breeze blowing the Bible pages across its binding with a sound akin to and absorbed by the stirring cottonwood leaves.

Standing now on the rise that gently puffed up a smooth dome on the prairie as subtle and unmistakable as the curve of a sleeping woman's breast, she said, "I feel like singing again." She turned to him and he, with the un-

easiness of beginning an unfamiliar song alone, bent at
the waist, turned his head a little and guided his hat brim
past her face and into the mist of yellow hair. He kissed
her with dry flat lips, feeling her return the touch as softly
as leaves turn to the sun. Like a wax figurine melting from
the bottom, she began sinking slowly to the breast of the
prairie.

Great God, Arron thought, feeling himself sinking with
her, I was rough, I am mashing her down, God, Arron hold
back, Arron hold back! He opened his eyes and was surprised to see her curled down into the grass. He had not
pressed her, he was standing with stiff knees, bending over
from the waist. She was sitting in the grass beside his fallen
hat, her eyes still closed and her head tilted up. He knelt
beside her as if she had been injured.

"Would you like to feel the earth turn?" he said softly
as if asking her to locate the pain. She opened her eyes.
"You do it like this." He stretched out flat on his back and
spread his arms out straight. He then twisted them and
took a handful of grass in each hand, pulling hard against
the roots. "Now you look straight up," he said, "and close
your eyes so you can just barely see through your eyelashes, so everything's fuzzy, and think hard about it,
then pretty soon you can feel it." He closed his lashes together and waited for her to speak, not thinking about the
world, but of melons, not like breasts but large body-sized
melons lying hot in the sun and of smashing them open
and crushing the hot juicy red heart against his naked
body, of closing himself inside an overripe hot melon and
twisting and thrashing around in its mushy heart.

He felt her move and almost opened his eyes but instead
pulled harder at the grass until he could hear the roots
begin to tear. And as if that sound was her tearing away
from the earth, she rose to her knees over him. He could
feel her long hair falling gently into his face like a shower
of damp wheat chaff. Her breath on his face smelled sweet

and rotten, like a skin of mildew on strawberry preserves. I will hold the grass, he thought, *I've got to hold the grass!* Her hair moved in his face and he could feel her breath quicken.

"Christ was like this," she said close to his face, "stretched out like this before they nailed him." Arron felt specks of spittle on his face. "Before they nailed him to the tree, quiet as you Arron before they dropped it in that Roman hole. Oh . . . Arron."

Her open mouth fell on his without lips without tongue, their teeth crashed together in violent and frightened innocence. He jerked his head to the side from the quick, cold pain of chipped teeth, abandoning the grass, rolling her under him without tasting the blood from her lip.

He closed his eyes tight and again grasped the grass, pinning her body flat against the turf. Her body pitched up hard against him and his visions of passive melons vanished. Somewhere from the back of his horseman's mind he knew himself invited and committed to a combat of flesh.

He felt her mashed fullness under him and, as if he were lying flat on the back of a horse trying to remove the saddle from under him, he struggled with their clothes. Then they were off, torn off, slipped off, ignored off. She was smooth and fleshy under him like a fat bareback mare. She jolted him like rough trotting yet he held her under. The first touch of his dry entrance into her killed the coltish trot. Then, coming slowly as blood from a puncture wound, he felt her again begin to move under him. As if she, the fat back mare, had fallen through the air into a river, her motions became that of a swimming horse; long deep movements under him, until without warning, the animal awkwardly burst into shallow water, stumbling, faltering, then exploding out of the river onto hard earth, dashing on.

Arron the rider, fighting for balance, for control,

smashed against her with vicious impact, hoping to stun, to stab deep. He held the grass and fought to hold her on the earth. He imagined his bull muscle plunging through her and into the earth like a mooring stake. He saw it penetrate her and the grass, and even the earth.

Then, still fighting to hold her under him, the driving power of the act changed, it became enormous. He could feel the earth trying to sling them off as he smashed against her, clutching the grass. Then she gave a death burst of pounding speed and exploded into spasms. And as if detonated by it, he ripped loose the fistfuls of grass, crushing her in his arms and felt the earth sling them out, whiplashed out, arching a fiery orange trail of fire dust across the black sky; out into the silent darkness falling.

They were a long time falling through the cool prairie air, sleeping until Arron's coughing awoke them, a violent spent coughing as he tried to cough up a long blond hair he had sucked down in his throat.

Now in the rancid bed alone, that cough in Arron's throat was not dry and firm as it was then, the years had flooded it with asthma, and on moist nights the wheeze came thin. Under his hoary fingernails that were yellow like rat's teeth, the dirt was greasy from scratching himself and not that moist clean loam from the grass roots. Not that sandy loam which packed under them as he ripped the grass trying to hold himself and her on the face of the earth. Not that earth which was still packed under them as he had waited for her to dress, tucking the torn summer cotton about her, raking the grass from her thatched hair with long fingers and wiping the blood from herself and her lips while he went for the last flare and the Bible, the pages of which were swollen and damp having absorbed the fresh clean night moisture and surrendered their brittleness to it.

That Bible over which they confessed and under which they, in false atonement, were married in the paling darkness of that same night before God at the headquarters house. Before dawn with Mae crying cool tears, the old preacher read from the still damp and flexible pages.

Arron stood for the first time in his life before Tom Parker without a puppy-fear in his chest, even when Tom had threatened a beating, offering the whip handle first to the minister. Before the others, Arron felt lowly and ashamed, but somehow looking at his father his pride rose with the thoughts of cream puffs and the smell of crushed grass that stained green the bruised spots on Sarah's skin as well as his own.

The old bed rocked on its springs as Arron coughed again, a long chest-contracting spasm which squeezed and twisted the thick cloudy mucus from his lungs.

Downstairs, Smith sat on the edge of his cot, then moved very slowly to get dressed. He pulled the scuffed high-top shoes on his bare feet, then sat for a long time in the rising bed warmth, listening to Arron cough and waiting for the dawn.

XI

Smith moved slowly about in the frigid kitchen. The night moistures mixed with the thick smell of cold cooking grease. He stood in the middle of the floor, hunched over a little against the grey morning chill, and rubbed his hands up and down along the sides of his legs as if pumping himself into action.

"Gots to feed thet ole smooth-mouth," he mumbled without moving or altering the speed or stroke of his slow plunging arms. "He gots to have his mash—if the worl quits right now and dis is all the light we gits—thet ole hoss gonna get his hot mash." His hands came up and stopped on his waist with his bony elbows stuck out behind him. Upstairs, Arron coughed. The Negro dropped his arms. He gonna hack up a gut one of dese mornins, Smith thought, as he went out the back door and walked toward the roofless barn.

The unpainted barn was the bleached grey color of the predawn sky. It was warped in every direction, its great sagging curves frozen in the brittle thinness of ageing and spent wood. Only the saddle and carriage shed had its roof.

Smith dragged open one of its doors, swinging it out like a hinged prop to hold up the building while he was inside. He came out with a rusty and battered five gallon bucket and hobbled back to the house, stopping at the foot of the back steps to run about a gallon of water in it from the dripping water faucet that stood knee deep in a clump of bermuda grass.

Inside he started a fire and set the old bucket on the stove. Arron coughed again and Smith knew he was getting up. Yep, he thought, he'll hack up a long red gut one ob dese days, then we gonna have ourselves a little set-to about pissin off the front porch.

He went now to get the egg. For Arron, upstairs, sleeping and waking were not divided by any physical act. He sank into sleep as if his prone body was being slowly submerged in liquid blackness. And he came awake as if that body were being slowly lifted from that same liquid and finally through its surface into the light where he would lay waiting. Waiting as he did now for it to drain from him. The imaginary sounds of it dripping from him urged him to get up and relieve himself.

He flung back the damp and heavy quilts. They landed against the wall like something recently dead. He pulled on his pants, then reached for his old scuffed boots. The ankles and toes, where a layer of the stitched leather had worn through, looked like work-abraded calluses on the thick hard skin of old hands. He pulled them on slowly, easing into them. The pull stretched his arms and back like a good deep yawn, then his heel hit bottom with a satisfying thud and he sat moving his toes in the snug tightness of these two old companions.

As he stood buttoning on a soft frayed shirt, he looked east out the window. The red sun was squeezing up through a thin slot along the horizon. It moved up flat out of the earth, a thin disk, encrusted with glittering granules of sulphur and ground orange peel.

Arron, looking through the cloudy window glass down

at the twisted sagging barn, saw Smith carrying the steaming bucket of hot oats across the yard toward the saddle shed. One hand held the bucket handle, the other stuck straight out for balance so he looked like a coolie water boy who had lost one bucket and was stumbling along awkwardly under a broken yoke.

Arron put on an old faded levi jacket and jerked the collar up flat against his neck, slowly hunching his shoulders and drawing his neck in with the cautious movement of an ancient turtle.

He turned and went out into the long hall and down the narrow path that these same boots had made over the years in the crusted dust which now covered the carpet. A layer of powdered earth covered all the upstairs rooms and sealed the thresholds of every door except the one he had just crossed. The thin path was close to the wall, a narrow passage that his steps had worn through the dust and wool, down to the brown cord of the matting under the carpet.

Arron walked down the stair without lowering his eyes. He turned without stepping on the first landing, where Sarah had lain cold with the blood washed baby. His foot did not disturb the cracking blanket of dust which now covered the stained carpet. It was marked only by the cracks and by occasional white bird-droppings from the sparrows which flew freely now through a broken pane near the top of the tall window.

Past the landing he stopped and stood with his back to the broad tall window and the dust-sodded stairs. His eyes did not lower to the remaining stairs, yet he did stop here on the second step of the lower staircase. Standing on the wool carpet (the Negro cleaned it up to the landing), he pulled his neck back and down into the levi jacket a little more and reached a horseman's hand out to the banister. Holding the railing with a light grip, he waited as if for the sky to lighten in the window behind him, waited for some signal, some evaporation of dew or clanking of a cold coffee pot that would begin the day.

He was still, with his shrunken hand on the broad, flat banister. At this moment with the early north light behind him in the tall window, he seemed to be an enlarged man, immobile and statuesque, scowling down at diluted descendants.

Smith came in the room from the kitchen, below Arron. He did not look up until he was in the center of the room. It was as if he felt himself walking through Arron's brittle unmoving line of vision. He walked through it; like passing through an invisible spider thread. Feeling it on his face, he turned, looking up at Arron.

"Will mister piss off de porch, how do the worl suit you today? Has it peckterfied you up dere to see dis ole nigger some where 'cept where you can show you true self? You can notice even from up dere dat dere ain't no egg. I guess thet ole hen knows what to do 'bout somethin likes you."

Arron did not move. "Get the horse," he said, "get the horse and when I am gone, kill the chicken. I want chicken."

"You wants chicken," Smith turned his back to Arron and leaned toward the kitchen without taking a step. "Thet ole hen been here eight years doin her best fo you breakfas and one time takes up fo dis ole head and you wants chicken. If in she laid it and I din' go get it, I guess he'd be wantin nigger—an if he got it he'd bitch and moan lookin fo de white meat." He slammed the kitchen door behind him.

Arron moved down the stairs and across to the tall front door, stopping once to look into the dining room at the thick oak table. On one end of the table a clean white tablecloth was draped almost to the floor, the rest and greater part of the table was bare. Washing the tablecloth had kept Smith busy until he discovered Arron did not care beyond his own place at the end of the table. Now Smith folded the long white cloth seven times, each day changing the fold and exposing a clean part of the whole.

Arron opened the door and saw the gaunt horse standing saddled at the edge of the porch, its head lowered slightly as if in profound disillusionment, the reins falling from its mouth straight to the ground. Bits of the hot mash that the Negro had hand-fed it were dried on its flat dark nose, sticking together some of the long grey bristles that covered its lower lip and chin like embedded cactus needles. The horse did not move as Arron relieved himself from the end of the porch. Finished, a shudder passed over him.

He stepped to the ground and over to the immobile horse. He gathered the reins and tossed the right rein over its neck where it dropped across the mane in front of the saddle horn. Before moving to the left side of the horse, he tipped the square topless can of water which Smith had put on the edge of the porch. Every morning Smith brought the water when he stationed the horse. The porch had rotted under the leaking bucket and tall bermuda grass grew up at this one spot in the dead arid yard. The toothless horse stood ignoring the lush, lonesome growth as if it had understood Smith the second summer after Sarah's death, when the bucket was still new and the grass on her grave was beginning to feel its first drouth.

"You, hoss," he had said, "get you head outen thet bucket —thet's grave water—don't you know thet we done took to gardenin grave tops now. Yes suh guess he done run out of tear watter or maybe it was too mean and salty—anyways thet ain't for you. And you better keep yo self offen thet grass thet it grows too—you eat grass offen thet grave and he's liable to be a leadin you up the stairs at night callin you Sarah—like he's been doin thet poor Miss Harvest—and you a stud."

Arron walked slowly around to the horse's side. He was about to enjoy the last pleasure left to him, the only act of living that had not gone flat, receded into bland dust.

Slowly he took the reins and grasped the horse's mane in his left hand. His other hand caught the rough ugly horn of the saddle. He lifted one foot to the stirrup feeling his crotch and back muscles stretch. He paused a moment squatting a little and feeling the tightness of his muscles. Then with the other foot he pushed off from the earth and swung hard yet with slow deliberate pleasure into the air and crashed hard down in the saddle, feeling the old horse shuffle a little under his weight.

As he leaned over out of the saddle to pick up the leaking bucket from the porch, Smith opened the door.

"So you wants chicken," he said, "you runnin off up dere to water yo wife and leavin me to look thet ole hen in the eye wit the knife in my hand."

Arron was now straight in the saddle, holding the dripping bucket out from his leg, out at the end of a stiff arm. Smith put his hand in his pocket and clamped it tightly around the blue jar of mentholated ointment. He could hear the drops of water patting softly into the dust at the horse's feet. Arron did not speak and the root hair wrinkles in his face were now deep enough to cast shadows into themselves.

"Alrightie," Smith said gripping the jar and taking strength from it. "If I'se gonna kill my old hen with the hands thet never lifted one ob her eggs to this ole mouth—and you won't say don't—if you playin yo self into thet mornin hex ahead ob time today and ain't talkin—we'll jest see how it is thet you're a hearin."

The water dripping steadily into the dust sounded like a large clock buried in a barrel of flour, its ticking muffled and immediate. Arron, though statuesque, no longer seemed of stone. In the dusty redness of the early sun the dumbfounded animal and Arron seemed to be of wax dusted too heavily with rouge.

In his pocket, Smith was gouging his thumbnail under the label on the small blue jar. "You jest sit up dere drippin the grave water on the yard and act hexed but what fixin to come outen dis ole man's mouth is some truth. Thet ole hen is all they is on this place thet's *doin*. She a makin eggs like she knows her bill from her butt. She is all there is here and mayhaps the rest of the worl

1 1 9

thet ain't got her head up her rump and cryin 'cause it's dark. You don't see her followin you down to the toilet and scratch 'round in yo leavins lookin for her chicks. An I ain't no better'n you—you hauls thet grave water every mornin—well. . . ." He pulled the blue jar from his pocket, held it in one hand and looked down at it, suddenly ashamed. With the other hand he began peeling off bits of the label. "Well . . . ," his voice sunk into him, "I'll tell you now, I *loves* thet ole chicken."

Arron did not move.

Smith stared down at the blue jar which he now held tight against his chest with both hands. He began to moan and now rocked back and forth slightly. Thick fluid began seeping from his eyes and the shrunken, twisted lump of grey flesh between the wide dark holes that had been his nose, glistened with moisture like a sweating wart. "It ain't right, Arron, I ain't never touched her, she clean as the day she hatched, I ain't used her Arron. Ain't nobody used her. She ain't no Edith Harvest. I never called her Sarah and took her to my bed. I never put no stinkin coal-oil torch in my room and almost burn down the place, callin her Sarah."

The dust-smothered ticking of the dripping water was slowing. The drops fell niggard and stingy. The battered can had not moved. Arron's arm was at the exact same parallel to the ground though the can, now almost empty, was ten pounds lighter. As the last drop fell and even before it spattered specks of mud on the hoof of the horse, Arron turned his head to the can, his arm raised slightly as if only now with the last drop gone was the total weight of that water severed from the rusty can.

He jerked the can to him and rested it on his leg as if it had now become too heavy to suspend at arm's length. He bent his head over it looking into the shallow can as if it were a deep well, holding his head close to it, squinting his eyes trying to see the bottom. The root hair wrinkles in his face deepened and extended themselves. He then pulled his face from the rim of the can and looked directly at Smith. The thin wrinkles shriveled deep into his face hanging almost plumb, like thin dead scars from his eyes.

He looked at Smith with an expression of ravaged astonishment.

"Well look at *me*, go 'head, like I spilled it, sit dere listenin to you gas bubble and look at me." He leaned toward Arron, his rocking stopped abruptly as if a stick of kindling had been shoved under the back of a rocking chair blocking it still at its forwardmost pitch.

The water-root wrinkles quivered in Arron's face. He blinked one eye.

"Dat's it," Smith said, "shiver you face at me. Well I ain't no gnat buzzin around you head." Holding the blue jar tight against him, he leaned out a little more at Arron. "They's only one thin thet kin stop dis ole gnat from buzzin yo addled head, an I done said it. Thet's it shiver again, but I'se tellin you this ole gnat's got a stinger like a hot railroad spike. You better say don't Arron, you better say don't. Thet ole hen is under dis porch rite now listenin for you to say. Thet egg she didn't lay out this morning is ahurting her but you kin bet she ain't 'bout to relieve herself 'til you say."

Arron looked quickly back into the can as if it had gotten heavier on his leg.

"Alrightie Arron," Smith said rocking back as if the stick of cord wood had been kicked from under the rocker. He stamped the heel of his stringless, high-top shoe three times on the rotten boards of the porch. "Hen, you jest go ahead on and relieve you'self, an as soon as I spikes a can over this fool's head, we gonna eat ourselves—I'm gonna finally get me some egg."

The noise frightened the hen and she fluttered from under the porch in a stiff trot, stopping as if snagged by a catcher's neck-hoop when she saw the small pile of fresh, grain aggregated droppings that lay steaming behind the horse.

"You get outen thet hen. We done enough of thet, you lay thet egg an we gonna eat fresh oats and egg on a white tablecloth."

Smith shuffled sideways down the porch to the bull-horn chair, which had been made for Tom Parker of horns and rawhide from the shaggy bull buffalo. He crumbled down into it slowly. Sitting on the hard rawhide, surrounded by the curving black horns, he looked like a shrunken, self-emaciated witch doctor.

"Yes suh," he said, "we gonna defold back thet white tablecloth one mo time and make a place for a good layin hen. I think I kin jest go into one ob them handy hexes myself. If you kin defold it back jest once fer thet Miss Edith Harvest and make thet tight lipped bundle of sour puckers be Sarah, an you leadin her upstairs callin her it, I guess I kin defold it jest the same. You ain't havin chicken Arron, I is—and I don mean to eat."

Arron was now looking directly at Smith in the chair of horns. The horse raised its head also, fixing its blank stare on Smith.

"I'd hate to choose," Smith said, "which one ob you two got the deadest eyes. I guess you kin tell how I means it or I wouldn't be sittin in yo daddy's chair, now unhex yo self fo one minute. I ain't killin thet hen and dis chair says I'se right. An since you done stood there and leaked thet grave water all out I'm gonna tell you where to get what it is you been trying to grow. She ain't come up through the grass 'cause she's like the rest ob dis place. Her guts is gone. You put her in the ground without her guts. You wrapped her up in thet saddle blanket and fought 'um like a grown man to keep her and forgot her guts. What was it you thought we scooped up offen de landin thet night? What was it was takin so much of Miss

Edith Harvest's time them four years—she was lookin after the guts—whilst she wasn't playin the whore comin like a starved huntin bitch ever time you hollered Sarah—*You forgot the guts, Arron!"*

Arron's eye was still, the thin wrinkles hung motionless. The hen scratched in the green manure behind the horse with quick, guilty motions. He had started listening but not to Smith. He would hear Smith but not yet, he had started listening to the chair. The memory of it and Tom were talking to him. He would after a while hear Smith. He listened to voices before Smith, knowing the memory of what Smith was now saying about Ronnie and the train would in time also come to him.

XII

Now Sunday was fixed in place over White Dove. The chaplain awoke at his usual time and waited in bed until he heard someone moving downstairs. It was Mildred who had been to the bathroom, which she'd left unflushed, and tiptoed back to bed.

The chaplain heard her and thinking they were getting up, eased out of the bed. He drew a hot bath and got in. As he sat there, the dead stillness of the strange house made the sounds of his bathing seem too loud. He felt isolated and exposed, as if in the silence below Buck and Mildred were listening as he washed himself. He bathed slowly and with the caution of a sneak thief. The noise of it frightened and excited him. With each movement of the water he felt more exposed. Finally he was absolutely still. He thought of prayer but could not bring himself to pray in the presence of his own nakedness. A desperate feeling of isolation and loneliness oppressed him as the bath water cooled and glazed over with an oily wax film.

The grey water was cold when he finally slid up out of it, trying not to drip. He dried himself gently and sat blue-nude and chilled on the toilet holding the soft bar of bath soap. Carefully and with absolute concentration, he began picking off the pubic hairs that were embedded in the soap, dropping them between his fat legs into the water below.

In town, the dogs knew it was fall. They stood close to buildings in the sun. They did not lie on the sidewalk, even though it was still warm, as on summer days. In the winter they stood.

Harry Eddens had already noticed it on Saturday but he had not thought about winter. But this morning, as he parked his car in front of the drugstore and sat looking in from the street, he thought of winter. Even though the sun through the car glass was hot on his arm, he thought of winter and hoped it would be a good one.

He got out of the car and walked to the front door of the store, stopping to pick up two small bundles of newspapers that the bus driver on the early bus from Amarillo had thrown off.

Inside, cosmetic and antiseptic smells were heavy in the air. The morning sun shining through the thick plate glass windows had warmed the store until it was almost stuffy. Behind the cigar counter he put down the papers, smelling now the moist tobacco.

He turned from the cigar case and walked behind the fountain, where he took a short Coke glass from the glistening pyramid of glasses and filled it with water. He lighted the burner under the Silex coffee maker, then walked back to the cigar case where he poured the water in the humidifier bowl. Putting aside the empty glass, he stooped slowly and picked up the bundled newspapers. Untying and spreading them before him on the counter, he picked up the black wax pencil that lay on the cash register and began printing the names of the subscribers on each one, without pausing to read even the headlines until he came to the end of the list and the extra paper that was his own.

He had not turned on the store lights and even though the wide door was open the empty store had still the dead air of something closed, abandoned. Harry moved from behind the counter to the end stool of the soda fountain. He sat cross legged and slightly hunched over as he waited for the coffee water to boil. The drugstore smells were the sweet toilet water, patent medicine and malted milky smells of a woman. To him it was so, not of sex, or love, or passion but of woman—female. And he enjoyed its company, enjoyed being alone with it. He had been in the same store for forty-seven years and in those years since his wife had died, he had come early on Sunday mornings to sit alone in the dim and pungent store where he would let his mind run free and sometimes his tongue as he sat smelling the fresh coffee brewing, occasionally chuckling or mumbling to himself.

No one came in on Sunday morning except once in a while a breathless child would dash in, having run to the drugstore between Sunday school and church service to spend the few cents that he had held back out of his offering on enough hard penny candy to see him through the long church service.

Harry had seen the grass, then the wheat land and the oil boom, in their time, and now it was some of all. Each had enjoyed its exciting bloom and was now gone. He was a little homesick for each of them.

The silence of the shaded store was broken by a distant ringing of the railroad warning signals down the street at the Santa Fe crossing. Without thinking of Ronnie Parker or of the train that was bringing his body home, Harry slid off the stool and crossed the store to the patent medicine counter.

He went behind the counter thinking, I got to get those flower orders off by six, they got to have time to get 'um ready. That's a new man on the early Amarillo bus—if he throws off the flowers like he done the papers this morning they'll sure look pretty. Maybe they'll say something at the greenhouse. He took the flower order book from the shelf under the counter.

Without opening it, he went back to the fountain, poured himself a cup of coffee and sat again at the end stool with the order book before him.

It was one of the old cloth covered ledger books from the First State Bank, the one that Roosevelt broke, according to the three Republicans in town. On the front, printed in letters blotched by the cloth's irregular absorption of the black ink, was, "Drugstore order book—Amarillo Greenhouse, Pho. 3976."

He thought of the funerals and weddings he had recorded in the book. There's just about nothin that happens that don't call for flowers. They's flowers for gettin born, gettin sick, gettin courted, married, healing up fights, dying, yes mostly for dying. It's the dying that calls up the flowers it don't matter who or how many let somebody die and sure as if that was the only reason somebody else had for living they show up and order flowers for that one who died. Like that Ronnie coming in here that day out of the rain, riding that horse in, not even knowing for sure she was dead riding through a rain that might have just come up to wash out and hide his tears to order red flowers. *"Mr. Eddens I want a hundred dollars worth of flowers."* He said it standing right there by the door shivering and wet like he had cried himself under a downpour. Ronnie all skinny in his wet clothes with his blue Parker eyes full of water too but blue like the sky when it rains with the sun out and not clouds. Edith Harvest died and out of nowhere but rain he comes in here dripping on the floor sayin, *"Mr. Eddens I want a hundred dollars worth of flowers."*

"Ronnie, that's too many flowers, you sure you want that?"

"*I want more'n that and I'd get 'um too if she could smell, I want 'um put in out at the graveyard, you send the bill to the Bank, maybe if they was red.*" And he walked out back to the rain so it could hide the tears, just standing outside the window with the rain falling on him washing down around his blue eyes as he stood bedraggled, lookin at me sittin here writing it in the book. A hundred dollars worth of flowers—that would fill any grave, even if they put her in without her box and maybe her clothes—those black clothes, widow's weeds. They said she was sure dried up, held only a quart and a half of embalming fluid, I bet her breast looked like dried apricot halves stuck on the front of something shrunk up to nothing. But I wrote it; I sat right here with him standin humped over outside that window in the rain watchin while I wrote it into the book.

Thinking that there is good money in flowers, Harry stopped turning the pages of the book at "Harvest Funeral," it was on the page across from "Henry Cole's operation." He read the short list of flowers under Harvest funeral. At the top of the list was, "order for Ronnie Parker, one hundred dollars worth of red flowers—to be put on grave." The handwriting was large and shaky as if it had been written very slowly. Under the penciled order written in ink in a hand that was slanted and fast was, "Bill to Bank, Crows Foot expense, one three dollar spray, ordered by Ronnie Parker."

Let them die and no matter, someone will turn up to put flowers around 'um. Ronnie too with his guts tore out by a gook lying in the ground over the water rotten tryin to be dead without flowers and Buck having him gouged up out of the ground so we can dump some flowers over him; like he wasn't dead without flowers, like Buck had to put him out of his misery with flowers.

Didn't take that skinny kid standin in the rain no seventeen years to know it was time for flowers, to come out of

128

the rain and away from old Arron for a hundred dollar flower.

She died of what she caught out there—they all die of it —its got 'um all—only Arron's still in the body—like a maggot, more'n one I guess in old Tom's body—when they come out in the light and air they die and now it's Ronnie, seventeen years late. Edith Harvest came out four years later after she went in if she hadn't gone in, Ronnie's page would be back with Tom's and Sarah's—or he might of just stayed in Sarah then her grave would'a held less flowers if somebody had'a wanted a hundred dollars worth for her. God—sweet Sarah—her staying just long enough to drop another blue-eyed Parker out there, droppin him just in time to suck in old Tom's last breath and be here suckin on dried apricot halves and bacon rind to keep here, but he stayed and grew and wanted a hundred dollar flower to cover two old dried apricot halves. Arron saw them I bet and tasted 'um some. Arron crazy Arron wild and crazy old man Arron Parker.

Harry sipped his cold coffee, shook his head to one side as if he had just remembered something he had forgotten to do. Standing up on the fountain rail, he leaned over the counter and poured the cold coffee out into the round copper sink. As he sat back down on the stool, he heard an engine racing at top speed up at the north end of Main Street. It sounded like an overture to a drag race. The sound got louder and nearer but it was out of balance; from the noise the vehicle should have passed out of earshot. He got off the stool and walked to the window to see what was holding it back. Sounds like it's tied to a post or got its back wheels off the ground, he thought. Then he saw Roy Turner's old red pickup easing down the street toward the drugstore, the motor running wide open but the pickup moving about ten miles an hour, as if it was pulling itself down the street with its radiator fan. Roy had both hands on the wheel and looked as if he

129

thought the pickup was moving as fast as it sounded. It pulled slowly into the curb in front of the store. He cut the switch and the Sunday morning silence smothered the noise. He had driven down Main Street from the Eddards Cafe in low gear because the notched stick with which he propped the shift into second gear had fallen under the seat.

The loose bumper rattled as the smooth front tire hit the curb and bounced the pickup back. Roy got out and slammed the glassless door. As he stepped up on the sidewalk, the old truck rolled slowly, almost timidly, back up to the curb. He looked back at it as if he had given it a command to sit and was seeing if it had obeyed.

He came into the unlighted store, looking up at the light fixtures.

"What's the matter, Harry, you got so much business this mornin you don't want nobody to know you're open?"

"Yep, I got so much I can't pay the light bill."

Roy straddled over the stool next to Harry, looked at his empty cup and said, "I guess it's pretty bad all right, when you can't even afford a second cup of your own coffee."

"Well, it's not that so much, it's just that I have to sell one to drink one—you gonna help me out? Understand I know it won't be as good as down at the cafe—not enough bullshit around here for seasoning." He poured them both a cup and returned to his stool.

"Harry, speaking of bullshit, what do you think of this circus Buck is having tomorrow?"

Harry eased the sugar over to Roy with the little finger-edge of his palm down hand. "Well, I guess that depends on how you look at it." He closed the flower book. "It's not hurtin my flower orders much, on the other hand it means I will have to close the store from two to four tomorrow."

Roy had poured about half of his coffee into his saucer

and held it with both hands, thumb and forefinger, to his lips and was blowing just over the edge in short soft breaths.

"Hell, I don't mean business, nothin Buck does is gonna hurt business, especially his. But I never seen him do anything yet that somebody don't get the short end of. And you can bet it ain't gonna be Buck. Look at that damn pickup out there, if he didn't stick a burr under my balls on that one I'll kiss your tail on Main Street and give you thirty minutes to draw a crowd." He turned his head back to the saucer, which he had not lowered, gave it a final blow, longer than the others, then took a noisy sip. "Yep, somebody's gotta take up the slack."

Harry thought, *what is it—what is it he wants—who am I today, doctor, lawyer, or priest, has he finally got Elmira with child, what would I be then, doctor priest—does he need money—want me to go to the Bank for him—*"I don't care if he's got Crows Foot money coming for a hundred years, he'll get it by the month," *that's what Will Sloan said and it's his Bank—don't matter whose money, he's got the Crows Foot checkbook. At least we did that much for Arron—we got Will Sloan appointed over the money.*

"Well, Roy, you don't think it'll hurt you, do you, I mean what are you figuring on it for?"

"Harry," Roy paused short as if his wind had been cut off by a sharp pain, "you know Buck hired me to go out to Lea Switch and clean it up—well I been thinking."

And here it comes, he's gonna vomit it out—out all over the fountain and I am gonna have to smell it. He'll get it out and feel fine but I'll smell it—I clean up after him and nobody'll know but me—everytime I make an eggmalt I'll smell it—"Roy, don't tell me you been thinkin—last time I tried it I think I threw somethin out of joint, better stay away from it—worse'n Johnson Street women."

"Well I allus said I wasn't paid to think but anyhow I done some an the way I figger it is, Buck is like a he dog humpin on your leg—he thinks he's doing somethin he ain't. The only thing I can't puzzle out is, who does he think he's a'doing it *to*."

"Well, Roy I can't see that it matters a great deal as long as you're sure it's not you."

"That's just it Harry, I ain't, I mean I ain't sure, you know about him sending me out to Lea Switch, well that ain't all——"

Here it comes, he's gonna do it—

"——yesterday when I took out the grocery order he told me to drive on up to the house—up to Arron and tell him —and then when I got back he never asked me if I done it—I hung around till he left the cemetery yesterday—close enough for him to spit on me but he never done it—he never asked me."

That's the retch.

"They all say the cemetery turned out real nice this year. I went out early and did Elizabeth's. I missed everybody," Harry said into his coffee cup.

"He didn't ask me, Harry—I stood right by him and he even introduced me to that army preacher he's got here, but he didn't ask me." Roy poured the rest of the coffee from his cup into the saucer and drank from it without cooling it. Harry picked up his cup and with a motion like a reflection of Roy's, he poured the coffee that had sloshed over into the saucer, back into the cup.

So I'll ask him, I'll gouge my finger down him—he come to me for it—he can't carry it—better to vomit in a friend's pocket but I'll charge him a little—make it cost him some— bend him a little toward Elmira—she needs that, I'll bend him a little.

"I spoke to Elmira yesterday as I was paying my phone bill, she said Buck called *Life* magazine in Dallas about the funeral. They may send out a photographer. She say anything to you?"

"She never asked me neither, she just talked, made coffee and talked, mostly about Ronnie and about Buck and how good he is to do all this. She listens to everybody so much on that damn phone she can't hardly make sense no more."

Harry got up. "You want to drink another cup, Roy?" He went behind the counter to refill the cups. *Of course she never asked him—wonder if she even tried.*

"Well, Roy, so Mr. Harris sent you out to trespass on the Crows Foot. My wages would be pretty high for a job like that. I bet I have used up a bale of cotton pluggin up holes in fellers like you over the years. And I just ordered a new bale for tomorrow just in case Arron was to get his head back and catch the funeral out there tomorrow."

"That's it, Harry, you got to ask me, Arron can't catch the funeral, he can't catch nothin. That nigger tole me that much. He took his whip to me when I tried to tell him they was bringing Ronnie home. I had to hold him to tell him; then he bawled and slobbered like a baby." Roy stopped short, remembering the old Negro's words, *I only tole him one thin 'bout that boy, an his eyes done bust in his head, I tole him 'bout Sarah. That old death telegram I used squattin 'hind a plum bush and it's been rained on and bleached out now with years and done gone in the grass like my pile.*

Roy hunched over the counter, not touching it, as if it were hot. Then he spoke to Harry in a strained whisper. Harry came back to his stool, Roy swiveled his body round, following him, a thin body that looked like a hand-scythe.

"Harry, Arron don't know, he don't even *know*. That crazy old nigger never told him—that's why he never done nothin when it happened."

Now I too know why Arron—crazy Arron with apricot stuck in his whiskers like egg—don't care—with mentholated ointment and apricot on him—don't care.

"Harry, that goddamned black drawn-up stinking old son of a bitch didn't tell him—sittin out there seein who's gonna rot first and he didn't tell him. Is it my worry? We pulled him off one windmill fan, I'll be damned if that seventy-five a month is better than my old daddy. You won't catch me grabbin up a slobberin loco coyote and hollerin in his face to come sane. They can sit out there till the world rots around 'um, I ain't facing Arron Parker."

Harry looked at himself in the fountain mirror, seeing a flaked and scattered image in that part of the mirror behind the coffee maker that the heat had caused to yellow and peel.

He has done it, he has come in here out of Sunday and done it. There's been a punishment buildin up all these Sundays that I been sittin here out of church. Now I gotta stand out there meetin that train and that boy and watch 'um put him in the ground beside old Tom—I gotta see all that and know I should'a wrong said it. Roy tried, at least he tried, and now it's me that's got the baby on my doorstep—he sure done it to me—like he thinks Buck is doing it to him or somebody.

"Now Roy you don't have to get all plowed up like this. There's a lot more to Bobtail Smith than you'd think. He's not like Arron, oh, maybe some of it has rubbed off on him over the years but he's gonna do right by Arron and the Crows Foot. Like I say, there's more to him than most people think, or care to remember."

Harry did not take his eyes away from the mirror. "You just go ahead on like always—you done yours, you told him or at least told someone to tell him."

Roy looked down at his cup for a moment, then without moving his body, turned his head sideways to Harry.

"Harry, like I allus said, I ain't paid to think but I'll be damned if Buck ain't just twisting the whole town's tail. I tried to figger it talking to Elmira and didn't do nothin but make her mad, and if you don't know, then I give up."

"Well, Roy, it's a cinch I don't know but the wagon's rollin in that direction and we're on it, so I guess you might as well stay on for the ride."

1 3 4

Roy stood over the stool, put both hands on the counter and pushed himself away and upright. "I guess you're right Harry but somehow I feel like somebody just offered me a ride to my own hangin instead of lettin me walk. You want to sell me a couple of these wood-tipped cigars?"

Harry got the box and held it out to Roy to pick out two. "Speaking of Elmira, I figger you are about due to hit bottom on that wild oat sack of yours. When you gonna put the town ladies at ease about Elmira? Buck tells me you got a regular footpath wore out from the hotel to the telephone office, along behind his shop."

"That damn Buck—you see it's things like that makes me care so much for him. I wonder what it is about his own business that's so bad that he has to mind everybody else's."

Harry rang up the money. "Probably good that he does. What if he didn't bother about anybody's but yours and his—he'd have you and Elmira married and with five kids, all in six months."

Roy had walked to the door. He called back, "Yeah and you know which part he'd be wantin to help with the most." He went out of the door and over to the pickup where he stopped just for a moment and looked at the smooth front tire to try to tell if it was going to blow out today, or tomorrow. Then he got in, having decided tomorrow. He started the engine, backed out, made a U-turn in the middle of the empty block and headed toward the highway.

With his feet out in front of him, Harry leaned back against the counter. As he watched Roy's pickup pass out of sight, he rested one arm on the counter and book. He stuck one finger in the book near the middle and squeezed it between the hard covers with the rest of his hand, allowing his mind also to penetrate the brief history recorded there.

And maybe he's right about Buck, but Arron and Bobtail Smith, that's something else—all this for Ronnie—him and Buck and everybody cussin Arron and calling Bobtail

135

Smith a crazy old nigger—a cuss grows up around a man quicker than weeds in a garden, jest quit tendin it every mornin and you got a weed patch—he was a hero—more'n Ronnie to my thinkin, that crazy old nigger—I guess I sold him enough mentholated ointment over the years to put a three-inch coat all over Main Street—it was cold and icy when it happened—forty miles in waist-high snow— there's a lot more to him than most care to remember—I remember—remember Tom bringing him in all wrapped in a blanket—nigger in the snow—he'd walked three days cuttin fences—and they found him froze inside the belly of an old cow he'd split open and crawled into to keep warm. Forty miles to the canyon with the Crows Foot herd fol- lowin him like Moses—and he led 'um, six thousand, over the rim and out of the blowin snow—and only ask 'um one for his trouble. They found him froze in her.

"I cleaned him—but it was Mae that cured him." Mae Parker, seemed strange for her—southern lady like her rolling up her sleeves and workin over him like that, but she didn't falter. Five times a day just like I told her, she put 'um on him—washed him and put a fresh green manure poultice on him—It was her that started the men- tholated ointment—she put it around his nose—and hers too—so he couldn't smell his flesh rottin off like it done. An I guess it was her he smelled, maybe still smells—he didn't use it when he healed up—but he was my first customer when I opened up the store that afternoon after her funeral. And I been sellin it to him ever since—yep, I guess it's her he is smellin and that don't sound too crazy to me.

And Mae Parker—Mae Batten Parker. Tom, young feller then, and she made him a good one—she filled his coffee pot at four o'clock every morning and lived in a dugout in the early years and give him Arron. And later he give her that house just like her daddy's—and the Baptist Church—had every brick hauled in wagons—then the rail- road came and she got her house—stuck out there on the bare grass—looks like the Ark before the rain—sittin out there naked without its swamp and cane fields—I guesss he'd of given them to her too if he'd thought of it or could, but he didn't.

Her funeral day old Smith took back to that ointment. Puttin her in the ground—she looked the same on the outside, still young—but like she didn't weigh nothin—pretty, a speckle blue robin's egg but empty like a cat had sucked it out—Just a bird's egg shell in an iron box. Nothin seems right when you start puttin 'um in the ground—I guess Ronnie's the same—puttin him in.

I've seen two of 'um put in and one dug for Sarah—poor Sarah with that empty hole waiting for her—we put Tom in on the same day and come to hers without nothin to put in—it was like an empty offering plate being passed by you—when we was puttin Tom in I looked at hers, all fresh dug for her and it almost sucked me in—almost sucked us all in, cause it was so empty—still empty, except for dirt and gravedigger sweat I guess.

And even now it sucks at us, all of us that let Arron keep her out there—and puttin in Ronnie now, it'll suck at us if Arron's not there, it'll suck at me. If Smith don't tell him—if Roy don't tell him, God if I don't—it'll suck me out my eyes if I look at 'um puttin him in without Arron knowin—Great God there's been a punishment building up all these Sundays.

Harry squeezed the book harder to capitalize Great God, and felt a numb pain in the finger he had stuck between the pages. He looked at it a moment, seeing the white, greenish color of bloodless flesh and thought, a dead finger in the flower book. Then he released his grip and with the cold finger, hooked the book open. It opened to a blank page. He waited before he looked down at it, hoping that it would be blank, and without remembering or thinking of anything else he got off the stool and walked from the front of the store to the back, pulling on light strings and rubbing his tingling finger.

XIII

A HALF block down the street the unpainted, shack house telephone office with its ever-present electronic buzzlike hum was almost quiet. Only the faint vibration of electricity passing through copper could be heard. And Elmira could not hear that, she could not hear it as she could not hear the blood passing in her veins. But she knew it was there, that it was in the air. She knew because there had been times when she had not heard it, times when the power was gone.

She remembered these times physically, as loneliness is remembered by the physical pain of emptiness, or of weight on the chest.

This morning she felt as if the power were off, as if the phone office were dead. She had put through calls and even listened to some to be sure everything was working —yet she felt the absence of something.

She had not dressed this morning. This was the first time in five years that she had not stayed up on Saturday night and ironed her Sunday dress, brushed her shoes and laid out her hat. For five years every Sunday she dressed for church. She had made a collection plate from an old tin pie pan by gluing green felt on it. She laid it out on Saturday night also, along with a black hymnal, her Bible with gold-edged pages and red ink Jesus words and a Sunday school quarterly. On Communion Sundays she prepared her grape juice and unleavened bread.

She would sit at the switchboard in her Sunday dress and hat listening to the sermon through the headset which she wore under her hat. She followed each movement of the service. Just standing for prayer at first, then the offering plate was added and for the last few years she had taken the Lord's Supper.

Today was a Lord's Supper Sunday. When she talked to Brother Morris over the phone earlier, he had told her about communion, that he thought it was fitting to have it today because of Ronnie's funeral and the fact that most of his Deacons would probably be absent planting wheat next Sunday. He had mentioned it in the prayer. He always led her in prayer just before he propped the open phone up on his desk and went out to give his sermon.

He would sit at his desk in the church study with the door closed between it and the sanctuary leading her in prayer. They were good prayers, long and passionate and sometimes personal for things or about things Elmira felt she had no right to hear. Then she would pray. At first they both used *we* and *us* but as Sundays passed it became *I* and *me*, forgive *me* O Lord. By some mutual, silent consent they heard each other's prayers. They felt the black instrument in their hand and heard the breathing on the other end, each feeling a private connection with God as if a Great Old Man sat somewhere on an alabaster throne in white robes, holding a black phone to his ear—intently cocking his head and nodding deep, solemn, sympathetic nods.

Elmira's isolated ritual was not secret, the townspeople knew and respected her for it. Their telephones became icons during the hours of worship. To use them at those times, even in case of emergency, had an air of blasphemy about it. Many times however, although she worshiped alone, her acts were not private. The older boys sometimes skipped the church service and sat in the tall weeds outside the back window of the telephone office and watched Elmira; listened to her sing alto by herself and pray out loud for sinners during the invitation.

But today they could not have watched. The water-marked brown shades were drawn. Today she sat at the switchboard in her faded pink bathrobe. She had not combed her hair and her mouth tasted musty. It was Lord's Supper Sunday but she had not poured out the little thimble glass of grape juice or made the flour and water bread. Today she sat there with a half-full bottle of the grape juice she had herself put up in the long-necked wine bottles. Beside the tall thin bottle was an empty soda cracker box.

"I'll use the crumbs" she thought, "just pinch up some crumbs and take a swallow of grape juice." She thought of the grape juice and was thirsty. She picked it up, thought of a glass, forgot it, and put the small mouth of the lean bottle to her lips and sucked. The juice was tart and seemed to cut the sliminess out of her mouth. She sucked again and the bottle sucked back, pulling part of her upper lip into its tight mouth. *Do this in remembrance of me,* she thought and sucked again feeling the bottle pull her lips against its mouth. She swallowed and the vacuum ruptured.

Take this cup and drink in remembrance of me. She lowered the bottle from her mouth. The suction had clotted her lip into a little purple flesh dome. She smiled faintly, showing bluish teeth in the half light and thought, in remembrance of me—*yes remember me and I will, little Jesus baby, you and Elmira and—yes, it's his Sunday too, Brother Morris so said it—today is Ronnie's Sunday too.*

140

She looked at the bottle and saw a little fleck of something floating on the juice. *Today is your day and his day and Lord—it's my day too.*

She got up from the switchboard, set the night bell and went back to the bedroom. The black earphones sang to each other in the empty switchboard room as the choir began "Praise God from Whom All Blessings Flow."

In the small bedroom under a sagging ceiling and on a sagging bed over the warped floor she sat, not hearing the earphones singing their duet. The floor, the bed and the ceiling seemed to be making saucers for each in its own turn to fall into.

The cheap, brown shades were still drawn. The light shone through them, giving the room a dusty tan air and the water stains on them were projected on the opposite wall by the sun. She sat back on the bed and watched the shadowy, watermark patterns splotch the faded wallpaper. A fly, trapped between the window and the shade, buzzed and bumped it, sending ripples of magnified shadows across the wall.

Today is Lord's Supper Sunday. She lay back on the saucer bed, letting her arm hang off the edge, not quite letting the long-necked wine bottle touch the floor. *Are you washed,* she thought, *are you washed in the blood of the lamb.* She lifted the bottle—*this is my blood, take it in remembrance of me—and they took it and He died. I took His blood, sucked it right out his shoulder—the blood of the lamb. I was washed in the blood—in the soul cleansing blood of the lamb—I sucked it right out.*

She put the bottle to her lips—*take this in remembrance.* She sucked hard and the juice came easy and warm, then harder. She plugged the bottle with her tongue and rolled her eyes back in her head, then moved the sucking bottle over her lips feeling it pull the blood to the surface of her skin—*oh God I remember the lamb—he kissed me and I was washed. He crushed me like the grapes and my wine*

1 4 1

and his blood ran together. She moved the bottle over her face, and forgetting the juice in it, she tried to move it to her breast. As it slid off her chin the vacuum broke and the hot juice drenched her. She lay back opening her robe, rubbing the thick purple juice over her scrub breast and down over the rest of her body. Then sucking at the empty bottle again she sang in her thoughts—*I am washed in the blood—in the blood.* She slipped her thumb into her mouth and over the bottle to hold the suction. She then slid it down onto her stomach—*they can remember Jesus and I will have service for Ronnie the lamb.*

Poor little Ronnie lamb born into this world with no mother—poor Jesus but at least he had a mama. But Sarah died. Died without even good-bye to that lamb. It was the fire. Arron was crazy to leave her—crazy dumb even before it happened and made him crazy crazy—the fires of hell could'a got him. But they didn't—it took that grass and those cows and old Tom Parker on to glory but not the lamb. Safe in his dead mother's arms, screaming and crying as loud as Arron done when he found them and went crazy. Crazy Arron they still say it—but not me. He wasn't crazy to have Miss Edith Harvest stay on out there to care for him. And she done it—raised him up for four years then she left. Left straight from Arron's house back to her daddy's with her head up high—sittin on a milk stool in the back of Bobtail Smith's wagon—right down Main Street —don't matter what they say a crazy man ain't a dead man but can't nobody say wrong about her without seeing that straight line she made riding down Main Street—that line is straighter and cleaner than all the dirty things they said.

Some years passed without her and she died—she died that I might live. He was riding from town in the rain where he bought her red flowers for her grave—and he come to me out of the rain into the hay—he come to me.

She gouged long red purple streaks on the pale mushroom flesh of her low belly with the bottle, and from her grotesque mouth of blue teeth came a moaning hymn— *out of the rain he come to me, pure lamb washed by God to me—and it crushed me like the grapes—sticky grapes and shoulder blood—and my wine ran red under him—Jesus God Ronnie and the blood of the lamb gushed from me— wine for the bottle, blood for the cup. Oh God-Ronnie-Lamb-of-God you are back—home from the fire—crush my grapes Ronnie God.* She gnashed teeth-blood marks in her own forearm as the long-necked bottle in the other hand penetrated and became God, Ronnie, heaven and hell. Her mind echoed, *are you washed in the blood of the lamb.*

The earphones in the other room united in silent prayer, as the watermark shadows of the window shades boiled and smoldered visions into focus on the faded roses of the wallpaper.

She hunched her back, raising her head, her bulging eyes fixed on the churning shadows in an adhesive stare and like dust dulling the life glint in the eyes of a fresh-killed rabbit she lost focus and the mind's eye was free.

It saw a mouth, Ronnie's mouth and hay then rain, then the rain-drenched bodies of a thousand boys coming to her in horse sweat and rain with molded hay sticking to their naked bodies. She saw lovers as railroad ties, lying in the throes of passion for miles on top of the track and the black locomotive with the laughing toothless face of Bobtail Smith bearing down on them—slicing across their bodies—and each body was hers and her lover's. Then the train was gone and she could hear the blood running and the visions softened and became real.

Ronnie spoke to her.

"You're bleeding Elmira. Did it cut you?"

"No Ronnie lamb, it didn't cut me."

"Are you hurt?"

"No."

"I—I guess I went wild a little."

"A little."

"The rain's stopped. Is Roy coming?"

"Not for a little."

"I tore your clothes. I'm sorry I tore your clothes."

"It's O.K. lamb. It's O.K."

"I guess I had a fit. I feel like I did. Like I had a fit and tore loose from myself. Like I slung myself to pieces."

"That's the way it is they say. A fellow said it was like a star-burst in the night of his soul."

"You tired Elmira?"

"Not tired, jest relaxed and full."

"Me too, only new. I feel new. Like all I was before was a carbuncle, all sore and rotten. Then I exploded out the core and all the corruption and filled back up with new blood, fresh new blood."

"It's raining again lamb, are you cold?"

"I'm running away Elmira. Tonight I'm tellin 'um and running away."

"Lamb, it's cold, don't you feel a chill?"

"I got my ticket to California. If you come to the train tonight—I'll—I'll say good-bye."

"Yes, lamb, tonight at the train. Now cover yourself."

The shadows dimmed on the faded wallpaper of her bedroom as a lone thunderhead covered the sun. Elmira was chilled as she lay in the saucer bed. The bottle was still and the saucer was filling slowly with the tide of her hemorrhage. She thought the chill was a night chill and the shadow was darkness because it was a late train.

She saw herself standing at the train depot in the shadow of the single lamp post, a shadow created by its own dim light. The building was empty and dark. The steel-wheeled mail carts were gaunt and impersonal, parked next to the freight room door. She looked back over her shoulder at the lights across the highway in the hotel. The light was

144

on in Roy's room. She did not think of him or of the room. She was cold in the fall night air. She waited for the sound of Ronnie. And the sound came. The sound of an old tin-covered suitcase slapping against the broad calf of his leg as he carried it up the track. At first it was a quick regular slap, slap, slap, as he stepped on every cross tie. Then the slaps came slower, the same rhythm only in half time, he had lengthened his stride to every other tie. He had alternated steps all the way from the Crows Foot fence, where he had turned loose his horse with a swat on the rump.

The slaps were farther apart now but approaching faster.

"Ronnie," she spoke in a normal voice but the sound seemed to jump to the iron tracks and carry down them like electricity, "is that you?"

"Elmira?" The spark cracked back along the tracks. She left the thin shadow and ran down the gravel siding.

"Has it come? Has it come yet?"

"No," she said, wishing his question had been "Will it come."

"I didn't know it would take so long to walk. I should'a took a horse."

They walked to one of the mail carts. The night air was chill and heavy with the smell of creosote from the cross ties and dead coal smoke. Inside the dark depot office the telegraph key chattered once, then again. It jerked their attention to it as it set off again for a long crazy mechanical laugh, rhythm without rhythm, like an insane, runaway metronome.

"It's the telegraph." Her whisper cut the darkness with a hollow hiss, like a cigarette dropped in a toilet bowl. Then it was quiet and the smells and darkness washed back to fill the hole in time blasted out by the noise. Ronnie rubbed the palm of his right hand on the side of his levi jacket.

"I done somethin else bad Elmira—somethin else than what we done this afternoon."

1 4 5

She did not move or speak, the word bad shot hot air into her stomach.

"What it was we done isn't bad Ronnie."

"What I done was—I don't want to go Elmira—I jest bought the ticket because I was sorry inside that Miss Edith died—but . . ."

"But what Ronnie?" A hope valve popped open and the hot air that had jammed her heart like a fist into her throat escaped, he's going to stay, she thought, he's going to stay.

In that same instant of thought, she married him, buried Arron Parker, moved into and made over the headquarters house, drilled oil wells, gave birth to sons and burned down the telephone office.

"I hit old Smith." He rubbed his hand harder on the faded jacket. "I slapped him down. Smell my hand, smell him on it; that ointment. He didn't get up. I cussed my own father and killed Smith."

He put the hand to his face. She pulled it away.

"I can't smell it, Ronnie, it don't smell like nothin to me."

He jerked it back and put it inside his open jacket as if it were deformed.

"Well I can and that ain't all that's on it. . . . You're on it, what we done is, and I can smell it. I can't keep from it, I can't keep it down. I can smell you, your juice like I was an old bull. It's been in my face ever since. I can't keep it down." His voice got tighter and tighter in his throat like a man screaming an oath as he was being strangled, "I don't want to go; I ain't never been; Elmira I ain't never been." He stopped and gasped in the darkness. It was quiet. Then through tight lips, "I'm a yellow coward, I hit an old man and took from a virgin." The hand went back to his face. The smell began its penetration, being carried along as incidental flotsam on the inward tide of pity, a tide rolling inward toward a glowing brimstone pit of guilt.

She touched him. "Ronnie."

"Get away," the words singed the darkness. "Get Away."
He threw himself on the ground, crawling to the track
and smashing his arm down across the rail. Face down on
the gravel siding he screamed, "Cut it off, the train can
cut it off."

His consciousness, the frail hunter, bolted into the night
and watched its ugly prey from the darkness with burning
eyes.

Elmira ran to the fire barrel by the station door and
dipped the cone-shaped bucket full of water. The oily film
on it glinted a single pinpoint reflection of the lone night
light down the siding as she knelt beside him. She splashed
water on his head and the back of his neck. The water was
warm and thick with soot and rust.

As she held the dunce-cap bucket and squatted beside
the track bathing Ronnie's neck, she looked up. The moon
had come full. The tracks shown silver, worn sterling lines,
sliding forward under the skin of darkness. Her mind
jumped to the track and flashed along it, she imagined
straight around the world, next to the earth, close as its
circumference; and held for an instant, possession, as solid
and fleeting as the slap of a tossed orange against the palm
of the catching hand. And Mother, that driving inertia
at the heart of the species, consumed her.

Forgetting the shape of the bucket, she set it aside
turning her head from the track, pulling her eyes away,
recoiling her imagination into herself.

"Ronnie, Ronnie Baby," she said toned like a lullaby.
The bucket lay on its side, the water running under him.
The wetness shocked him and he lifted himself. She sat
him up, holding him close. She was now possessed. Time
had accelerated or it had stopped. The female instincts
with the time intervals jerked from beteeen them,
slapped together as beads on a string—now she was mother.

"Sit up lamb, sit up and let me wipe you off."

He was sick and frightened, the conspiracy of *she* was
working against him. He was being thrust out even as

from the womb. Man stands unwilling, tricked into being, taunted into bravery, facing life, as the grim co-conspirator, mother earth, turns under him, bashing him into it.

"Elmira, I can't go, I—I got to stay and tell, I got to tell what I done—I got to make up. I'll buy you something —anythin—they got to do what I say—the Bank has got to —I ain't like Papa—they got to do it." He stood up. She stood by him wiping the gravel off his clothes with her head scarf.

"No lamb you're not like Arron."

"Some of 'um say I am—Smith says it—that's why I hit him, he kept saying it and nasty things about you—saying it, callin me crazy—and telling me he's my mama 'cause Papa said it. I can't go, even if I am, I can't go."

She drew him to her whispering—whispering nature's pragmatic lies of reassurance, those lies universal to mother-absolute, lies communicated by bear and bird alike to the young, lies whispered just before the abandonment.

"Show man Ronnie, show us some man. Get strong, come back and show man." As she spoke, the round yellow headlight of the train broke the surface of infinity down the silver tracks.

Outside the telephone shack, the grey thunderhead moved on, exposing the sun. The trapped fly, feeling the heat magnified on it by the age-dulled glass of the window-pane, buzzed again against the glass and the watermarked shade. The shadows smoldered on the wall.

Elmira felt the last chill. The slight shiver and the erection of chill pimples broke the thin dry skim on the pool of cooling coagulating blood with a sound like tearing spider web. Her thoughts were now in dim sound. Her mind saw the shadows but the image had not been relayed by her eyes, for they were in death focus on the browned ceiling paper. Her ears reported the sound of the night telephone bell.

Harry Eddens trying to ring her to call Amarillo to

place the flower order. Then the long distance key began to chatter and one of the country party lines rang its three ring code. The shadows dimmed to black and her ears squeezed their focus in between sounds and relaxed in that void, hearing only death which is constant, and the drying blood.

In the other room the switchboard keys chattered and call lights blinked like red and white insect eyes.

It could have been an insane old man, winking and giggling at some joke his vision told him. Winking and laughing through his chattering teeth at the joke of isolation.

XIV

Harry gave the phone crank a final, irritated spin. Well if that ain't somethin, he thought, as he banged the ear piece into the little black wishbone hanger on the side of the old wall telephone. I guess she's so fired up with soul saving she can't even say number please. I could be dying. I could be dying right here in my own store; just barely able to get to the phone—to turn it once, much less enough times to wind every clock, watch and music box in the damn county.

It's a hell of a note, he thought, when you have to run down to the office, wake up central and run back home just to enjoy the convenience of having a telephone in your house. He stepped a half step outside and looked at his watch, then up at the sun, still holding his shirt sleeve back from the face of the dial.

He came back inside, looking again at the wall phone. Its nose was always pointed down and the black bells mounted above it gave it the eyes of a somber, long-faced old man waiting with the patience of death to deliver bad news.

Ten to twelve, he thought. I got to get that flower order

in before noon; church is gonna be out and they'll be coming in. That must be a damn fine sermon if she can't hear my ring right before her eyes. Maybe she's got 'um closed; a prayer maybe. I don't want to disturb her praying; but dadburn it. . . . He paced back to the door. Well I don't want to interrupt her church; Lord knows that's all she's got, that and Roy Turner sniffin around at night like some stray hound trying to disaddle his brain long enough to decide where to wet down a fireplug.

He looked at his watch again, then back over his shoulder at the phone, decided it wouldn't do any good to try again, and went quickly to the back of the store to get the keys. He walked fast and with guilt, feeling already the exaggerated urgency that possesses the storekeeper during his infidelity. He took the wad of keys from the pocket of his suit coat which hung on the peg behind the door.

He hurried back toward the front. The closer he got to the door, the faster he sorted keys, until he dropped the jangling wad almost in the doorway. He stopped short, not moving, and just looked at them. Then he bowed grandly and plucked the wad from the floor by the right key. Pulling the door closed, he looked at the postmaster who had just come from meeting the eleven-thirty mail train and had backed his old Chevrolet coupe up to the curb in front of the post office next door. The postmaster got out.

"Mornin Harry, comin or goin?"

"Neither one—I just got to run over to the phone office and try to talk Elmira into answering the phone."

"Isn't she listening to church about now?"

"How do I know what she is listening to? All I know is that it ain't the phone."

"Well, that's one thing about the U.S. Post Office—like the inspector said, 'she's a jealous mistress'—if she wasn't I'd be in church myself this mornin."

He pulled up the trunk lid, jiggled it to test the support

catch, then put his left hand to his back and straightened up. Inside, the three dirty canvas mailsacks looked empty, yet each was locked. They looked locked against something getting in, rather than out, like protecting the chastity of the mails.

"I never thought of it as being bad women that kept you out of church, Wendell, but I guess that's as good as any." Harry stepped off the curb toward the telephone office, "If anybody comes up to the store tell 'um I just went over to the phone office for a minute and I'll be right on back."

"All right, but don't say nothing to me about bad women when in the same breath you are askin me to watch the store while you are makin a mornin call on an unwed lady." He bent over, picked up the locked end of the mailsacks and dragged them into the post office. He dragged them because they were not empty. As long as they contained one post card he dragged them; if they were unlocked and empty he carried them.

Harry rushed diagonally across the empty street to the phone office. He pushed open the limber front door of the outer office. It dragged at the bottom, then, giving away, opened wigwagging, rattling loose glass panes against shrunken putty.

The room inside was narrow and dim. It had about it that lifeless, impersonal, wasted air of all unused public waiting places. In one corner a toll booth stood brooding like a rejected casket upended and forgotten. Beside it a curve-backed jury chair sat with a dirty pillow showing through the bottom of its ruptured cane seat. The one outside window was on the north side of the room. Through its sooty glass a waiting customer could look up the main street that Harry had just crossed.

Across the room from that window was another, a small square interior window set in the wall between the waiting room and the one next to it where the switchboard and banks of telephone apparatus were. It was chest high, the size of a bathroom medicine cabinet and open. There was a counter-like board across the bottom where checks could be written when bills were paid.

Inside, Harry paused listening to the chattering switchboard and the long ring of the night bell thrusting into the other dry insect noises, withdrawing to silence then thrusting again. He closed the warped door softly and crossed the narrow room to the high window.

The switchboard was empty, the earphones lay on the prickled bank of key switches. He could not hear the hymn. The entire room, even the air, seemed to be chattering, grinding and buzzing. The switchboard seemed alive outside itself, like a dead body swarming with ants, maggots and buzzing flies. Harry stood silent before the frenzy of sound. He could smell the over-heated wiring.

"Elmira," he called through the opening into the empty switchboard room. "Elmira, are you there?" Hell where else would she be, he thought, you idiot, she must be sick, maybe passed out back there.

"Elmira, it's Harry," he shouted louder over the noise. No answer. Now he could feel the heat on his face coming from the switchboard. He pushed himself away from the service window and went to the door beside the toll booth. He stood before it for a moment, looking down at the crack underneath as if he expected a sign of welcome or moral easement.

Then he grasped the knob as if to hold it shut, and knocked hard on the center panel.

"Elmira, you all right?" He yelled and knocked at the same time as if one trespass were an excuse for the other. "Elmira!" He paused for an answer, waited long moments listening. Each time he knocked and shouted it was harder. "Elmira, are you all right?"

He turned the door knob, still pulling. I'll ease it open, he thought, she may be asleep—asleep hell, what's the matter with me, she's either dead or gone or maybe both. Just as he started to ease forward on the door, the bell in the toll booth sprang out at him. It startled him and he shoved hard against the door, banging it into the back of the overstuffed chair in the bedroom. The door opened about five inches. Harry's eyes turned to the booth, an angry sickness balled up in the pit of his stomach. He kicked the booth door shut. The violence and noise felt good and he turned back to the opening in the bedroom doorway.

He saw first the greasy headrest of the chair that was holding the door, then across the room the end of the bed, and a bare foot crazily pointed out.

"Elmira," he called. The foot did not move. He pushed the door but it did not give; the chair was wedged between it and the bed. He squeezed his head through the opening. His face was down, the door and its jamb scraped his ears. He forced his head on through and turned toward the bed.

"Great God." He saw her in the pool of drying blood and violently jerked his head back through the narrow crack, cutting his chin and bruising his ears. He did not feel it, he did not feel anything except a dull ache at the roots of his teeth as the angry ball of fear from his stomach spattered the waiting room floor and burned the inside of his nose.

He stumbled from the waiting room, wiping his mouth and nose, slinging the gorge away from him with violent nastiness.

"Great God—great God," he repeated, "she's dead."

The outside air and Sunday silence sobered him. He began to taste his mouth. Stopping in the middle of the street, he heard himself once again say, "Great God she's dead." It seemed as if it were a voice outside himself. A dialogue ricocheted inside his head.

How do you know, did you feel her pulse? *Hell, no, would you—you saw her in that blood—if you are so god-damned interested why didn't you feel it?* You know I couldn't get in. *Well, I guess you call puking on the floor respectful, what about the back door?* What about it? *Try*

154

the back door—feel her pulse—mirror under her nose—puke
in the back door.

He turned, shook his head, took out his handkerchief, and blew his nose, moving slowly through the high weeds around the shack.

He opened the thin, unpainted back door. Tension jerked a net of wrinkles around his eyes and mouth. He went directly to the bed, and paused a moment to notice a large green fly stuck, with one wing vibrating, in the thick, red-brown, chocolate syrup mess which framed her white body, a whiteness not white but somehow blushing apple-green. He placed his hand on her forehead. It was cool as morning earth.

He walked around the bed, looking for something with which to cover her, compelled to cloak in modesty the vulgar fact of death. He looked down at her as he walked, and his foot hit the grape juice bottle, kicking it crazily like spin the bottle for a kiss under the chair. He did not try to pick it up, he didn't even know what it was.

After finding a blanket, he paused long seconds at the edge of the bed looking down at her, fascinated by this babe in death almost like a father, before he flung it out over the bed and watched it settle over her body.

The breeze created by the blanket puffed a wisp of mouse colored hair across her open mouth. He raised the blanket from her face and with finicky fingers, lifted the hair, like a speck off milk foam from where it lay across her purple teeth. A sunset of loneliness and old man's sadness settled over him as he lowered the thin tattered edge of the blanket over her face.

He sighed a long quivering sigh and started to straighten up. Then he stopped. Half bending over the bed, he softly and slowly, as dust falls to dust, laid his hand on her covered breast and after a moment moved it slowly down her side to her waist, drowning the trapped fly.

XV

Harry did not go back to the store. He walked the block and a half to the nightwatchman's house, woke him, and standing on the ground beside the large concrete block that was the step up into the house, talked through the screen door. Standing in the doorway in just his trousers hurriedly pulled up like a fireman's over his long underwear and with his wide suspender straps still twisted where he had jerked his thumbs from under them, the nightwatchman knew it was something urgent before Harry spoke.

"Mason, I just found Elmira over at the phone office—she's dead."

The old man's thoughts stumbled. Killed, he thought, somebody robbed the phone office and she's killed—I didn't sleep, I swear I didn't sleep—like I told 'um don't sleep anymore anyways, good job for man like me.

"Looks like she died sometime this mornin. Hemorrhage of the female parts."

The watchman ran his thumbs under the suspender straps at the waist, then up to his shoulders. The straps snapped straight and flat.

"Hemorrhage of the female parts? Should we call a doctor? I'll call the Sheriff, he can drive over and bring a doctor."

Harry squinted up through the screen wire and spoke slowly, each word sprouting a brittle fuzz of irritation, and with more force as if the screen wire was straining the reason from his statements, and only the skimmed words were getting through to the old man.

"We can't *call* nobody, Mason. The switchboard is chasin its own tail. I got to get back and try to cut off the power or there's gonna be a fire. You go get Buck." He turned to go, then stopped in the middle of the yard and called back, not to give any more information but to try to replace with a direct man-to-man statement the props of respect his harsh words had kicked loose.

"Buck's up at church, see if you can get him out and down to the phone office." He turned and started across the vacant lots toward the shack. His strides through the tall dead weeds were long and fast, but his movement seemed slow as if the thick brown weeds were a knee-high current against him.

Mason watched him through the rusty screen wire. Then he focused his eyes on the screen, moving them down to a long narrow piece of cloth that had been sewed with red mannish stitches over a tear near the hook to keep out flies. "Hemorrhage of the female parts," he said as he turned slowly back into the house.

Mason dressed, took a swipe at his hair, buttoned the top button of his blue collarless shirt, the one he would have worn to church if he had gone and if he had owned a collar for it. He went to the small, tightly packed closet near the door, reached in and peeled a drooping brown double-breasted suit coat out of the squeezed billows of old clothes.

It's hell to be so poor you can't throw away stuff you never use or wear, he thought, as he put on the coat and walked out the door.

The screen door banged shut. The noise stopped him on the brick walk. He listened to the knot in the door spring vibrate out a taunting countryfied echo of the slam, and realized how quiet it was on Sunday morning. Already he felt uneasy about having to walk into the church house in the middle of a sermon to get Buck.

The old red brick church stood on the corner of a vacant block. With all the empty cars and pickups parked close around, it looked like a huge fortress into which the occupants of the abandoned vehicles had recently fled.

Inside it was different. It was wide-eyed and serious. It seemed a moist cool place—a place out of the sun and driving wind of the prairie. It smelled like starch and clean cotton whipped fresh by the wind on breezy Mondays when each fiber dried suspended in sun and country air. The smells were fresh and joyous like echoes of happy flapping clotheslines. They were mixed with the resident odors of oak furniture polish, floor sweep, and of old hymn books and forgotten Bibles; all mixed like bakery whiffs into the fresh mustiness of sealed rooms. High on the walls, next to tall windows with frosted bathroom windowglass, black electric fans slowly nodded back and forth like disapproving widows.

On a back pew four boys, old enough to sit away from their families but too young to be in the choir or to sit with girls, silently amused themselves, taunted each other to the brink of noise by turning through the hymn book and showing hymn titles which followed the predetermined mental prefix or suffix, "between the sheets."

> Love Divine—*between the sheets!*
> God Will Take Care of You—*between the sheets!*
> Take My Life and Let It Be—*between the sheets!*
> Nothing But the Blood—*between the sheets!*
> Why Not Tonight—*between the sheets!*
> *between the sheets*—Softly and Tenderly

It was an old game and had caused many in their own

158

time to become conscience-stricken at the end of the service, during the long and pleading invitation, and step out in the aisle, walk to the front and give the pastor their hands, confessing blasphemy and marking at that point the beginning of an awareness of sin.

The preacher, Brother Morris, was not a table-pounder; he seldom shouted. He had been chosen by a pulpit committee of rough-skinned Deacons, men who were battered or threatened constantly by the elemental wrath of God, their guilt beaten from them like dust from a rug. It was without guilt and often with a sizeable debt of the Creator's mercy owing them, that they came on Sundays. The noise of the corral at branding time or the loud and monotonous roar of farm machinery left them in no mood to be preached at. Brother Morris was a quiet man. But he was also a crier. Like some of the old men who broke into great sobs during prayers they were asked to lead. Men who, when called on for prayer, would with slow deliberate strength like Christ rising under the cross, get to their feet and speak directly to God. Great long soul-rumbling prayers, as if they were themselves the earth, trembling from deep internal quakes and upheavals.

Today he spoke of death and in memory of Ronnie Parker.

Sitting between Buck and Mildred Harris, the chaplain was hot. The winter uniform directive had arrived three days before he left the Ruley Base. Texas weather put the Air Force quartermaster at a disadvantage. It was ninety degrees at Ruley the day the order was posted.

The wool in his trousers pricked his legs. A trickle of sweat scurried crookedly down his leg, dodging around hairs and now and then stinging quickly like a small hot needle. The pew was crowded. Mildred had leaned forward to give them more room but he still felt pressed. Hips nudged against him on both sides. Several times he looked up at the wall fans just as they nodded away.

He had spoken briefly to Buck's Sunday school class.

The idea of these men in a Sunday school class seemed frail even to him, something less than manly, as if they were there because their wives made them attend. But the wide noncommittal seriousness of their eyes when he spoke disturbed him, and when he finished he had felt thin, aware of some vague silliness, almost a feeling of trespass.

He felt depressed and uncomfortable. Through the sermon he picked and argued with the preacher, mentally grading him, taking some pleasure in his mispronunciations of biblical names. Yet he could not make the satisfaction last, the pile of bones he was picking seemed to crumble and disintegrate as soon as he snatched them out into the light. He felt he was the only one in the whole church who ever blinked his eyes. The congregation seemed like a school of fish suspended, stationary, held without motion facing upstream. Their eyes and mouths open, letting the natural current of the stream flow in, bringing food and air as it rippled in silent eddies over their gills.

He held his eyes open as long as he could, until they burned, until the angry wool and sweat wasps buried a volley of stingers in his thigh. Then he clamped them shut, detonating a prayer in his mind toward heaven with the velocity of a curse. God in heaven, his mind spat out on the hot iron of his misery, what is it—what is it that You torture me thus? What am I that You withhold from me?

He opened his eyes. Mildred looked at him and leaned out a little farther. He could feel the deep wrinkles in the squint of her girdle. His eyes were red and watery. The preacher may have noticed and felt the holy spirit, for it is the eyes that give the first indication of a soul-burst. He knew the signs, for even in his stumblings he had lanced many spiritual pustules. He was saying: "How big, brother, just how big is your soul, just what size is this thing that you're givin the Lord God Almighty? A man don't come to his neighbor with a teacup to get a gallon of oil—you don't rope a thousand pound steer with a cotton clothesline, and brother, when you throw a rope around Christianity you got holt of somethin wilder and stronger than any bull that ever set hoof to God's green earth. And, brother, your soul is all you got for a lariat rope.

"Every man born of man comes to this earth with his soul coiled in his hand, already ankle-deep in the quicksand of sin, and any of you that's been up on the North Canadian River knows what I'm talking about, a two hundred dollar cow will sink out of sight before you can get your rope off the saddle. Well Brethren, there you stand.

"Some men won't throw their rope 'cause they're afraid of gettin skinned up by bein dragged out through the shinery and mesquite bushes. And they're right. Christ never said it was easy. You might get dragged a half mile up a rocky gully, but it won't hurt nothin but your pride and, besides, it'll scrape a little of the sin off you."

Is that it Sir, the chaplain thought, are You being abrasive to scrape the sin off me? He looked at his watch. He's going to hang himself if he keeps extending that rope example, he thought, as Buck grunted an "Amen."

He had forgotten about Buck, even the hot flank pressed against him and the wad of change in Buck's pocket. He shifted his leg slightly and it felt hotter. He wondered again why Buck had elbowed him gently and almost proudly earlier when the preacher was talking about Ronnie. It was during a prayer. A prayer that contained what he had always called a sermonette, something the preacher ricocheted off God to come screaming back like steel off flint to pierce the sin-encrusted hearts of the congregation.

"Lord, we know that being saved don't run in the blood. The fact that this boy's Granddaddy had every brick in this very house of worship hauled in by wagon and team and had it put up and dedicated to your work in the name of this boy's Grandmother and that she lived and died in this church. And that his Daddy turned his back on it when

1 6 1

his bride was taken home to God. Lord, even though this boy never saw the inside of this sanctuary, we pray for his soul—that some man of God out there on the field of battle led him into the fold." It was at this point that Buck nudged him. It was not that he had done it but the way he had done it. Two quick times, like indicating the punch line of some unknown joke or slander. He listened to the rest of the sermonette in his mind, looking for a clue.

"And Lord we pray for Arron, the very mortar in these walls cries out in sorrow for him—call him back, Lord, open his eyes. Show him that by turning his back on God and the world he may have condemned his own son to an early grave and an eternity in Hell. And Lord help us when we commit the earthly remains of Ronnie Parker to final rest tomorrow to find in our hearts a Christian compassion and reverence that will reveal the value of faith in Jesus Christ to Arron Parker and the Godless. In His Blessed Name we pray—Amen."

The rerun in his memory of the sermonette ended, and the chaplain moved his leg again to stop the harassed skin on the inside of his thighs from twitching.

The preacher was closing his sermon. "And like the old cowboy who, on his deathbed, told the rest of the boys who had gathered to watch him die, 'Like I say, all you can do when you come to the end of your rope, is to tie a knot and hang on.' And in my own satisfaction, that God-fearing old cowboy was jerked out of the sinful bog of this life right into the stars.

"Shall we stand for the invitation? The invitation hymn will be number one, oh, two, 'Why Do You Wait Dear Brother.' "

There was a slow pause like coffee soaking up through a spoon of sugar, then the congregation stood with a certain bashfulness, hanging their heads down into the songbooks.

As the chaplain stood, he felt his underwear pull away from his buttocks like adhesive tape, then the cool air like an alcohol sponge. While they sang the preacher repeated the words of the verse. "Why do you wait, dear brother? Why do you tarry so long?" All through the singing the chaplain kept his eyes straight ahead. Should I pray for them, he thought, would it help if I bowed my head—is someone watching me, some boy back from service sick of Christ and officer-club chaplains? He kept his eyes on the crude, stiff, lifeless painting on the wall behind the baptistry, a painting done by a woman of the church who had never seen a waterfall.

For a moment he again felt thin, as if his soul was thin. He felt for the first time since his youth lowly before God. Surrounded by the absolute openness of these men as they submitted their strength and integrity to God for judgment and blessing, he felt the enormous power of the spirit. His shrunken soul was swelling in his chest. I've been touched by God, he thought, the firm hand of God has been put upon me.

His eyes turned slightly from the baptistry. He heard slow uncertain footsteps in the back coming down the aisle. As they came nearer, he thought, it's started, Great God an avalanche for Christ has started—and I shall go— I will return to the wellsprings of my youth—I will run ahead and lead them.

The preacher walked slowly from behind the lectern, holding himself back, trying not to seem eager in victory, a smile of relief and empthy on his face.

The steps stopped, they were very near now, they were beside his pew, in the aisle, beside his pew, on the other side of Buck. He's stopped, the chaplain thought, stopped for me to go with him—and I will—yes Lord I will. He turned to step out and saw Mason Holton, the nightwatchman, whispering to Buck. Buck nodded his head, stepped out and followed the old man back up the sloping aisle and out of the church.

XVI

Now *I will know Arron, you, me, myself, and I will know,* Arron thought. He was riding away from the house, holding the can out, not hearing the dripping water as it fell to the grass, with evenly spaced sounds that were as slow and rhythmical as the sound of the walking hoofs that crushed into the turf.

Behind him the big house looked haggard in the light of morning, like an ill-used old woman.

Smith had taken the bucket from him and refilled it, stopping only to chase the green-footed hen gently away from the manure. "Ain't thet gonna be a fine thin fo you to be a trackin on thet white tablecloth," he had said to the hen, then looked sharply at Arron who sat heavy as defeat on the old and broken horse.

The horse plodded along the deep path its hoofs had worn into the grass and even the ground beneath it. The path was narrow and uniformly wide and deep. The grass on one side, the right side, was taller, and still, this late in autumn, flecked with green. The leaking water had grown a thin line of green parallel to the path on its right side, a line greener and thicker near the gate to the house, and gradually diminishing in size and weakening in color as it moved away.

The can was lighter now, dripping less water into the fading grass, and the house was out of sight. Again Arron did not feel the water going. His arm did not move. The narrow dust channel in front and behind him was the only mark on the miles of surrounding empty grassland. He listened to the soft screak of the leather under him and held the reins with a dead hand.

I will now hear the chair, he thought, Smith is talkin but not yet. First I will listen to the chair.

I stood by it tall with my hand on the black shaggy hair 'like long nigger hair which was still then on the buffalo horns and they was black too. Papa said and they said, standing on the ground and not on the porch. They were short from the porch, up to their waist in something— Papa said again and they squirmed in the yard like they was sinkin, then they said, "Mr. Parker I tell you there's enough to buy all the good grassland in Texas." *The one from the company said it.* "We'll put a well every twenty acres and I'll buy you a hat if in six months after, you can show me one footprint where we been that ain't growin grass." *I seen Papa in a hat three times. Then Papa said again and his eyebrows moved forward like two black dogs on chains at the gate.* "Gentlemen, I am sittin in what's left of a deal like you're offering me, a deal that was made to them that was before me on this land. Show me an Indian rich from the royalties off buffalo hide and bone." *One of the times was the hat he wore to watch 'um put Mother-Mae in the ground. They squirmed some more in the yard. Then his eyebrows begin to settle back like the dogs had recognized the sound of our wagon even before they could see it. And Papa settled back too in the horn and hide chair.* "I am about to tell you somethin. You'll hear this too Arron." *I took my hand off the long nigger hair on the*

1 6 5

black horn that went back of his head. "You," *he said at them two that was sinkin in the yard,* "You won't laugh until you get beyond my front gate. This earth that you are now standin on is a woman, this same earth that you want to punch into, and siphon out of, is the body of a woman. Down in her guts somewhere she finds it within her to take compassion on this life that crawls upon her. I will not permit that part of her allotted to me for my time or for the time of this boy standing beside me or for the time of that part of me and him which now rides in the belly of his wife to be violated. So it turns that the part of her allotted by sweat to me shields her vitals which you would suck out. I would no more allow what it is that you suggest than I would have torn open this boy's mother, selling her tubes of fecundity as worms to the buzzards." *They didn't laugh and could have sunk out of sight there in the yard while I was lookin at Papa's black brows and white side hairs. I don't think I knew they was white 'til the door slammed on their company car that had a picture of an oil derrick right on the door in the same place where the Star of Texas on the sheriff's car door is. It was the sheriff that caught them later after the fire, or caught who it was they hired.*

The horse stumbled softly in the dust of the path, the grass was now brown and dry below the suspended can. Arron's dead hand did not feel the little jerk of the reins, yet his eyes responded as if the tug from the horse's mouth had jerked him up short, kept him from falling into the darker thoughts.

Arron saw the giant and lonely cottonwood tree on the rise three miles in the distance. The sun was high now and there was a hot-house stillness over the land. The unruffled blanket of brown grass draped over the horizon on all sides of him. In the distance was the knoll and the gnarled, unvanquished tree. He could also see five different isolated windmills, miles apart on the empty grass,

166

their dead towers rotting like skeletons, their fans broken and deformed like smashed birds wings. Only one still turned, its fan had missing blades which made it like a snaggle-toothed old man grinning. It was the one where Roy Turner brought the groceries.

Ahead, he could see the fence posts that enclosed and marked the garden-sized burial plot beside the tree. The posts were spaced evenly and stood like tall thin pall-bearers surrounding the plot. The strands of rusted barbed wire sagged between them like heavy bands of mourning. There was no mound. In the center of the small enclosure a rusty flare pole leaned out of the ground like an Indian lance thrown from a running horse. A dead and unin-habited bird's nest filled the rusted-out oil pot on top of the pole. Long strands of grass and weed hung from the nest. At the base of the pole, the ground hollowed slightly like a tightly stretched, empty hammock.

Arron rode through the gate, the deep path marked the exact center of it. The horse walked unguided to the grave. Arron eased down to the ground, taking care to keep the empty can level. The grass in the low place which indi-cated the grave was thick and smooth. It had been care-fully transplanted and tended in those years before the can began to leak. The horse followed the path on past the grave. That part of it was shallower. Arron had never ridden over it. Its depth measured only the weight of the horse and saddle, it was that much shallower.

The horse followed it to the tree, and stood now in the shade of that tree with its tail turned to Arron. It stood head down in the shade, not grazing, standing still, almost rigid, in an air of relaxed apprehension as cattle with their tails to the north, stand waiting the impending and unfailing arrival of blue northers. The horse stood thus, respecting the private reverence of the man behind it.

Arron carefully lowered the empty can to the ground. The stiff dry grass made a hollow scratching sound in it as the tin bottom mashed it down. He did not hear the tinny sound nor did he look in the can. The tall sun was hot on his head and the top of his shoulders.

Now I will know. Arron, me, myself, and I will know. These were the steps down into himself, steps he knowingly took. Each step down and back in time was more difficult. He was now like a diver without ballast, forcing himself down submerged steps, feeling himself grow increasingly weightless yet forcing down another step deeper.

He had not yet sat in the grass nor had he touched it with his hands.

So Smith is now sitting in the buffalo chair sitting and talking. Papa wore a hat. He held it over his front when we was standing watchin Mother-Mae go into the ground, over his front like he had a hole in his shirt, then sittin in the horn chair three nights under the hat which was uncreased on his head like risin dough. We was standin over the grave Sarah's belly was already big and she stood at the edge of Mother-Mae's grave all rared back like her big belly was pullin her over into it. I put my hand on her shoulder up under her hair. It was after that, after those three nights, on the morning of the third when he slapped both hands down hard on the black horn arms of the chair and got up. We heard it and Sarah got out the white tablecloth that her mother sent her saying it come from Ireland with her Grandmother. The edge of it caught and draped across her big belly as she fanned it out over the table like a bed sheet. "You'll smother that boy," Papa said when he come through the door and she set off one of her tingling laughs that sounded like a willow tree stirrin, a willow tree that had little silver bells instead of leaves.

Arron heard falling water and turned to see the horse hanging down its black elephantine member and relieving itself. The yellow foam under it ran back down the dusty path like a flash flood in the arroyo.

He stepped to the bucket and looked down into it, his

head bowed over as if in prayer, his eyes moving around over the dry tin bottom. *It's gone, the sacks are dry.* He stepped quickly back to the grave, ducking and jerking. He threw the arm that had held the can over his face and felt the tall hot sun burning his head and shoulders. He squatted abruptly, finally sitting flat beside the grave. With the other hand he rubbed long strokes flat against the ground, combing the thick dead grass between his fingers.

"There's a fire!" She had screamed it from the bedroom where she was now already confined, lying flat under her big belly with her unseen feet to the north window. She had seen the angry orange glow over it like sunset behind a hill. "There's a fire!"

Tom had been in the horn chair smoking and watching the bent sliver of moon thread itself up through the prairie. Arron was in the wellhouse gettin cool water and a cloth for Sarah who was already feeling the pains though she did not know what it was. "There's a fire," she screamed down again before the pain pinched it off, leaving her trying with open gasping mouth to scream again.

Tom was out of the chair and to the north end of the porch in one movement. She tried to scream again. Smith was running toward the cake house for burlap sacks. "They did it," Tom thought out loud. "Those greedy, horse-fucking, blue-eyed son-of-a-bitches have set me on fire."

When Arron came out of the wellhouse holding the cold dripping cloth, he saw his shadow on the tank wall and looked north. The sky was boiling orange. From east to west in the night, the churning glow billowed like a dust cloud ahead of a norther. Above him he heard the tail of the windmill screak, swinging to the south. The wind was rising. Tom was saddling horses, Smith had thrown twenty gunny sacks in the horse tank.

"Arron," Tom yelled. "Arron!" Smith ran to help with the horses.

In the north now Sarah from upstairs saw the flames

burning low at the point where the grass entered the black sky as if the earth was a sheet of flat paper burning from its edge toward her. A pain shot up her womb, contracting her spine, jerking her head up from the pillow, and she saw the fire coming fast over her belly.

Arron dropped the wet cold cloth as he ran to the corral.

"We'll meet it," Tom yelled.

The wind was rising and frightened cattle were now running south past the house. "Smith," Tom yelled again as a bawling cow running blind from the north crashed into the board corral fence, "backfire the house." He was now on his horse with wet gunny sacks draped over its neck and behind the saddle. It looked like an armored war horse. Arron swung up on his saddled horse and a thought of the cold cloth crossed his mind as Smith threw the wet sacks across in front and behind him, hastily tying them with the saddle thongs. The bunkhouse emptied like a barracks under attack. Horses armored with dripping sacks carried their half-dressed riders dashing out against the darkness and fire.

"Get me a rope," Tom shouted to Smith.

More cattle were crashing through the yard, bellowing and crazy. Smith brought the rope. "Stay north of the house," he said, as he roped a board gate and spurred his horse, ripping it loose, dragging it out northward into the orange night.

Arron turned to follow and a running cow cut in front of his horse; her hide was smoking. The air was getting thick with heat and dust. Bawling cows, blind from running, splintered the board fences around the barns, some were running headlong into the buildings, making thundering booms. Arron spurred his frightened horse after Tom, north into the fire.

A tidal wave of fire was running in at them, running before the rising wind. Tom ran his horse into it, dragging the gate, cutting a black and dead swath in the fire. Arron spurred his horse through the thin wall into the blackened grass, he could see the ground glowing like spent tinder and he heard the agony of burning cows. He wheeled and dashed back through the running tide. He looked south to the house and got off the horse, dragging the sacks with him. With one wet sack in each hand he began running and beating out the flames.

The black ashes covered him, blending him into the orange night. He fought running, slinging the heavy wet sacks over hand against the flames. Retreating, running at an angle, slapping the ground, breathing the thick white smoke, he thought of the cold wet cloth. The fire was sweeping past the house, hitting the backfired strip as if it were a sunken boulder and eddying around it. Arron was past the house too now, fighting the line of fire. The sacks were dry and black, as light as ashes without the water, yet they felt heavier. He clenched his teeth, feeling the carbon grit between them and kept the dogged pace.

The line was curving, he was now almost a mile past the house and it had begun curving northward. He was fighting almost due north before he realized he had rounded it on the east side. His angry red eyes were deep in his carbon black face, they were dry, exhausted of tears, bits of ashes stuck and ground into them; he could not blink. He slowed to a walk now, keeping still the grim, flailing, overhand stroke. He could see the line burning itself out on the edge of a shallow gully.

He stumbled, falling into it before his churning arms were still.

Smith heard her screaming from the landing as he fought the backfire and dodged the running cattle. Heard her on the landing where she had carried the big belly, where it finally dragged her down to the carpet with the fire glistening on the tall window behind her like sunshine.

It dragged her down and she, crazy and screaming in internal agony, fought it, slinging her head from side to side, smashing her small fist into it, feeling herself being ripped inside, ripped and slashed by the yellow teeth of the fever-crazy and hungry rats she knew were inside her, tearing and slashing to get out. She rolled and smashed at them, struggling finally to her feet, tearing her own tight skin with broken fingernails, clutched it to her and in a diving fall forward she smashed it against the floor, rupturing her taut womb, releasing the water and blood and slimy twisting rats.

Dying, her body shook with spasms of birthing, violently contracting, shaking her buried fingernails out of the now loose skin of her belly, and the final spasm and contraction, when she was no longer dying, squeezed out the last rat. His tiny foot now free, Ronnie Parker was born, lying in the gush of jellied blood, making invertebrate swimming motions toward her hemorrhaged and cooling breast.

Smith had heard her as he was catching Arron's horse which had returned to the barn. He threw more wet sacks on and mounted, spurring the horse east into what was now smoke-filled, singed darkness.

And out of the darkness Smith yelled "Arron" to me. "Arron, I can't see where you is at." I tried to move, tried to say where but all I could do was think about the cold wet cloth from the wellhouse. It was quiet and I could hear Smith coming calling "Arron." I could hear the cows, the burned and broken cows bawling and grunting somewhere. I got to get the cloth, they're burned with broken legs, we got to get them the cloth.

Smith could also hear the isolated and distant moans of animal agony out there bawling, independent and ubiquitous. He found Arron lying still and face down in the shallow gully. He took a wet sack from the horse and squeezed dirty water on the back of Arron's head, then lifted it gently by the hair and wiped the rough, wet burlap over his black, puffy face.

"They ain't nothin broke is they Arron?" he said. Smith

raised him to his feet, then set him down on the edge of the shallow gully. Then Arron, as though bitten in the small of the back by a snake, jerked rigid and grabbed the wet sack from Smith. He threw his head back and howled a dry sound at the bent sliver of a moon. The cooked skin on his lips cracked like old leather. "The cloth," he howled, clenching his teeth against the pain, "the cold wet cloth." The thought of it racked him with trembling violence.

Smith took the wet sack from him and draped it around his neck.

"I got more on the horse Arron, now get up, you got to get up, yo Papa ain't come in yet, we gots to find him." Arron got to his feet holding the wet sack tight around his neck.

They rode double, Smith in the saddle and Arron on the wet sacks behind. Smith reached one arm around behind him, holding Arron to him and on the horse like a papoose. The wet sacks soaked through Arron's pants, driving a chill into his fevered body.

When they reached the house the air was desolate. In the darkness a burned cow which had blindly run headlong into a raised horse tank was bawling, trying to get out, thrashing her broken front legs in the water and slowly drowning. Smith slid Arron to the ground near the tank. "Go get the guns," he said, "we got to end them critters' misery, I'll get the other horse, you go get the guns."

Arron started to run to the wellhouse. "Arron, in the house, get the guns." Arron changed his direction, heading for the house, still looking at the ground and holding the wet sack tight around his neck.

In the house Arron stood still for a moment shivering, then ran to the guncase in the hall and jerked out two rifles from the rack. Then he ran through the house to the back door, running for the wellhouse. Smith heard the back door slam.

173

"Out here Arron!" he yelled. He was drowning the cow in the horse tank, holding her weak head under the bloody water. Arron ran toward him, still looking at the ground.

The sky was beginning to bleach in the east, fuzzy shapes were beginning to appear, shapes with no form. In the bleaching of black before grey, the shapes were like clots of black smoke suspended, billowing out of nothing.

They rode out west, away from the new light into what was still darkness, a darkness that sullenly retreated before them. They were now able to follow the black edge of ashes. They rode close to its edge on the brown unburned grass. In this light, the black grass to them looked as if they were riding along the edge of a sheer endless drop-off into black emptiness. And the dying moans of burned cattle came as if suspended somewhere in it.

The darkness was running before them now and sliding out of the sky, slowly first then falling quickly down and into a western slot behind the dim horizon.

The charred acres of blackened grass spread out to the north like a giant black boar's skin staked to the ground. They turned their streaked faces from it and saw ahead of them the smoldering gate.

Tom Parker lay between the charred gate and the fallen horse. One of his arms pointed a fist, still clenched around soft powdery rope ashes, at the broken horse. The other arm stretched behind him toward the smoldering gate; its fist also clenched full of the same grey ash.

The rope had broken or burned in two as he had dragged the gate across the flaming grass. He had jumped to the ground in the fire cursing and commanding the horse to "stand" as he, with one end of the parted rope in each hand, fought to knot it. The horse had obeyed until the shallow fire washed under it, then it bolted wild into that fire dragging the man who in turn dragged the gate holding the ropes as he now held the ashes of them; in a grip as final and irrevocable as death's own.

174

The burning grass abrasion had taken his face. Arron watched Smith dismount and cover it with a damp sack. He was shaking inside himself, feeling the burlap around his neck and thinking of the cloth. The bowels of the broken and burned horse involuntarily moved, drawing Smith's attention from the man. "God's poor critter," he said, going to it. It was marked like, and descended from, the one he had ridden in the snow.

The shot from Smith's rifle exploded, then whispered away into the stillness. And as if it had entered his brain Arron jumped stiff-legged up, standing in the stirrups. He arched his back and as if his head were being slowly pulled back by the hair, he squeezed out a long, bloody wail, thin, grotesque and defeated.

He wheeled the frightened horse, dropping the sack from his neck and, smashing his burnt fist against its foaming neck, dashed from Smith toward the house. He pounded the running horse's neck now with both fists, letting the reins fall over the horn. He stood hunched forward in the stirrups beating the walleyed animal, who was dashing airborne over the ashes, its frantic hoofs suspended, immobile, inches above the shrunken black grass, dead still, in a moment of sheer savage velocity, carrying something awkward and hunched; a man running and stumbling in the stirrups on its back.

Papa wore a hat three times.

Arron, kneeling now squaw-legged at the edge of the grave, rubbed the grass in front of him with both hands palm down like an Indian grinding corn. He followed his thoughts to a dark cool place. His reeling mind had run ahead of itself and was still; panting and exhausted, in some dark cool hollow, away for this short time from the running.

He had followed himself into himself, down past me, myself, and I, and now sat still, smashed into the silence of shock. It was as physical as it had been on the night of the fire when he ran the horse full speed into the low, narrow, wellhouse door.

As the horse entered Arron was slammed against the outside wall and scraped off. The horse was carried through the narrow door by its momentum, where it thrashed itself to trapped death, smashing jars of canned corn and pickled peaches as the shelves of widemouth jars collapsed over and around it, finally saturating the dead horse stillness with the pungence of canning spices, watermelon rind preserves, horse sweat and sweet cloves.

Arron did not feel the pain. Though he struck the brick path to the wellhouse flat on his back, he neither dropped the rifle nor guessed that he had been unhorsed. He was a robot hitting a wall, bouncing from it and abruptly changing directions.

He ran, still looking at the ground for the cloth, toward the front of the house. There were men and horses in the front yard, men and horses and Edith Harvest. The men were gathered around the Sheriff's car, looking at the two men in the back, men handcuffed together.

Arron burst into the yard like a black hunted animal. The men turned from the car and, following the Sheriff, started toward him. His eyes were swollen, red slits drawn up at oriental angles by the burned and shrunken skin of his carbon-black face.

Facing the approaching men, he was instinctively still, a cunning lizard-like flash of absolute immobility held him. Then, as if he were being electrocuted, his body began to contract and was racked with long jagged tremors. And again something like a hand in his hair was drawing his head back, something outside himself was trying to break his neck, turning his face up into the hot morning. His quaking body excreted another long wail, ugly and thin, through his black teeth.

The men stopped short. The Sheriff's hand dropped to the runted gun on his hip. They watched him as they would a dying dog, snarling and snapping at its own death throes. They were stunned by the obscenity of his agony. Just as he was about to fall on his arched back, Edith Harvest burst through the line of men in front of her.

"Arron!" she screamed, "Arron, where's your father?"

The gut-wail stopped. And as if a bow string had been cut, he snapped forward, springing upright with the rifle level at her, pointed perfectly and beautifully at her stomach, pointed with the sureness of a blind man, as if the sound had come from there.

"Arron!" she screamed.

"Arron!" her voice was prickled with spines of hysteria.

He suddenly cocked his burned ear to the wind. Then like explosive memory, he dashed, running low toward the front door. Edith Harvest, in long skirts, ran after him.

Smith rode into the yard with Tom's faceless and charred body bent stiffly over the saddle in front of him. The men, still silent, ran to the horse. There was no sound. They slid the body down in silence, each man trying to get a hand on it. They carried it to a tree near the house and as if the grass itself had let out an outraged and defiled cry when his body touched it, they heard a baby's indignant and absurd wail punch out at the emptiness of the house.

The men around the body, each from his different position, turned only their heads quickly and in individual unison toward the door as though their separate names had been whispered.

"She's dropped it," Smith finally said, "she done dropped her chile. Get Arron, where's Arron?"

The men stirred and began to talk softly at first. Then they were all shouting commands to each other and running out from the circle, and back to it, talking and shouting at Smith. Before anyone of them could listen to the other, Edith Harvest appeared in the door holding the naked runt to her. The outraged cries echoed through the empty house behind her. The men, frightened and em-

177

barrassed, were impelled toward her. The moment before they moved, while they yet only leaned toward the house, Arron from the inside smashed a hall window with the black rifle and watched them settle back into their tracks in the dusty yard. The jagged glass spines framed his black face as he crouched, watching them with puffy, crimson eyes.

The men lowered their eyes to the body on the grass, all except Smith. One of the men took off his hat and covered the matted hair and blood, black now with grass ashes, that had been Tom Parker's face.

Three times Papa wore a hat, he wore it three times and they took him in it the third time he was under it bent like a dog's leg and smellin bay rum when they took him without a cold cloth he went out with them.

Arron stopped rubbing the grass.

The smooth-mouthed horse (Arron's horse, still alive and old, for it was Smith's horse he had driven into the dark wellhouse) was not trying to graze the tall grass under the tree. He could no longer rip off the grass. He would take a mouthful and, trying to tear it off, feel it slide through his smooth gums. The grass was spotted around it with foaming saliva-soaked tufts which hooked up, combed by his gums and lips up like spit curls.

A breeze sent rattling whispers through the yellow leaves of the cottonwood tree, releasing and showering down a thin cloud of lint. The seed-carrying fuzz caught white in the grass like early snow. Arron felt it brush his face and snare in his thick black eyebrows, clinging like spider webs. He brushed his hand over his face and turned to the rusty can.

He dragged it to him and, without looking in it, he reached down inside for the cloth. His nails scraped on the rusty bottom running to each corner. He was not surprised or disappointed to find the can empty. He rose to his knees and pulled his shirt from his pants. The tail of the shirt was long and of a different color and cloth from the shirt. A large piece of red bandana had been sewn to it just below the waist line. The large mannish stitches of black thread gave way easily as he pulled the red tail from the faded orange shirt.

He did not break the black thread. He held the red cloth out with one hand and unlaced the thread carefully with the other. He dropped the cloth in the rusty can and tucked the thread and orange shirt back in his bleached levis. Waiting for the cloth to soak, he put his hands on his grounded knees and turned his deep wrinkled face to the horizon, letting his eyesight run out of him over the brown dying land.

Yes Smith is in the chair, in the chair with a chicken and no hat. I will eat that chicken.

That same breeze of the leaves and lint now stirred the trailing remains of the bird's nest which hung down over him from the leaning flare pole, bits of the cottonwood lint were sticking to it like flypaper.

He reached in the can and with both hands began wringing out the dry cloth. He twisted it tight, shaking it over the can, then folded it neatly like a pad and began wiping his face with it.

Yes my melon the torch is dead even the birds are gone. I brought the cloth I've been to the wellhouse I found a dead horse I'll bring you his tail but now the cloth the cold cloth.

He unfolded the red cloth over the head of the grave and with stiff bones and dead muscles he lowered himself prone into the hammock-like hollow. He felt the clumps of grass against his chest and burrowed gently against them, pressing firmly also the matted flat cluster at his crotch.

You are warm my fruit I feel your heart—Oh roll under me my mare roll under me.

He buried his face in the cloth, biting the grass through it, straining to move the earth. *The chicken is cold my*

179

heart dry and cold Smith let her blood out—was it her guts?

"You forgot her guts, Arron you forgot to take her guts," Smith was laughing, screaming from the horned chair, "You wrapped her all up in thet saddle blanket but her guts—we got the guts, you left 'um on the staircase and we got 'um. And while you was suckin at Miss Edith's dry teat like a starved calf and callin her Sarah—the guts was suckin a lamp wick thet dis ole man cut up and stuck in a bowl of sweet cream—while you was suckin at her ears, the guts was suckin some bacon rind. It was them guts Arron you forgot. An my chicken ain't dying on account ob you forgettin 'cause dis ole man knows where dey is, he knows where de guts is."

The wind in the tree was getting stronger and along the northern horizon a pale grey line of haze had appeared. The strands of hanging bird's nest were whipping about the leaning pole like the tangled hair of a hag about her skinny neck. The horse looked up from its futile sucking of grass to see Arron spring up on all fours. The grass he had bitten through the cloth was still clamped in the cloth and the cloth in his mouth. He got to his knees and began twisting that part of the cloth which hung out of his mouth, twisting it frantically around the bite of uprooted grass, twisting and sucking on it like a sugar-teat pacifier. Then he plucked it violently from his mouth, looking at it, spitting and rasping out high chuckles, looking at it knotted in the red cloth like a quarter's worth of nickles.

It's the guts, I hurried to get you warm under the tree and I forgot the guts.

He was excited now, biting the wad in the red cloth, then burrowing it into his crotch. Winking at the baffled and profound horse, he grabbed up the can, hugged it to him and ran toward the tree.

Smith loves a chicken and the melon moving is mine.

He stabbed the red cloth sugar-teat back in his mouth and awkwardly mounted the horse, still hugging the can.

He kicked the old horse into a rough trot. His teeth were clenched over the grass pacifier. One arm hugged the rusty can, the other hand, holding the loose reins, came to rest on the dried and cracked scrotum covered saddle horn. Laughter exploded in his head, erupting green mucus from his nose which blew back along his face in cloudy streams as he rode north into the freshening dry coldness of the coming norther.

XVII

Buck had gotten to the phone office just after Harry found the power switches. He had started for the front door, followed by the constable. Harry, hearing the car door slam, came out of the back door in time to motion them around to the rear.

The shack was quiet now and the waxy odor from the overheated wiring thickened on the cooling air. Harry could smell the mess in the outer office and remembered having been sick once into a wax milk carton.

"She's in here," he said and turned back into the bedroom. They followed him in.

"When did you find her, Harry?"

"'Bout half hour ago."

"Was she in bed?" Buck asked as Mason walked around the bed and through the kitchen to the switchboard room.

"Jest like you see her, 'course I covered her."

"Mason said it was her female parts—you mean she bled to death?"

"Best I can tell," Harry said.

Neither man mentioned looking at the body. Mason came back through the kitchen.

"From the looks of them wires, we almost had a fire on top of it all," he said, and turned to Harry, "you been out in the waitin room? She must've tried to go that way for help, cause there's fresh vomit all over the floor."

Harry did not speak, his mind stalled for a moment. Mason walked around the bed and squeezed through the door into the waiting room. He called back, "I'll jest lock the front door 'til we can get somebody in here to clean up."

Then it was too late and Harry became fiduciary to another unsolicited secret.

"We'll have to send to Roan for the funeral home," he said.

"And get word to the phone company," Buck added. "I hate to say it over her like this, but I'm expecting an important long distance call from Dallas. You know, *Life* magazine, about the service tomorrow."

As they walked outside and stood waiting for Mason, Harry was quiet. In this week's issue of *Life,* he thought, see *Life*'s own true-to-life, life-sized issue of death—that's it, see Death in *Life*—subscribe now to your very own year's subscription of death. He looked at Buck, then out past the alley trash barrels at the old, tipped-over outhouse whose open bottom faced them, its two holes stared back at him like black eyes.

They sent Mason to get the Santa Fe depot master who sent telegrams to the funeral home and the telephone company. While Buck waited, Harry returned to the drugstore. He hung the closed sign in the window and took the Sunday papers next door to the post office and laid them on the public writing table. The postmaster was still putting up the mail. Harry rapped on the frosted glass of the parcel post window and told him about Elmira.

"Buck's over there now, but he can't stay. He's got that army chaplain staying out home so he's got to go."

"Well, jest let me finish here and I'll run home and grab a bite to eat and come sit with you till they get here."

1 8 3

"There's no use, Wendell, nothing we can do now. I guess one's as good as two."

"Well, I'll come back anyhow, I can bring you some lunch."

"No, that's all right, I'm not too much on lunch as yet."

"Yeah, I guess that's so, but I'll come back anyhow. You might want to go get coffee."

On his way back to the telephone office, Harry stopped at the corner. Up one street he could see that the Methodist Church was emptying. About time, he thought, and glanced up at the sun. The teenagers who were allowed to drive the pickups and work cars to church were racing the engines and speeding away. The older people stood about in groups, the men talking about the price of calves and the prospects of winter wheat pasture, the women about the sermon and who was having the new preacher to dinner. "You know he's not married."

He'll tell 'um, Harry thought, when they come to get the mail, and he walked across the street and around back of the office. Mason was gone and Buck was standing outside.

"Harry, I hate to leave you like this but I told Mason to stop back by and to come get me when the telephone man gets here."

"It's all right Buck, it won't take long for 'um to get here with the ambulance, you go ahead on."

Buck started away, then stopped, turning back to Harry. "I don't guess there's anybody to notify, I mean if we could."

"No, Buck." Harry felt a shiver of fatigue sift down over him. "I guess not."

"Well," he said, "I guess I'll go on then."

Harry waited until he heard Buck's car door slam, before he walked to the back door. He stood outside until he heard the church kids racing up Main Street. I don't guess they need to see me standing out here, he thought, and went

184

inside. He left the door open and sat down in the over-stuffed chair, sat there looking out of the back door, over the bed and Elmira's body which the blanket covered like drifting sand covers rotten and warped floors in vacant houses; smoothly, anonymously.

She was a good woman, he thought, a good lonely, poor-didn't-have-a-pot-to-piss-in woman. He slumped and looked hard out of the back door, straight into the outhouse eyes.

That's right, born and lived right under the shithouse of what's happened to her. I'd give 'um both to see that one explained. And her voice was always pleasant. "Number please, sorry Mr. Eddens, I think he went over to the court house," *and young too—gonna be funny for 'um to look in at her and see an ugly, half old, dead woman.* "The line's dead out there Mr. Eddens, I guess last night's wind hung a tumbleweed on it." *That's just about it, last night's wind blew in here, broke a fly's wing and hung up a few tumbleweeds and the phone is dead—By God, you can call 'um from here on if you'll show me the prescription on this one.*

He could hear the cars passing in front, slowing down to look. Then a pickup full of boys driving fast came down the dirt road that ran alongside the building. He did not move his eyes and the dust drifted across the weeds in back, dimming the charmed fix that the skull eyes of the privy, staring in out of the gleaming brightness, held over him. He looked around the room, rolling his shoulders and neck as if he was trying to ward off a thin glaze of chilliness.

The shade on the side window at the head of her bed was raised about three inches. He looked at it, rolled his shoulders again, got up and went to the window. He leaned over the high iron bedstead and, taking the edges of the brown watermarked shade between the thumb and forefinger of both hands, pulled it down below the window sill. As he moved back, his leg nudged the mattress. The

1 8 5

rusty bedsprings creaked softly and a momentary fear of waking her went over him.

He thought of a cup of coffee and looking down he saw her Bible on the night stand. He picked it up and stared for a long moment at the spider web crocheted doily and the faded blue ribbon woven through it. Then he carried the book back to the chair.

I'll just look it up, under God's all merciful justice. He sat down, holding the book flat against his leg. *Maybe it's under widows and orphans or ugly two-headed babies.* He pulled the old book up to his side and the pages flopped over, sliding away from each other, the gold edges shading into different hues. He turned back the cover; inside was one word and its definition, "Faith: Keeping on, keeping on."

He turned the pages in half-inch bites with his thumb. They slid over quickly, patting against the open cover. His thumb slid quickly past the technicolor Bible pictures and stopped in the middle, at a page entitled "Our Blessed Family." In the top blank of this page was, Elmira Rose Gent, Born: October 24, 1917, Year of Our Lord. The rest of the blanks were empty. The paper was white and slick. Harry wet his thumb to turn the page. As it touched the paper his wet thumb slipped and left a dirty streak.

Well, that's what you should be doing, now that you've blasphemed yourself into hell, leaving your dirty fingerprints all over her Bible—He felt himself sinking as if he were standing in the scalepan on the great balance of God's patience and his sinful words and thoughts were tipping the scales and he was sinking. A puff of fear tightened his stomach as he rethought the questions he was about to look up, and he cast out some ballast prayer thoughts. *God knows how I stand. You know how I stand, God.*

He held the place with one hand, holding the dry thumb straight up as if a thorn was in it, and reached for

186

his handkerchief with the other. He rubbed at the smudge, then held it up to the light. It was then that he saw the erasure. He tried to read what had been erased by holding the page even with his eye, letting the outside light reflect off it. He forgot about the smudge and as he got up and walked to the door the handkerchief fell to the floor. He held the page at different angles to the light, then without thinking, without even remembering how he had noticed it, he rubbed his other thumb over the erasure.

The thin trail of a tightly-held stub pencil showed in the smudge, like worm tracks in the dust.

On the line below her name, the one that began with fancy black script, spelling MARRIED, in a cramped hand that was yet somehow widely spaced and open, was the name, Ronald A. Parker and the date, September 19, 1951.

He looked over his shoulder at the body, then outside through the screen wire. He squinted his eyes as if he were trying to squeeze all his sight through one of the little square holes in the wire. He slapped the Bible against his side making the sound of a loose spattering cow flop. *I guess I'll ask some more questions before I die; just to insure myself a good seat in Hell.*

He sat down with the Bible on his lap, the back side up. He turned it upside down. *Maybe I'll manage not to read somethin I don't want to this way.* He started flipping the pages. He did not know he was sweating until the breeze made by the fanning pages felt cool on his face. He ran past the place the first time through, as one might decline a lethal cup the first time around, only to accept it for less reason on the second offering. He started again and the pages stalled; the book lay open and widening before him like the swollen belly of a dead cow after the first long and deep-easy pass of the skinner's knife. Between the pages were a post card and two letters without envelopes. The letters were on thin paper, thinner than a Bible page.

With the Bible spread-eagled on his lap he pushed his head back, against the dingy headrest of the old chair. He closed his eyes, letting out a deep sigh as if to blow away the thick cloud of musty, gloom and sorrow that was set-tling over him. He was seeing death in reverse—first the corpse and now the cruel vicious body blows that had crumbled her.

He opened his eyes, not moving his head, and looked long minutes at the puffy ceiling where the water-stained and dust-loaded paper had pulled loose. Still with eyes on the ceiling, his hand found the post card. He forced the edge of the card under his thumbnail, pressing down, disappointed that it was not painful, cramming the card even tighter into the binding between the pages and curs-ing the lewdness that was driving him to commit these acts of unholiness against her.

He lifted the card; his eyes met it halfway. It was a picture of the Kansas City stockyards. There was no mes-sage. He was relieved as a man is when looking through a house for death opens a door on an empty room. The relief reassured him. They'll have to look at everything, he thought, when they settle her affairs. He picked up the first letter. It was in two pieces, broken at the fold. The edges were fuzzy as though it had been worn in two by folding and unfolding, bent back and forth until it crystal-lized and broke like sheet tin. It was USO stationery. The hand was small and each line melted at the middle in the same spot. They drooped off the page in unison, indepen-dent yet identical.

Dear Elmira

I hope you got my card. I didn't write on it because I don't want nobody to know. I would have said thank you on it otherwise. I sent it from the train. I met a feller there who is in the army and has a good job. He is a chaplains assistant helps a army Preacher. He said he would help me to get in the army. I think he had drunk a little before I met him or something as he slept with his head in my lap all the way to St. Louis Mo. He did and now I am in and he is out. He got me in and they say I got him out. I joined for six years without telling them anything but my name.

I thought I was out almost before I got in good the sergeant feller who helped me got put on trial for being like Jimmy Singer and they called me and ask about the train. I haven't thought much about home—except when my hand sweats you know what I mean as it did in the trial.

If you was to write don't put my last name on it only my first and the number they gave me. RA 54 181 486 Fort Leonard Wood Mo.

Your friend

Pvt Ronald A. Parker

P.S. I know I can trust you.

Harry held the two pieces of paper together; the fuzzy seam made a ridge across the paper. He folded it, trying not to break the seam, and picked up the other one. It was in one piece.

Dear Elmira

I haven't written you to much and this I guess will be the last time for a long time. I am on a ship going somewheres. They spoke to us about writing home as much as we can while we are on the ship. I guess I would have anyways because the ocean looks alot like there since it is so flat and open. Only here it always looks like you are in the middle of a little low place where as there it always looks like you are on a little rise.

They spoke about other things to here when they talk to us. If I was to get killed I am leaving word for them to send my remains back there in care of the bank. Not that I care about coming home it is just that I would kinda like to be on a rise and it might give you some place to go on Sunday afternoon if you felt like it. I don't know that you would but I thought about it and I would if it was you. I don't think it will happen and I kinda hope it don't as I like it here even on the ship you can trade your sheets every week even if they are still clean. They are good to me and I hope to do a lot of killing for them.

I got your letter and what you said about God. And I am gonna try—I guess I can love somebody or something but I don't think I'll have to much time from now on.

Your friend
P.F.C. Ronald A. Parker

Harry let his hand fall limp on the Bible. His head fell back on the chair. He closed his eyes, opened his mouth and took a deep breath, trying to give room in his chest for something that was pushing upward from his stomach jamming his heart.

Lord, Lord, I've had enough—enough dying and living —don't stumble me onto no more. I'm bowing my head this minute and I'm holding it bowed. I'll scratch around down here doing the best I can but I don't want to see it happening to us.

He bowed his head over his lap, then slowly raised it. With his eyes on the body, he felt a new side of sadness, a pity and embarrassment as if he had not covered it. That sadness when old men stumble to their knees on Main Street, mixed with the chagrin of seeing an injured woman awkward and ugly with pain.

Then, without knowing specifically what he was feeling for in his pocket, he removed his knife. It was as if the knife had been carried all these years for that one small click in the silence.

I wiped her nose as a kid; well not exactly her nose.
It was Gather Hughes that kissed her at post office up at
the school Halloween carnival and the next day she gave
down her first blood and come running to me to take out
the baby like a splinter in her toe. "You fold it like a hot
dog bun—it only means you're not a little girl anymore."
And she loved me for it and maybe even Gather Hughes.
I guess if I done that then and maybe woulda done more,
I won't let 'um bury her with her fly open now.

He tossed the knife loosely in his hand, then held it
firmly with his forefinger, reinforcing the blade as if he
were about to dig and loosen the earth around a plant.
Then, with gentle precision as a surgeon performing a
lobotomy, he severed the family page from its binding, almost expecting the old Bible to bleed or ooze sap.

He crumpled the page and the tissue letters in his hand.
He got up, replaced the Bible and walked to the door,
then turned back to look at the room. He saw the handkerchief that had fallen from his lap lying next to the
chair on the floor. He went back and, stooping to pick it
up, saw the bottle under the chair.

He carried it to the trash barrel outside in his handkerchief, even though the brown chocolate syrup film on
it was dry. He smashed it on the rim of the rusty barrel,
tossed in the little white ball of paper like the first clod
of graveyard dirt, then looked straight into the sun. *Please,*
Lord, don't stumble me again——

The sun burned his eyes. He almost used the handkerchief to wipe away the water, then stopped, dropped it in
the barrel, and wiped them with the butt of each hand as
he walked back to the door.

The postmaster drove up, pulled his old Chevrolet over
to the ditch and got out. Harry was still outside.

"You think I wasn't coming?" he said as he waded
through the weeds in the ditch. "Nobody's showed up yet
huh, well it won't be long—you go ahead on, I'll sit 'til
they get here."

191

Harry's tongue felt dead in his mouth.

"No," he said, "it won't be long now. Mason ought to be back anyways."

"Naw, Mason ain't coming back. I jest met him on the road, Buck sent him out to the cemetery to be sure Deafy Jon don't start on her grave until after tomorrow, jest in case he heard about it. You know how he is about finding out almost before anybody tells him and going ahead with the diggin. He don't give a damn about the wishes of the family. He's liable to put it anywhere on the lot. He plants that graveyard like it was his own garden, jest where ever he damn pleases and thinks it looks good."

Harry felt a swarm of bees swoop down on his liver, stinging and crawling.

"I guess the church will make the arrangements," the postmaster went on, "that's about all she had. However she used to write a good many letters to some feller in the army, but not since the war. She never put on no return address, but I guess I know everybody's hand, me being postmaster. Probably some pole climber for the company. Say, you better go eat, there won't be nothin left down there."

The bees were still crawling and stinging.

"Yeah," Harry said, "I'll get a cup of coffee."

XVIII

THE night was warm as new soot as it filtered down over White Dove. Elmira's death was a part of every house. The black phones by their very presence brought an immediate sense of personal loss. A simultaneous experience of sorrow, transmitted through an inanimate system of wires and switches by the passing of Elmira who had no one.

It was after evening church now and many were in bed. They had eaten cold chicken, left from Sunday dinner, and gone to bed, only to be startled by half rings and abortive chatters of the black phones. Some, mostly the country party lines who had not heard the news, answered, listening hard, hearing only their own breath in the receiver as from a sea shell.

The telephone company repairman was at the phone office, tracing out the shorted wires, and at Buck's insistence testing the long-distance lines. His company car was parked on the sloping side of the ditch, tilting as if it had been suddenly abandoned: the lower door hung open, spilling out the harsh detached commands and information from the two-way radio. In the back seat of the car sat a lonely rootless woman, a replacement operator from the Amarillo office. She was frightened by the strangeness of night in a new town and had refused to enter the office after she'd heard what had happened.

Mason reassured her that even though he hadn't slept all day he would be near all night, that he didn't need sleep anymore and would park at the phone office end of Main Street tonight.

She sat in the car, knowing Elmira, knowing this small town as she knew the past towns in her own life, towns and times that were now smooth worn knots in the shortening cord of her life span, smooth from being fingered like beads. She too, like Elmira, had sat decomposing with loneliness.

In the back, out by the trash barrels, the mattress smoldered. Buck and Mason had carried it out, doused it with kerosene and set it on fire. It glowed in the darkness as the cotton wadding burned slow and orange, without flame, brightening and dying back with each gentle puff of breeze.

Inside, the bedroom was empty, the body was gone, and now the mattress. The room seemed much larger and less crowded. The exposed springs, fuzzy with spider webs and house lint, seemed to add space.

The repairman found the mesh of switchboard wires curled and brittle as singed hair; they crumbled when he touched them. Buck stayed with him, watching him work, sitting on the high switchboard chair, his fat buttocks bulging over its edges.

"You see, I'm expecting a very important call from Dallas," he said.

"Mister, this outfit is so burned out Jesus Christ couldn't get a direct line to God Hisself, they're so shriveled up they wouldn't carry a prayer," the repairman said as he hung his pliers on the crowded belt of tools he wore around his waist; a sagging tutu of electronic paraphernalia.

194

"If I was you and really wanted to talk, I'd drive over to the next town that's got service."

I can't be called in a town where I don't even live, Buck thought. Then he got up. "Well I guess it's a little late for that, anyway it's Sunday, they'd have to call me."

The repairman came out from behind the bank of connections. "I'm sorry I can't help you, but in a way you're lucky—I don't mean the girl, God rest her, but this mess ought to put you all at the top of the list for gettin a new dial system. But if you do, don't be like the feller I was talkin to in the last town where we put one in. He said he had to crank the pencil sharpener a couple of rounds every time he made a call, just so he'd feel right."

Buck laughed his Ford-salesman laugh, a dead chuckle that ended abruptly without the coasting momentum of real humor.

"Well I don't know about that," he said, "but I'd be willing to gamble not feeling right for a few days to get one. That would mean we could tear down this eyesore. I bet I've written the company, as Mayor, a dozen letters just trying to get 'um to paint it."

"My guess is that it won't be here to paint much longer." He lit the cigar stub he had been chewing on and sucked in his stomach so that he could unlatch the heavy belt of tools. "Well, what this outfit needs is a gravedigger not a doctor," he said as he rolled the belt.

Buck thought of Elmira as they went out through the neat kitchen. He was glad Harry had volunteered to sit with the body tomorrow at the funeral parlor and that Roy Turner was taking his turn tonight. Like Roy, he thought, even when she's dead, taking the night.

"This overtime's good," the repairman was saying as they stepped outside, "but the wife gives me hell if it takes too long, especially if I'm takin out a replacement operator. I can't figger why she thinks I'd chase around all night for a little of something that I got more'n I can take care of at home."

195

Again the Ford laugh from Buck. "Well I'm a little behind myself, I'd better be gettin on too," he said. "Thanks for comin out. And see what you can do about that dial system."

As the repairman walked to the car, listening now to the two-way radio, the woman in the back seat did not move. She kept her eyes on the man standing across the dirt road, a man almost hidden by the tall weeds, standing in a footpath which cut through them like a trench.

She did not know it was Roy Turner, nor did she feel the sadness of the dead weeds around him. She could not see his clean-shaven varicose face or the pressed levis and fresh shirt. Yet she knew who he was, that he was a man of the night paths. She could not see the stillness of his eyes, nor did they reflect her or anything save a bewildered, passive sorrow.

Roy stood across the road in the weeds, but his weather-rasped body felt nothing nor did he smell the smoldering mattress.

She had seen only the image of Roy Turner in the shadows, yet later when the repairman drove the company car down a country road, turned off the two-way radio, and crawled to her in the back seat without throwing away the dead cigar stub, it was this shadow in the weeds not the job insurance rape that brought tears (for she had once tried to become a whore, sitting three successive nights in the lobby of a cheap hotel waiting, like an abandoned child for a bus, for a "white slaver," until the Negro night porter sent her home). She knew the path was there, that it was a night path—she knew of night paths that stuck out like insect-feelers from the back doors of loneliness. But this one, this trench through the weeds, was not empty even after loneliness was gone—yes dead—he was standing there. It was this unknown shadow that she clutched, hunching out cries like a virgin, feeling the cigar smash against the seat and the dead ashes and crisp dry tobacco particles stick to her sweating back, sifting down between her and the leather seat with each absorbed thrust. For these same night paths in her life were empty. She had not received even the tribute of bewilderment.

And Roy Turner, who had dressed slowly, felt strange, as if he were standing on a slight incline. He wore now a pair of two-tone, low-quarter shoes. The low heels made him feel tilted back. Even though it was a warm night, his ankles were chilled and his thin socks were stickery with the thorny seedpods of dead winter grass. He could not remember being without his boots. The low-quarters had been in the closet of his room when he moved in. And tonight, as he dressed to go sit with the body, they became important. He had blown the dust out of them, wiped them off with a dirty sweat-damp sock and put them on.

Damn my soul, he had thought when he mashed his finger between his bare heel and the shoe, trying them on. I'm gettin dressed up like I was marrin her not burin her. There ain't nothin she coulda done to get 'um on me, but jest let her die and I can't keep 'um off.

He stood watching from the weeds until Buck and the repairman were gone. Buck had turned on all the lights. They were to be left burning each night until Elmira was buried; a small town custom, an effort to distinguish the dark houses of the sleeping from that house of the dead.

When they drove away, Roy turned his back on the gleaming shanty. The lights had destroyed the solitude of the weeds.

Later, driving toward the funeral home, he tried to open himself to sorrow, forcing himself to think of Elmira. But sorrow would not come. The chilling wind blew up from the floor of the pickup and made him curse the low-quarter shoes, and swear to burn them, "If we ever get a day or two off between buryin's."

XIX

O NLY a streetcar or maybe a steamboat parked in front of the drugstore Monday morning could have been stranger looking than the yellow taxi cab. No one could remember ever having seen a taxi in White Dove. It looked lost, strayed from somewhere, gaudy and superfluous.

"I couldn't get what it cost to hire it out here from Amarillo for my whole pickup," Roy Turner had said, "even throwin in my solid oak stock racks to boot."

"You'll see stranger than that before the sun sets on this day," said the skinny cowboy across the table from him.

They were sitting over empty coffee mugs at the corner table in the hotel cafe. They had watched the yellow cab turn off the highway and park in front of the drugstore. The man across from Roy was lean, his age was barely marked on him. The cowboy adolescence defied time to mark it. He was scarred, but not with age, battered and shrunken by harsh and rough weather and brutal work, work that became sport, its brutality sustenance. Like

Roy's, his face was slick under shrunken, tight skin that was ruddy, with root hairs of purple varicose veins marking it like a road map. When he drew his thin lips into a tight pucker, his mouth was round and gathered like the top of a Bull Durham tobacco sack. To these men pain and hardship were a joke, to be endured if it was one on them or laughed at as it fell to others. The current of humor that crackled under their tough hides was a logical extension of a simple joke, funny only because it was absolute; the laughable fact that you live only until you die.

"You goin out to Lea Switch?" Roy asked as he slowly put his hand over the top of his empty cup, catching a fly that was after the sugar in the bottom. The cowboy lowered his head to look under the large red lettering on the cafe window and stretched his mouth wide in a humorless flat smile.

"Well, if any more oddballs like that'un show up, I might jest go on out there." Roy did not speak for a moment. He held the cup between his hands as if it were open at both ends, finally lifting it to his ear and listening to the fly buzzing against his hard palm.

"He's from a magazine," he said finally.

"Well, thet's good."

"This fly says he's a cocksucker, and he wears that beard 'cause he heard you country boys like 'um."

"I'm glad you tole me thet, I knew all along thet ole Buck hadn't been able to get Jesus Christ here for it, but anyhow I'm so glad you tole me thet."

"If you go meet the train you might get your pitcher took." A smothered smile lay dead in Roy's eyes.

"I'm damned if I can think of anything I'd rather have, 'cept possibly one of thet bastard's beard hairs hanging out of a biscuit I jest bit off of."

Roy spread his fingers and the fly buzzed louder for a moment in the cup, then escaped. The Mexican girl behind the counter was running her fingers through the

199

change in her apron pocket and fanning herself with a red plastic fly swatter.

"You want another cup?" Roy asked, bending his head down to see out of the cafe window. The yellow cab had not moved.

"Naw," the cowboy said, "I'd better haul another load of water—my monkey says an Eskimo's ass'll feel warm to the hand by mornin." He pushed the cane-bottom chair back from the table.

"Radio says they's a front movin in," Roy said.

"Well," the cowboy got up, stretched tall and lean, pressing both hands against his hip pockets in back of him, and leaned back, still looking down at Roy. "If the train's late—I guess you and thet magazine feller can invite everybody on out to old man Parker's for coffee. What's he mostly interested in anyway, the crazy or the dead, or is it thet he jest loves to write about family life?" He tossed a worn buffalo nickel down on the counter by the cash register. "I'd buy you coffee but I know how you hate takin from the rich," he said standing at the door.

"All right, go on and haul water," Roy said, "but don't come around here tonight tryin to get at the head of the line, 'cause I'm rentin thet feller out on a first come first served basis. 'Course I got to get a rope on him first."

The cowboy went out the door and Roy watched him walk to the dripping water truck. He started to think about windmills and the Crows Foot, then stopped. "Isabel, you're scratchin that money like it itched, how about warming my coffee?" The waitress looked at him with sullen eyes, scabbarded the plastic fly swatter in her apron sash and moved toward the Silex coffee urn. As she moved she examined a handful of small change for a nickel with fingernail polish on it, a free one for the juke box.

Outside a high thin haze was building in the north. The sky was bleaching. It was the light blue of cheap blotter paper and it was growing lighter and grey as if it were blotting up skim milk where it touched the northern horizon. The milk grey eased across the absorbent sky, diluting and chilling it. The winds had not come nor was it cold, yet three lazy dogs scattered along Main Street were standing. One of them, thin and homeless, moved from the street to the south side of a vacant building, pausing to sniff briefly the front wheel of the yellow cab.

Inside the drugstore at the back booth the chaplain sat talking to the man from *Life*. Buck and Harry were at the front, near the wall telephone. They stood hunched and confidential.

"Dammit Harry, I got three used cars over there that I can't get forty dollars on and I wouldn't trade one of them for that damn taxi cab. And he ain't even a reporter, all he does is take pictures. He missed his partner that does the writin somewheres and now he thinks he's gonna have to do both jobs. He's mad as hell about it."

"Buck that cab's got a clock in it and it don't tick seconds, it ticks pennies. You better go pay that feller while you still can."

Buck looked out the window at the taxi as if it were something about to attack him. The driver was trying to start it. Buck watched him hunching over the wheel grinding the engine.

"If it don't start," Harry said, "you could give him half money and half repairs." Buck turned his eyes to Harry with a glimmer of frustrated hope. He looked back out the window just as the motor started.

"Shit," he said and went out the door. Then he turned and stuck his head back in and grinned toward the back booth. "Take good care of him Chaplain," he shouted, "I'll settle the hack and be back in a minute. I got something over at the office I want him to see." His voice was loud and hollow, Harry looked at him blankly as he closed the door. As he watched Buck hurry across the street his face felt empty as if he were prepared for a smile that had failed to materialize.

To avoid going back to the booth, Harry went through

the double screen doors that separated his store from the post office. He walked to what he already knew to be an empty P.O. box and looked in, waiting for the smile which refused to appear on his face.

Back in the empty drugstore, the photographer sat facing the chaplain across the booth. His beard made the chaplain uncomfortable, a little embarrassed, at his own thought that the hair looked so exactly pubic. He was made uneasy also by the fact that the photographer had not yet blinked his eyes, eyes that were absurdly round, hinting of goiter.

The photographer removed a ball-point pen from his shirt pocket, reached across the table for a paper napkin and began wiping the point. "Under water, O.K.," he said looking at it, "but stay the hell out of airplanes."

"It's the hole," the chaplain said.

"What's the hole?" the photographer said suddenly, holding the pen dead still in the napkin and looking up at him.

"The pinhole in the pen that allows the pressure to equalize," the chaplain said defensively as if he were about to be quoted. "It stops up sometimes, have you got a pin?" The reporter's face sagged into forced blandness. He offered the pen to the chaplain without removing it from the paper napkin.

"No, no, I don't mean that pen, wait a minute." He began fumbling nervously with one of his major's insignias.

"Never mind, Major, let it stay clogged, I'll get it the next time I change the baby."

"Oh, do you have a baby?"

The photographer's face became more bland, what little expression there had been in his absurd eyes drained down behind the beard.

"Yes, two girls and a boy, or vice versa. Now, why don't you begin and fill me in on what it looks like to you—as an outsider so to speak. Just what you have seen and heard since you arrived."

"Well it has been pretty busy. The telephone operator died yesterday," the chaplain said uneasily. Again the eyes floated up from the paper and met his. "The town has been without communications," he added, feeling again that vague misgiving at being quoted.

"Yes, Major, the man who drove the cab I was forced to take out here because of that fact told me." He put his fingers to the hairs around his red, wet mouth.

"Perhaps if I ask direct questions," he said into the air just above the Major's head. "Major, are you to preach the funeral?"

"No, no, I will bring a prayer at the grave side."

"Before or after the body goes in?"

"Well, I really can't say just yet. You see . . ."

"Have you conducted services of this nature before?"

"Well no, not exactly on the order of this one."

"Do you *know* the order of this one, Chaplain?"

"Yes, it seems . . ." He looked toward the fountain, feeling himself made, by his ignorance, an accomplice to the conspiracy of silence that surrounded the events taking place around him. "Would you like more coffee?"

"No, thank you, but what I would like is just one or two small details about what the hell is happening. Am I in the right town, or am I the one that's lost. Is this White Dove, Texas, population six hundred and seventy-three? Did an ex-soldier by the name of Ronald A. Parker live here? Is he being brought here today, this afternoon, to be buried? Are the flags flying today because it's the day this town chooses to dry the mildew from them or does it in some subtle way have something to do with the arrival of a soldier's body that is almost addressed C.O.D. to the First State Bank, White Dove, Texas. A bank which is just coincidentally closed today for a funeral."

As the startled chaplain began feeling for an answer, Buck opened the front door. The chaplain could see a mechanic working under the hood of the taxi.

"You all want more coffee?" he asked as he passed the fountain walking toward them. The photographer turned his eyes up and sighed like a tired woman sitting.

"Well now," Buck said as he squeezed into the small booth beside the chaplain. "Well now, where were we?" The photographer was silent, slumped back in the corner of the booth.

"I guess you want a fill-in," Buck said, trying to remember the cute way they talked in the magazine. He unrolled a long photograph that was yellowed and almost without contrast. It was a picture taken of the town forty years ago. It showed a small cluster of stark frame houses. There were four stores with thin, brittle-looking false fronts. There were no trees, yards or fences, the merchants were standing on the high front porches of the stores above the rutted dirt street. They were without coats and in wide strap suspenders, standing in arrogant poses as if it were their wedding day. The town took only the middle third of the long narrow picture; on both sides of it a plain of grass emptiness extended to infinity, the contrast of the horizon having long ago faded from the old print.

"Who is that?" the photographer asked pointing to a man on a black horse in front of the Harvest Hardware and General Mercantile Co. The ball-point touched the blotter-like print under the horse's neck, leaving a blue dot.

"That's the grandfather of Ronnie Parker," Buck said, "Tom Parker."

The photographer sat up. "Can I talk to him?"

"He's dead," Buck said looking up.

"So's your telephone operator, I hear," the photographer said slumping back.

"That's true," Buck said, "but don't worry, it won't interfere, her funeral's not 'til Thursday." He leaned forward toward the photographer, squeezing the chaplain farther into the corner. "Now you just tell me what it is

204

that you want to know. I checked the train, it'll be here at 4:59."

"Alright, I'll try again," the reporter said. "The train will be here at 4:59, right?"

"That's right, it'll be *here,* but that ain't where we all are gonna meet it. The funeral will meet it at Lea Switch out on the Parker ranch, the one where his daddy is, the Crows Foot. Then we will come to town in caravan, everybody behind the hearse. Then to the grave. Reverend Morris will preach at the depot at Lea Switch and Major Sutton here will reward us with prayer at the grave site, after we have caravaned down Main Street between the flags."

The photographer was drawing on a paper napkin as he listened. He had drawn a coffin wrapped like a parcel post package. It was addressed, "To: White Dove Body Works. From: Department of War and Human Disposal. Contents: One used soldier. Parcel may be opened for postal inspection."

"I was thinking maybe you could use this old picture of the town to start out with, that's his granddaddy there on the horse, then maybe end it with us all standing under the new flagpole out at the cemetery. We can put the flag at half-mast and get it in the picture."

The photographer didn't speak or even look up from the skull stamps he was drawing on the parcel post coffin.

"Mr. Harris," he said slowly, with a subdued force behind each syllable, "there is something we must understand, both you and I and the good chaplain seated here with us. I, or the twenty-seven million readers of my magazine, do not give a sugar-coated goddamn about this lovely and isolated hamlet. I am here to do what is commonly known as a human interest story and it has been my experience that the less human it is the more interesting my twenty-seven million thumbclicking readers find it. It must be simple enough to be thoroughly comprehended and absorbed from the page before the spit dries on the thumb that turned it."

He had not yet looked at them, he was shading the design on the napkin. "Thus far this morning you have given me information about everything *except* the soldier you expect to receive and bury here this afternoon. Is it possible that this coffin, named and addressed to the bank of this town is a product of drunkenness in the graves registration branch of the U.S. Quartermaster Corps?" He let his absurd eyes float up from the napkin, and looked directly at them. "I want only one thing, gentlemen, one small request—please direct me to one person who *loved* Ronald A. Parker—carnal, spiritual, platonic or perverted—classification does not interest me." He folded the napkin and placed it under his empty cup in the saucer of cold coffee. The three men, for Harry was there now standing at the end of the table, were silent as they watched the paper turn brown, absorbing the spilled liquid.

They waited, each with his own thoughts running out to meet the photographer's approaching question. Harry fought the late-coming smile he felt rising to the surface of his face. He turned his eyes to Buck just a beat before the photographer asked, "You say the *ranch* where his *father* is?"

"Yes," Buck answered without lifting his eyes from the soggy napkin. He felt Harry's gaze and put his hand across his slick head as if feeling for something.

The chaplain thought about it later in the upstairs room of the old Harvest house where he had gone on the pretext of meditation and now sat fat in his government underwear nervously listening to the first winds of the norther wheeze and cry through the weather stripping. *God loved him. God loved him. God and the government loved him. I will prove to them that he was loved, I will in my prayer speak as agent for both.* His mind began racing blindly through a wild defensive prayer, he saw himself standing at the grave side; *you who still contain your souls witness this soulless box which we now commit to eternal rest.* Cut that, he thought. Again the windows howled high and reedy. He fumbled to start his thoughts over again. I must pray to love or to whatever it is they feel for him. He could see them, the weather-beaten men wide-eyed by the grave as they had been in the church and he felt lost—standing at the edge of an abyss with nothing but the nervous urge to urinate.

XX

It's three o'clock, Major," Buck shouted up from the foot of the stairs where he stood having just come out of the bath. He held large cufflinks in one hand and a tie draped over his arm. Standing too clean, a little powder in the chafed cracks around his nose, in nothing but underwear, black socks, and a stiff white shirt with French cuffs flat and unfolded over his hands like paddles; from the rear he looked like a fat albino penguin with black feet.

He did not wait for an answer. He waddled back down the hall and into the bedroom where Mildred was dressing. She was twisting her body in a sluggish squirming motion into her girdle. When he saw her struggling against herself this way, Buck felt like grabbing the top of the elastic sack and bouncing her down into it.

The wind was also wheezing through cracks around the doors and windows downstairs. It was a moaning wind laced with the reedy tin vibrations of the weather stripping.

"An that furry faced S.O.B. didn't even offer to pay the taxi," Buck continued, "like he thought *we* ought to pay *him* for coming out here to do his job. Harry says he acts like we called him out here to take out an advertisement in his dadburned magazine. Anyway, I told him he could see Arron at Lea Switch when the rest of us did."

Mildred was sitting on the edge of the bed threading her leg into a stocking. The large rolls of fat at her waist were like the bulges between the bands on a cotton bale.

"You told me all he wanted was to talk to somebody that loved him," she said licking her index finger and twisting a loose thread on the heel of the stocking. "Now that don't sound too queer to me."

"That loved him," Buck said fumbling with the large cufflinks, thinking: *Loved him shit.* "We'll see who loved him after while, it's gonna take a pretty warm feelin of some kind to get people out with this norther blowin in. Especially to stand around out at Lea Switch with no heat. I guess that'll show that citified S.O.B. how this town feels about Ronnie Parker."

She was almost dressed now. "Do you think I should take a thermos of coffee? You know what a headache I get when the cold gets on my sinuses."

"It ain't a picnic Mildred. You can sit in the car if it gets that cold. Now get a little high behind, this is one time I don't want us to be late."

Mildred's eyes were cold and set deep in her florid face. When she looked at Buck, they glazed over with a hard film. Last night, she had finally received an insult for which she had been waiting, an insult distilled by that waiting.

There had been in her mind, during all the years since her barrenness began to advertise itself with pets and clubs and migraine headaches, a haunting tinge of disgust. It was something she felt when Buck called her "My little girl."

She had not been able to hate him for the easy manner in which he had accepted his failed prospects for heirs. Unable to goad him into provocation, she had languished in the subtle agonies of unrequited guilt.

The insult had come not out of his appetite as she had feared or hoped it would, but came rather as an aftermath of impotency. He had been unable to stiffen himself when he had to come to her from the whiskey and hot bath. After mauling her around in the bed until both their bodies were slick with sweat, he had given up. "Too many people in the house," he said, referring to the chaplain, and got up to stand with his back to her while she remade the ruined bed.

Then in the darkness of early morning the insult came. She had gotten up and returned to bed. Just as she reached to turn out the bed lamp, Buck began to mumble in his sleep. He stopped and after a moment, giggled a sluggish, drugged laugh. She looked over her shoulder at him and pulled the light. Before she could lie back against her pillow, Buck rolled over and pulled her to him, giggling and mumbling. He jabbed his hard little penis against her back, jabbing and mumbling, "Vacant, she's vacant, ole mother Crows Foot run out of daddies." He giggled a long time, jabbed again against her back and held her. "I'm her daddy now, says I'm her daddy now."

Mildred stiffened her body; he fell away from her and lay quiet on his back. Her body was rigid in the dark bed. She had not understood him say "Crows Foot." To her he was having an adulterous dream, in which he not only scorned her, but whispered and laughed in a harlot's ear about his barren wife.

Her eyes were wide; stunned open. It was not until the room was fully light that she blinked, realizing the sun had risen.

Upstairs the chaplain was dressed. The wool uniform felt good to him. He stood at the north window looking out at the sky that was now a high thin grey. His stance was rigid, military. The ashen light dulled the cleanliness of his scrubbed skin as if the window were covered with wax paper. He listened intently to the dissonant wind, straining to hear in it a hint of the something he felt himself becoming a part of. His mind was retching with the urge to pray, yet he did not pray. He held his prayer back, like a growing moment of courage, until he could kneel there before that wax paper window without thinking of the sharp creases in his pants or the polished toes of his shoes. Then sinking under the weight of that moment, he dropped to his knees near the window sill, feeling on his face the jet of cold air that the wind was cramming through the cracks of the buzzing weather stripping.

How could you do it Lord God? How can you keep so unrevealed? I am on my knees before you to be filled—God pour the spirit into me, my body and the clothes I now still wear are tarnished with blood but inside Lord I ask now for a clean lining—take away my sin the sin of blood I will no longer serve two Gods I now repudiate and foreswear the very cloth of the symbol I wear, I shall not kill nor shall I advertise it. My mouth is your mouth my body your body and when they, those unflinching people of that church, turn their wide unblemished eyes innocent of doubt to me over this boy's grave I will only pass the words that you have sewn on my heart and tongue, nothing more. If words do not come, then nothing—I will hollow my mouth to the wind.

The blade of wind under the window sill was cold on his damp forehead. He raised his bowed head and felt it sharp against his hot eyes. A slow excitement was coming over him. He felt like the exhausted distance runner whose cells have consumed too much oxygen and are themselves now being consumed. There was a burning micro-sting in his flesh that was building rapidly into a hot flush of excitement. I am *saved!* he thought, *Redeemed!*

He stumbled toward the bed and began tearing off the uniform, ripping at the tie, tearing the shirt open, the buttons hitting the oak floor like spilled beads.

Naked now in the chill room he began digging in his

shoes out of it to the floor where they landed on their suitcase with both hands. He tossed a pair of worn golf nubbin spikes. A white wadded athletic sock bounced from one like a cotton boll. Then a floral nylon sport shirt arched through the air to the bed and a wrinkled pair of cotton pants with green stains on the knees were in the air at the same instant. He scavenged through the white underwear flinging each piece away as if it were soiled when his eyes found the stamped military serial number. He rose from the ravaged suitcase, sweating a little now and feeling against him the cold invisible jets that laced the stillness of the room. He stepped naked into the wrinkled cotton trousers and jerked up the zipper.

The floral nylon shirt was icy against his damp skin He tucked it in the stained trousers and hobbled into the golf shoes, leaving shallow pits in the waxed oak floor with the spikes.

Dressed now and beltless, he began searching the cluttered room for the Bible. His eyes crossed it like a beam of light in darkness, then returned to it lying on the night stand. A look of astonishment bloomed slowly, then jerked full as if he were hooked to some morbid vision. He grabbed the Book as though from the fire and ripped the blue Air Force binding from it. It tore loose evenly and cleanly. He looked at it raw, without its binding, and the flowering astonishment in his face began closing, puckering into itself. He tucked the Book under his arm, pressing the still cold floral nylon of his shirt to his tepid skin, feeling his raised and hard nipple already beginning to chafe. He walked across the oak floor, the shoes making a sound like gritting teeth, to the howling window where the bland sky made it seem to be covered with wax paper. He stopped, striking an ursine silhouette against it, casting no shadow into the darkening room.

If nothing, God of my reborn soul, if nothing I will hollow my mouth to the wind. I will stand grave side

waiting the Holy Ghost and my mouth shall be as a
slender trumpet set to the lips of the wind.

Buck came again to the foot of the stairs. He did not
call to the chaplain. He was retracing his steps through
the house, looking for his glasses. He was dressed now
except for the tie which was still draped over his arm, the
French cuffs were neatly folded back and fastened with
the large cufflinks, miniature Ford hubcaps like the ones
he had sent out to his customers last Christmas. The harassed urgency with which he now searched for his glasses
seemed to turn in him that ratchet which since the death
of Elmira had been clicking tighter with each new, splayed
event.

Back in the bathroom he saw the glasses on the window
sill behind the commode. As he put them on the back
door slammed, the noise coming at the same instant that
his fuzzy vision cleared.

The screen door had not slammed shut. The wind had
snatched it from the chaplain's hand, catching it full and
banging it open wide against the house. Buck listened to
its slow erratic knocking, the spring pulling it out from
the wall into the wind and its being slapped back against
the wall.

He knew as he listened to that wind, spooking hollow
whispers down the vent to the hot water heater, that the
banging screen door had been opened by the chaplain
going to wait in the car. He knotted the tie, feeling choked
even before he slid the wide gangster knot up to his throat.
He glanced through the open door into the bedroom
where Mildred was leaning into a mirror wetting her
thumb and forefinger and pulling at her eyelashes.

"Better get a heavy coat," he said. "I ain't hooked back
up the heater hoses yet."

She turned to him, one eyelid still held out by the
lashes, and even with the distortion, was able to give him
a look of utter and complete agony, an insulted female

2 1 3

despair. She let the eyelash slip through her moist finger-tips, wiped the face powder and moisture from them with a Kleenex and slipped into the fur coat that had already been laid across the bed.

Outside, the high overcast sky was veined with grey scars. The wind buffeted the station wagon, rocking it like a small boat tied close to a pier.

The chaplain sat in the back with his eyes closed, the tears still wet and now cold in his lashes, tears not of rebirth but involuntary tears that came when the dry cold wind hit his eyes, with a pain like having hairs jerked from the inside of his nose.

In the dark behind his closed lids he could hear the final harassment of the norther beginning to invade the land, the marauding dust driven by, and suspended in the arid cold of the no longer invisible wind. Grits of moving land struck against the waxed metal of the station wagon with the sound of flying needles being shot through taut tissue paper. Though his eyes were closed to it, the bland sky was being smothered. Dust billowed from the barren wheat fields in great boiling suspirations.

The sound against the rocking car changed slightly and was like burning cellophane. The chaplain opened his eyes, breaking the adhesiveness of the drying tears in his lashes. He was startled by the change effected by the dust. The tan air had contracted the distance, the cold, wind-swept openness was gone. The dust had filled it, and the comfort of enclosure filled him. It was as paradoxical yet complete as children find in ducking their heads under bedcovers, an act separating friendly from hostile darkness.

He relaxed enough to be cold. The grit blasting against the swaying car, although unrelated to the chill, seemed to be the cause and even the sound of the prickles of goose flesh that were rippling over his skin. His nipples were hard as bird-shot.

The back door opened, though he could not see it, and

214

Buck stepped out on the porch. The wind struck him as from ambush. His coat and other loose clothing unfurled behind him, his hat brim blew flat down against his face. He put one hand to the hat and extended the other across the threshold to Mildred. Abruptly she was with him on the porch, standing bowed a little into the gritty onslaught, her scarf and coat angrily whipped out from her body. They turned their backs to the wind. It pressed their coats against them, outlining their bodies dimly through the cloth.

The chaplain raised himself from the back and reached over the front seat through the steering wheel and opened the door. He closed his eyes to avoid the dirt and bits of trash that the swirling wind erupted from the floorboards of the car.

When he opened his eyes, they were in the car. Buck slammed the door and they sat still for a moment breathing heavily. Finally Mildred began brushing at the dust and lint that was settling on her black dress. With one hand she held the grey silk scarf over her mouth and nose, almost refusing to breathe, trying to avoid the dust and cold air.

Buck and Mildred had yet to look directly at or speak to the shivering chaplain. Buck sat hunched over the wheel, looking at the windshield, watching the dust sift across it like ground cinnamon, piling minature dunes between the wipers and the glass. Then he began talking. The car was rocking less now with the added weight in it. He spoke to the windshield as if what he said was being rocked from him by the motion of the car.

"That's it, a dirt storm, a norther and a dirt storm—wonderful thing—hero nobody gives a damn buried in Texas dust bowl."

"Buck, start the car," Mildred said, slamming the air vent on her side closed.

"The heater ain't hooked up."

"Does the heater have to be hooked up for the motor to run?"

"No, Mildred, no it don't."

"Then start the *car*, if we're going let's get it over with. This dirt is choking me to death; close your vent."

He slammed the vent. A fringe of aggravation sprouted around the pupils of his eyes, something personal and subversive. As he hunched tighter over the wheel reaching for the starter, the chaplain's bare arm extended over the seat, a cold tense hand gripped Buck's shoulder, not tightly, more like an embrace of something mechanical.

"Brother Harris, before we go. . . ." Buck turned in the seat as if he had been burned. Mildred did not turn to his face. She dropped the scarf from her mouth and looked only at the bare arm which was a purple-pink, the color of old bruises and rough with chill pimples. The astonishment had flowered full on the chaplain's face and it did not wilt as he met Buck's uncomprehending eyes.

"I have walked in your house with the Lord. I have been reborn. Before we go to do this thing which falls to us as men, I would like us to have a prayer."

Buck could not close his eyes nor could he speak. He turned slowly back to the wheel. There was a chill spot on his shoulder where the chaplain had touched him. Mildred clenched her eyes as if expecting a blow in the face. The chaplain's voice began to fill the station wagon. It was not loud yet it seemed to inflate the space.

Buck was not compelled to lower his head. He stared blankly at the cinnamon dust drifting across the barren glass of the windshield feeling the wind rock the car, thinking, a coat, we gotta get the poor bastard a coat.

XXI

Even now as they drove toward town, the station wagon felt pressurized. Both Buck and Mildred were hunched forward staring down the macadam as if driving an unfamiliar road.

The chaplain was quiet; his eyes were closed and his pale lips moved from time to time, their movement almost like twitching. The heavy tweed overcoat Buck had gotten from a trunk under the stairs was lying across his lap. It filled the cold air with the smell of moth-balls.

Mildred coughed, and Buck without looking at her opened his small window just a crack. The wind screamed past as if he were driving ninety miles an hour. He looked at the dash and watched the shaky speedometer needle hovering just past fifty-seven. Mildred put the forgotten scarf back to her face and he returned his eyes to the road.

As they entered town they could see lights in many of the houses. It was still early afternoon but the dust had darkened the sky. Although the sun was still high, it shone dimly, like a ball of smoldering orange yarn, glowing through the suspended tan grit. Buck was driving slowly as if already following the hearse.

The street lights were on. The automatic sundown device had been deceived by the dust and they were burning also orange in the tan, arid mistiness. They were evenly spaced and tall, lining the blank wind-swept street, standing stiff and absurd. And between them, sagging slightly across the street like clotheslines, the Christmas decorations were also burning. The strands of colored lights were snaggled and ragged with dead bulbs. The wind swayed them like leafless overhead vines.

The post office flag was pressed full by the wind, blown out rigid about two-thirds up the swaying pole.

As they drove past the drugstore, Buck saw Harry inside. The store was empty and Harry was locking the cash register. Buck made a U-turn and pulled into the curb in front of the store. The dust and lint boiled up again from the floor as he opened the door. He got out quickly and slammed it, bending over immediately to look through the glass at Mildred. She did not fight the settling particles. She looked full at him, still leaning forward away from the chaplain, and fragments of terror swirled up like the car dust in the cold smoldering fury of her eyes.

"I'll see if Harry wants to ride out with us," he shouted, ducking lower behind the car to break the wind. Then, holding his hat, he straightened up into the wind and walked leaning sideways against it across the barren sidewalk.

As he opened the door the wind scurried in ahead of him blowing down the Greyhound bus timetable that had been leaning against the inside of the large window.

"Let it go," Harry called. "No more buses today." He looked across the store to the Coca-Cola clock. "What do you need, Buck, you got about forty-five minutes 'til train time."

"Nothin, I just wondered if you wanted to ride out with us, we got plenty of room."

"Well, seems a little early but then again I always seem to be early to funerals and late to weddings. It's because of the flowers. I'm gonna handle the flowers for a wedding sometime just so I can get there on time." He was not looking at Buck. "It sure picked a fine time to give us a duster. I'd thought it would'a saved one like this for the spring, for the county track meet or something like that."

Buck was staring out the window and across the street where he could see through the Ford showroom and on back into the shop. The yellow cab was hanging up by the rear bumper from a chain hoist. Harry followed his line of vision.

"That cab driver has been in here most of the afternoon, says the transmission was about to go on his cab."

Buck did not answer.

"I told him it sounded pretty bad to me. I figure he's got about forty dollars worth of transmission trouble, 'course I didn't say that to him, I just said it sounded bad."

Buck turned from the window. "That's about how it sounds to me," he said, " 'Course that's listening from here, across the wind. You can't tell it might be worse."

Before Harry turned from the window he saw the chaplain in Buck's car. "Is that the Major you got in your back seat?" he said as he waved to Mildred and watched her lift the grey scarf back to her face.

"Harry, that's it." Buck walked quickly to the cigar counter. "It's the Major all right but something has happened to him—he's gone off his rocker—me and Mildred come out to the car and the poor bastard was sitting out there in the cold in nothing but a silk sport shirt and some dirty summer slacks. Just sittin there freezin his ass, looking like some damn fish that somebody had scaled before they killed him." Harry looked sideways out the window. "Says he walked with the Lord in my house." Buck's voice was more miserable and confidential than it had been when he had first come to Harry about the

2 1 9

hemorrhoids. "The train's comin in thirty minutes and he's supposed to give a military prayer. It's gonna be great with him standin out there like a goddamned scaled fish."

"How do you know he didn't?" Harry asked, feeling another creeping manifestation of the punishment that he was now convinced had been building up around him. And also enjoying an aftertaste of the pleasure he still derived from watching Buck squirm in his own snares. He squatted down behind the cigar case and was pouring water from a Coca-Cola glass into the homemade toilet paper humidifier.

"How do I know he didn't what?" Buck asked, almost whispering now.

"Didn't walk with the Lord," Harry said, shooting a look up at him that seemed to leap out thin and sharp.

"Godammit, Harry, how do I know anything?" Buck hunched over the coin scratched glass top of the cigar case and watched Harry through it. "All I said was that he *said* he walked with the Lord in my house. Then he prayed out loud in the car just before we left to come to town, all about dead soldiers and the people that loved them, about how they was like having an arm cut off then after it was gone still fanning yourself with it, not even movin the stub but still feeling the breeze on your face."

Harry stood up and closed the case. "Buck, all this has got your nerves tight," he said starting toward the back of the store, setting the empty Coke glass on the marble top of the soda fountain. "Come on back here."

Buck followed him through the swinging door of the prescription department. Harry set two clean graduated beakers on the counter top next to the small set of balance scales. He turned to the wall of shelved bottles and took down a tall flat brown bottle with a red skull and cross bones on its label. He reached in his pants pocket and tossed a small square packet of Sen-Sen breath fresheners on the counter between the glistening beakers. Setting the brown bottle beside them, he said, "You pour while I get my coat on, my nerves may get a little tight before this is all over myself."

Out in the station wagon Mildred crouched away from the chaplain whose eyes were still closed, though they quivered mechanically from time to time as a spasm set his lips into jerky motion.

The sky and air had lightened slightly, the sun was now able to cast pale shadows. The blinker light at the end of Main Street hanging from a cable stretched across Highway 60, bobbed in the wind over the bare, houndstooth intersection, its amber light flashing in the dust.

In the cafe Roy was still sitting at the corner table next to the window. He had been watching the blinker light and drinking coffee. The ash tray in front of him was full of butts from his handrolled cigarettes.

At a booth in the back corner away from the window, the bearded photographer sat alone, hunched over a borrowed typewriter. The Mexican girl had taken him coffee and he had given her fifty cents. "For the coffee and to stay the hell away from the juke box—*por favor.*"

But for these three, the cafe was empty. Roy sat listening to the typewriter and watching the highway and Main Street. The girl was behind the counter leaning against the screened-in pie case with her hand in the large low pocket of her uniform. She pressed the fifty cent piece against the inside of her thigh, feeling the silver getting hot to her touch. She had read but was not thinking about the caption she had watched the typewriter bang into the clean sheet of yellow paper—*Dust to Dust, White Dove Tex, Oct. 9.*

Looking down Main Street toward the drugstore Roy saw Buck and Harry standing on the sidewalk pressing themselves against the wind while Harry locked the door.

A Cadillac hearse crawled slowly across the intersection following its yellow fog lamps. As it pulled into the cafe curb, the driver cut the lights. The undertaker got out and the wind billowed his heavy black overcoat exposing a long chromium thermos with a bright red plastic top. He covered it, quickly gathering the black coat around him.

The typing had stopped and the waitress was edging toward the juke box. The tall undertaker walked past the window toward the door which was around the corner. Roy noticed a difference in the man's face. At the funeral chapel he had looked young, naturally well-preserved. Now his face was drawn and grey; even though the wind was cold, no color showed in his skin. Away from the soft theatrical light of the funeral parlor he was bloodless and ashen. It was as if he had watched too many arteries cut, too many draining bodies, and his color had drained also to the wet slab, flowing with the cold water and dead blood down its drainboard gutters to nowhere.

Roy did not look at him when the door opened. He could feel him in the room. He heard the door shut and felt the low gust of cold air swirl around his legs under the table. It sent a chill up the outside of his legs and over his thin buttocks, stopping at his belt. He looked past the hearse after meeting briefly the darting eyes of the scrawny driver, who was barely visible over the steering wheel.

There was now more traffic on Main Street. The cars moved slowly under the swaying Christmas lights. The cinnamon air had thickened again and the sun was lower.

The photographer had closed the typewriter and sat watching the undertaker paying for the thermos of hot coffee. She gave him his change and he quickly put each of the several coins in a different pocket so there would be no danger of money jingling in his pants during the performance of his solemn duties. He took the thermos, tucked it under the long black coat and walked smoothly to the door. Roy again felt the low gust of cold air. The photographer swung his camera case over his shoulder, snatched up the cased typewriter and followed him, almost running. The girl went to the back booth, picked up the salt shaker he had dragged off the table with the typewriter, tossed a dash of salt over her left shoulder and began clearing the table.

Roy watched the photographer outside standing at the door of the hearse talking to the undertaker, who had lowered his window about two inches. The wind blew the lip hairs of the photographer's beard into his mouth as he talked. The undertaker shook his head gravely, a negative gesture yet done with such profound smoothness there seemed nothing negative in it. It was at once negative and hopeful. A green ten dollar bill was flapping alive on the wind, about to escape from the photographer's hand. The undertaker rolled up the window and the hearse eased back off the slanting drive like a boat ungrounding itself. It crawled back across the intersection and turned north, across the false levee that supported the railroad tracks, toward the Crows Foot road and Lea Switch.

The photographer stuffed the bill in the side pocket of his flapping coat. Roy watched the wind sucking curses from his mouth and hoped it would not blow the ten dollars out of the pocket.

When he came back in the cafe he put the typewriter down near the door and sat on one of the stools with his back to the counter and leaned against it. Roy slid his chair around so he could see him.

"You want to get shed of that ten dollar bill?"

The photographer was pushing the hair back from his pink mouth with his thumb and forefinger. "It's possible," he said, putting his hand into the coat pocket as he should have done to protect the money from the wind. "Can you get me to Lea Switch, wherever that is, before the four fifty-nine train arrives?"

223

"I think I can," Roy said getting up from the chair.
"Do you know where it is?"

"I think I do," he said, picking up his empty coffee cup and bringing it to the counter, something he always did in lieu of a tip. "But you better get another cup of that hot coffee 'cause the ride may be just a little chillier than you like it." He ducked his head to look below the lettering on the window and down Main Street toward the drugstore. He saw Buck's station wagon backing away from the curb. "I'll get the coffee out of that ten dollars and charge it to expenses," he said, as he walked toward the door without his hat.

Outside, the wind snatched and curried his fine hair. He turned his back and leaned his weight against it as smoothly as old sailors judge the deck roll of tossing ships. Buck had driven to the highway and was obeying the bobbing blinker light. Roy waved him across and over to the curb in front of the cafe.

Mildred rolled her window down a little, grimacing. Roy hunched over, speaking into the open slot. "I jest hired out to take that young hair face out to the train, so he won't be needin to crowd you all up."

Buck leaned over almost into Mildred's lap so he could see up into Roy's face. "Well, get him on out there, it's suppose to be due in about twenty minutes."

Roy could not see the faces in the back seat. "Where's the chaplain?" he shouted looking at Buck. Buck straightened out of sight, Mildred shut the window with a fast turn of the handle and Roy bent his knees to look in the car. He saw the chaplain's dormant face. Harry in the back next to him smiled a wide slow smile and waved an inverted salute as Buck drove away, spinning the back wheel a little in the pea gravel that the wind had swept next to the curb. Roy returned to the cafe.

"You get your coffee?" he asked, brushing back his hair with the flat of both hands.

"I don't think we have time," the photographer answered looking up at the wall clock, "if that's correct." He nodded toward the clock above the serving window to the kitchen.

"It's close enough," Roy said, taking his hat off the deer horn hat rack. "Jest a minute and I'll help you with your rig," he said, holding the hat and taking up a notch in the leather hatband which was made like a miniature western belt. "You better cinch down anything you got that's loose, that wind is getting pretty thick. Lots of real estate bein swapped today."

"Is this normal weather for this part of Texas?" the photographer asked, checking the straps on his camera bag.

Roy watched him remove the ten dollar bill from the coat and stuff it in his pants pocket.

"Yes and no," he said, "it don't blow like this all the time, like this morning it was still as a rotten egg, but then on the other hand, I guess you'd call it normal since it don't never surprise anybody. In fact we kinda expect it in the fall and spring. You can't tell, it may blow itself out tonight and tomorrow it'll be so still you'll be calling yourself a liar for rememberin how bad it was today."

The photographer hoisted the camera bag over his shoulder where it hung by a long strap, and stooped carefully to pick up the portable typewriter. Roy took it out of his hand and opened the door.

"Put that last coffee on my bill," he said to the waitress who, hearing the wind howl past the door, instinctively flattened her hand against her skirt.

Roy led the way to the battered red pickup. The photographer stopped halfway, leaning into the pressure, and listened to the wind whine and moan through the telegraph wires which ran alongside the railroad tracks. As he approached the old truck, Roy shouted from the other side.

"If it don't seem windy enough for you inside you're welcome to the saddle." He pointed to the saddle that was mounted on the top slat of the high stock rack on the bed of the pickup. Empty, the stock rack made the truck look as if it were loaded with a small square cage made of oak boards. The old saddle was mounted near the front on the driver's side.

"I'll take the inside," the photographer answered, shouting into the wind and fighting to open the door by jerking at the drooping door handle. Roy got in and leaned across to the wedged door. With a vicious straight-arm thrust he hit the loose tin door panel with the heel of his hand, knocking it open. The photographer got in and slammed the door. The wind blew straight through the cab. There was no floor mat and under his feet he could see the corroded battery and, past that, the immaculate wind-scoured ground.

Roy started the engine and a fog of oil fumes and gasoline vapor filled the cab, defying for a moment the wind. He backed out onto the road and headed into the norther.

It was some time after they had crossed the railroad tracks before the heat from the engine was felt in the cab. The wind carried it back to them through the open floorboards. The photographer's feet were hot while the cold blast from the vacant window made his face and right ear go numb. The silence between them was filled with the photographer's discomfort and Roy's manipulation of the ancient and eccentric truck. Finally, Roy propped the short stick against the dash board and down to the gear shift, wedging it tight to keep the transmission from jumping out of high gear, and relaxed.

"It sure don't look much like a day for picture takin," he said, pulling a sack of tobacco from his shirt pocket. "Jest what is it that you figure on taking pictures of out here anyway?" He leaned over the cracked steering wheel, using his forearms to hold it steady, and began pouring the dry flaky tobacco from the sack onto the white paper, holding them close to the windshield out of the wind. The photographer did not answer even when the tobacco was neatly spread and rolled into the paper. Roy licked the seam of the thin cigarette as delicately as a cat licking a long scratch, stuck it in his mouth and began feeling the outside of his pockets for a match. The photographer fumbled for his lighter. He felt it in his pocket but did not remove it. Roy had found a kitchen match and struck it under the dash, cupping it in his hands where he held it a long time as if defying the wind, before leaning the splinter of a cigarette down into it. He held it for a few seconds after the tobacco was lighted as if waiting for some-one else to light, then whipped it out with a snap of the wrist. He put his thumb against the hot extinguished tip and broke the match in half, pausing then for one more second before dropping it out the window.

"Of course there won't be near this much dirt in the air when we get on the grass. That should lighten it up a little for you," he said, returning one hand to the wheel.

"Actually the amount of light doesn't matter a great deal," the photographer said, trying now to light a long filter-tip cigarette. He looked at the silver lighter with disgust, reading on it the engraved name of the camera store that had given it to him. He was about to speak again when Roy held a flaming sheltered match over toward him.

"I'd say without meaning nothing else, that all that hair you got there looks to me pretty much like a fire hazard," he said extinguishing the match and breaking it with the same automatic ritual. The photographer took a deep drag and laughed a thin laugh that was blown away and disseminated as quickly as his exhaled smoke.

"The chance is less, as a matter of fact, than cutting your own throat shaving if you happen to need to envision disasters."

Roy turned west off the macadam onto a dirt road. Now the wind no longer carried heat from the engine into the cab. It blew across them through the open windows, almost taking the long cigarette from the reporter's mouth.

"We jest turned west," Roy said, "we'll be on the grass in another two and a half miles. My advice is that you either hang onto that smoke or put it out before we get there."

"You mean a *cow ranch* prohibits smoking?"

"I mean we don't want a fire. Jest let old Arron see another fire and the shit will hit the fan sure enough."

The photographer put out his cigarette. He had not enjoyed it. He could not see the smoke. He never smoked in the dark for the same reason.

"Look, Turner." He paused as if inserting a comma. "What the hell is this Arron? What does his pyromania have to do with a dead soldier being shipped to a five and dime bank and why in the name of forty-three major gods are we driving out into the wilderness to meet a train that has a regularly scheduled stop in the town from which we have just left?"

Roy was startled by the ragged outburst. He looked across at the harried photographer, who was again picking the hairs out of his mouth.

"Ain't you talked to Buck?" he asked finally.

The photographer was holding his hand flat against the beard around his mouth. Brittle leaves of harassment and antagonism were showering dead across the black pupils of his eyes.

"I have talked to him, pleaded with him, and somehow failed to get past the fact that the telephone office is out of order and the taxi in which I arrived is in a sad state of disrepair. Oh, yes, and the train is due at four fifty-nine." He dropped his hand from his mouth. "Now, I would like to impose a few direct questions on you, hoping you will, out of your knowledge as a native, answer them in the simple declarative sentences for which the men of your breed are supposedly so well known."

They were now driving down the last mile before enter-
ing the Crows Foot. The weeds were tall and dead in the
barrow ditches. The brown wheat fields on either side
were alive and moving, the dust swirled and drifted across
them with fury and forlorn lack of contrast. Now and then
a giant tumbleweed would be ripped out of the choked
fence-row and sail, bouncing and tumbling across the field,
leaping and running blind.

The gaunt black oil derricks stood straddling their
moving walking beams, catching now and then one of the
bounding weeds in their rigging.

"They call 'um prairie goblins," Roy said evasively,
nodding with a hooking motion of his head at the large
pumpkin-shaped weeds springing across the dirt road at
the intersection fifty yards ahead of them. "You don't
believe it 'til you see 'um moving like that on a windy
night when there's lots of moon." The photographer
slumped back against the seat mumbling something about
"a goddamned nature tour."

Now they could see ahead of them the expanse of grass.
The barbed wire gate was thrown back. It lay rusting
in useless spirals, entwined and woven now with the dead
weeds. The pickup bounced loose-jointed and docile across
the rutted crossing. The photographer at that moment
could not remember the meridian he had just crossed. His
mind for the moment was as one reincarnated, the past
fields and derricks and town did not exist. The full bearing
of his mind was being drawn out of him, following his
eyes that now shot ahead knowing the temporary madness
of hallucinogenic pursuit, the madness of being sucked
toward a nonexistent dimension.

He recovered when the stick that wedged the truck in
gear bounced out. He reached down to pick it up and saw
the passing grass through a crack in the tin floorboards.
He straightened in the seat and handed the notched stick
to Roy.

"My God, Turner, what happened to the world?"

"Mister," Roy said, taking the stick and jamming it into place, "you jest left it."

The photographer turned violently in the seat and looked out the back window. He saw the boiling fields and gaunt black derricks framed like a wide angle photograph in the dirty rear window. "Stop the truck," he shouted, twisting the disconnected door handle. Roy began stopping. "Reach out to the outside handle," he said. The photographer reached out, pushed down the handle and threw his weight against the wedged door. It opened and he slid out almost jumping, dragging the camera bag out behind him by the long strap. He knelt in the grass and dug in the bag. His movements were quick and excited as if he were afraid that the wind would suddenly stop and the whole scene would disappear before him.

"How much time do we have?" he shouted at Roy.

" 'Bout twelve or fifteen minutes," Roy answered, watching several small yellow leaflets blow out of the bag and across the dust colored grass. The photographer slung two cameras over his neck and ran back to the door of the pickup. He tossed the bag on the seat. "Will that saddle hold me?" he asked, looking up at it straddled and cinched to the stock rack. Before Roy could answer, he ran around in front of the truck and up to Roy's window.

"I guess it will," Roy said.

"Good," he said climbing up the side of the oak cage. "You drive on toward the station, I'm going to shoot from up here. All you have to do is drive slow and try the hell to remember that I'm up here." He climbed the rest of the way up. He mounted himself backwards in the saddle, locked his feet in the stock rack and hunched over a small black camera as if he were protecting a small flame from the wind.

In the cab Roy leaned across the seat and slammed the open door. He listened for a moment to the wind slapping the tail of the reporter's coat against the top of the cab, then put the pickup in motion.

At least the son of a bitch had enough sense to stick that ten dollar bill in his pants, he thought, as he guided the wobbly goose-necked gear shift roughly through the gears.

XXII

THE crumbling depot at Lea Switch, with its maze of abandoned stock pens, looked even more useless and isolated with the automobiles parked near. Under the overcast of dust they glistened in contrast to it and the cured grass.

The wind, now that the boards had been removed from the broken windows of the depot, blasted in. Shingles were leaving the roof in flocks, fluttering low on the wind like grey winter sparrows.

The few cars parked at the east end of the scaling building represented the hard core of the Baptist Church. Those same cars could be seen huddled in the otherwise empty church parking lot on each Wednesday prayer meeting night. The black hearse was backed up to the loading dock. Its driver was reaching over the seat into the empty rear section, shaking the settled dust from the dark maroon velvet that draped the rear windows. In one of the cars parked near, a soberly dressed woman was spitting on a handkerchief and scrubbing at a long black smudge across the ear and cheek of a small boy who had dashed from

the car to the tracks and on hands and knees put his ear
to the rail to listen for the train.

There were also several official cars from the county
seat. The Sheriff's empty prowl car was parked in front of
the hearse. Its dual radio antennas were bowed over and
secured to the low top and the two red spotlights, one on
each front fender, were lifeless.

The Sheriff was inside the depot waiting room working
with the rusty potbellied stove. He had gathered the rain-
rotted and fallen stovepipe and assembled it into a makeshift chimney. He connected it to the stove and stuck the
open end of sagging pipe out of a broken window on the
south side of the room. A skinny deputy was outside,
gathering an armload of the shingles which had fallen on
the grass. The Sheriff walked into the littered station-
master's office and returned with a wad of paper and the
bucket half full of dust-covered coal.

Outside, on the west side of the building, Buck and
Harry stood in the center of a group of men dressed like
soldiers. The men were uncomfortable and gaudy in their
ill-fitting uniforms. They looked as if they were attending
a masquerade in rented, imitation military clothing. Several of them wore plaid civilian socks and all of them
were in civilian shoes, except one who wore a pair of fancy
stitched cowboy boots. They were bareheaded and the
brass on their lapels and belts was green with the cloudy
scum of oxidation and neglect. These were the pallbearers,
eight men from White Dove stuffed into their World
War II uniforms, hunched against the wind, telling war
stories.

". . . and I figger to be even," one of them was saying
to Harry. "I got somewhere in the neighborhood of twenty-
nine of 'um, close as I can tell." He looked down at the
pointed toes of the boots sticking out from under the
cuffless olive drab pants. "An you know I'm about like ole
Tom Parker when it comes to killin breeding stock, so

233

we hadn't won it more'n two hours before I started working on my debt. In the next six months I was seed bull to sixty-three of 'um poor young frauline widder women —I don't say they all stuck, but my new hat against a doughnut says a fair majority of 'um did—at least twenty-nine. So like I say, I figure to be about even." He spat on the wind and watched the splintered clear liquid land ten feet away. A couple of the men laughed.

Buck seeing the smoke said, "Looks like the Sheriff's got a fire goin, let's move inside." He looked at his watch as they filed in front of him and into the waiting room. The last fat ex-soldier passed as Buck looked out north across the grass. He saw Roy's pickup slowly coming over a rise about a quarter of a mile away. He could see the photographer sitting backwards in the saddle on top of the stock rack. As he watched, the pickup stopped and the man in the saddle climbed up, perching for a moment on all fours on the saddle like a goat on a stool, then he turned around, forking his legs and dropped down into it, looking toward the depot. Buck saw the cameras and paused undecided in the doorway, then joined the ill-fitted platoon which was now gathered around the smoking iron stove.

Even with the wind eddying through the ruptured and open room, Buck could smell the army wool, pungent with dissipated moth balls. The rusty stove hoarded the puny heat from the shingles which were kindling the frigid coal. It gave off only the acrid odor of scorching dust mixed with the smell of burning cobwebs and iron rust. Some of the men held their hands out flat over the stove as if they were resting them on the back of some gentle animal.

Buck walked back to the door and looked at the approaching pickup and its rider.

"Well here he comes," he said to Harry who was standing at the door. The refugee soldiers heard him and turned in one motion to look out the other window, the one which opened west and down the empty track. Their talk and memories had made them nervous.

"How about us all gettin outside," Buck said, hunched and staring out the broken window. He had begun to sweat even in the cold wind, and barbed spines of pain were making a red and swelling pincushion out of his hemorrhoid.

"Get around the mailcart like we practiced, he may want a picture of it before we get the casket." He looked at the watch again. "I make it about six minutes 'til train time."

The men pulled at their short Ike jackets, trying to cover the gap between them and their tight pants. Several of them could not button the top button of their flies and worked at the muddy brass belt buckles with nervous fingers.

"You take the tongue, H.A.," Buck called to the one in boots as they passed out the door. "Remember you got to hold it down, if you don't she won't roll."

He followed them out. They placed themselves around the steel-wheeled cart. The wind flapped their hair and short army ties. Around the mailcart with its high bed, made to mesh with the railroad cars, they looked stunted.

"When she passes the mile marker, I'll go tell the folks in the cars an you start rolling the cart up the siding. I figure the baggage car will stop up yonder—between here and the pens."

The men were silent. H.A. pumped the tongue of the cart every now and then, which would stir an occasional joke or comment from them but only temporarily pulled their eyes from the track.

Buck walked away, expecting to meet the pickup at the crossing. As he hurried along the trackside of the depot, a high school boy ran up to him carrying a black trumpet case.

"Mr. Harris, Mom said for me to ask you agin about Taps. Do I do it here or are we still gonna wait 'til out to the cemetery? She don't think anybody will hear it here with the train and all."

Buck stopped. "Eddy, like I told you, when we get out to the graveyard. I'll show you when we get there. You blow it jest as the coffin is going down. When they take off the flag you start blowin it. And remember to blow it slow like I told you. You saw it in the movies—slow like that."

The boy nodded, taking a silver mouthpiece out of his pocket and putting it in his mouth like a sucker.

"Tell your mother it's about time for the train," Buck said, looking up to see the pickup pull up and park out by the stock pens. The boy ran back toward the cars, leaving him in the chafing wind looking toward the pens which were now being photographed. That son of a bitch, he thought, that hair-faced son of a bitch.

He was about to turn back to the depot when the undertaker called to him from the freight doorway of the building. Buck walked over to where the mortician had been standing sheltered from the wind.

"Mr. Harris," he said, as Buck approached, "I am aware that this is hardly the time to annoy you with trivial matters but we had a most regrettable experience this morning in our effort to prepare the grave to receive the interment."

Buck's mind was still at the stock pens cursing the photographer. In the middle of his speech the mortician had noticed this and he put a hand on Buck's arm. Buck looked down at it as if it had come from nowhere. The moment it touched him his attention jumped to the undertaker. It brought him a chain of sensations: the cosmetic smell, the bones in the grip, the dead eyes like weathered lead and the chafed red skin on the fingers. Buck had heard only "to prepare the grave."

"Perhaps you could persuade the Sheriff. . . ." The lead eyes dropped and he removed his hand from Buck's arm.

"The Sheriff," Buck said. "The Sheriff, what the hell for?"

"Mr. Harris," the undertaker's eyes rose slowly "this is of great embarrassment to me personally and to the Home."

The boy who was to play Taps ran past them toward the track, without the black trumpet case. He saw them and yelled back as he ran. "She jest hit the one mile marker, Mr. Harris."

Buck winced but kept his attention clamped to the immaculate undertaker. "Get the Sheriff to do what?"

The mortician stood hump-shouldered drenched in humiliation. "It's the gravedigger," he said. His voice had lost its professional resonance and was now strident, finding its pitch by the dissonant wind.

"We found him sitting alone in the grave, we tried everything to coax him out. We set up the canopy without him. He wouldn't even speak to us. When we spread the grass carpet over the pile of dirt at the grave's edge, he leaped up and snatched it off, pulling it back down into the grave with him. The driver prodded him once with a shovel handle and he screamed as if he had been stabbed, yelling about bayonets and Germans."

"Well, shit a brick!" Buck said, turning from the undertaker. He paused in the warehouse doorway; then as if his crossing the threshold had pulled the cord, the train whistle spurted out its distant warning. The sound was mournful and distorted by the wind.

People in the cars began gathering their wraps and the car doors opened erratically.

Buck without more words started around the building toward the waiting room. The undertaker signaled his driver and the starter of the hearse ground its cold motor into whispering action.

The Sheriff ran past the warehouse door followed by the skinny deputy, who squatted like a woman at the edge of the loading dock before jumping to the ground. The running lawmen, and their swift exit from the siding in the prowl car with its red lights blinking and rear wheels spinning on the loose gravel, excited the people and they hurried, some half running toward the depot.

Another blast of the train's whistle punched out at the

wind. The photographer ran up the track from the pens to the depot building. Down the track the black engine looked as if it were coming out of the ground.

The bizarre platoon of masquerade soldiers rolled the mailcart down the siding toward the pens. The photographer passed it, then wheeled to take pictures of them. Buck ran toward the mailcart and the photographer darted away.

Out in the grass to the south of the building the chaplain and the preacher rose from their knees, and arm in arm like walking wounded, they began slowly to walk toward the track.

The train snorted to a protested standstill in front of the depot. The baggage car had glided to a stop exactly in front of the building's bay window. Steam spewed from its couplings. The sliding door opened. A conductor was running up the siding from the rear of the train. Buck saw the door open and motioned the platoon to come back with the mailcart. They tried to turn it around on the narrow siding, found it impossible and began pushing it backward toward the baggage car. People were gathered around the door and could not hear the steel wheels of the cart as it approached. Buck ran around them to the cart and began shouting and shoving them aside with a harassed gentleness, a violence barely suppressed.

An army sergeant appeared in the doorway of the baggage car, an American flag folded in a triangular bundle under his left arm. The mailcart was butted to the doorway and the sergeant stepped out on it. He knelt quickly as if taking cover and spoke to the men pushing the cart. Four of them climbed up on the cart and followed him inside the car.

There were no sounds from the tight clot of people surrounding the doorway; it was like waiting for a bride to appear. When the straining backs of the two men who carried the end of the grey coffin appeared, there was a general sigh and stirring of feet.

They carried it out, each with one hand holding the bright new flag which now draped it. The wind billowed the flag, almost tearing it away. Two of the mock soldiers jumped down and four remained, one at each corner to secure the undulating flag. They pushed the cart away from the baggage car, the men standing at the corners of the coffin swayed, trying to keep their balance on the high cart. From the end of the train a conductor called "All aboard" and the black caravan shuddered in response.

The chair cars began to slink past. They were almost empty. The four men standing high on the cart at the corners of the coffin could see through the train. They watched the windows pass slowly and through them saw the open grass on the other side. And over the white tables of the empty dining car they saw the wagon. One black mule hitched to a cock-eyed double-tree pulling a wagon. They could not see the Negro or the White or the rifle sticking up like a stubby lance. They saw only two men and a crazily hitched mule jerking a rickety wagon across the dead grass toward them. Through the passing train windows its motion was even more spastic like a silent movie film.

One of the pallbearers on the cart knelt and spoke to Buck. The wind snatched the corner of the flag from his grasp as he talked. He stood quickly and thrashed his arms in the wind across the coffin to recover it.

Buck pushed his way out of the small crowd and dashed along the track in the opposite direction to the passing train. Running and squatting, he moved along the siding, looking under the moving cars.

He stopped running and dropped to his knees in the gravel, ignoring the pain of the green goat-head thorns which drove into his hand and knees. He inhaled the pain of them and held it. The passing trucks under the Pullman cars clacked past, gaining speed.

The wagon seemed to be jumping toward him. He could see Arron sitting like stone beside the hunched Negro.

239

Smith lashed the slack-skinned mule with precise rhythm, savage blows repeated with perpetual, tumbling violence.

The last car of the train passed and the wind swept down on Buck. He jumped upright, feeling the goat-heads pinning the knees of his pants to him. The wagon was closer now and Buck saw the rifle.

Arron was without a hat and the north wind from his back swept his long white hair about his face.

The train was gone and the small congregation was silent. Every eye was turned into the cold abusive wind watching the spastic wagon move toward them. It was close enough now for them to hear the sharp blows of the whip split themselves across the protruding bones on the mule's back.

The photographer broke from the congregation, running toward the wagon. He stopped halfway and like a gunfighter caught in a crossfire, he turned, fired the camera at the isolated little crowd around the mailcart, then wheeled back to photograph the approaching wagon.

Buck crossed the track, walking toward Arron and the Negro. As he approached, Arron lowered the rifle barrel at him slowly with massive and heavy deliberateness, like a mono-span drawbridge swinging down.

"Get back, Bucky," he gut-yelled out of the mass of wind-rummaged white hair. Smith did not look up. His falling blows on the mule missed no beat. He drove the wagon past Buck who was now oblivious to the wind and felt as if his blood had drained from him into the grass and congealed, welding his feet to the spot where he now stood.

Arron, the moment he spoke the name *Bucky* had raised the rifle like a guidon. Among the clot of people around the coffin the sound of that voice struck a prismatic fear. Those who knew him were torn with shame and with fear of the Parker blood. Those who did not were confronted only with his madness and felt their fear like women.

Smith halted the wagon in front of them, parallel to the tracks. He bowed his scarred head and became fascinated by the sanskrit of grey scars on the mule's rump. The wind carried the rancid smell of men and mule across the tracks to the frozen crowd.

The army sergeant was standing next to Roy. "Who's that?" he asked out of the side of his mouth. Roy heard him and without turning his head from the wagon where he was searching for Arron's eyes, felt a moment of courage. With his eyes directly on Arron, he answered:

"That, Sergeant, is the remains of Arron Parker, owner of the land and daddy to whatever it is you brought him back in the casket." As Roy spoke Arron turned his grizzled head toward the crowd. Again the wind whipped his hair into his face like frosted hemp.

The sergeant, a stranger to the blood and no party to the madness, left Roy and began walking through the dumb crowd toward the wagon. He crossed the tracks and Arron did not speak. As he approached the wagon he could see under the morass of white hair the thick black brows which hung over the ledge of his sunken eyes and under them in the dark caves, the blue eyes, glistening gemstone chipped from the heart of a glacial outrage.

He stopped next to the warped front wheel of the wagon. A whiff of the ointment reached him and he thought of napalm. Arron looked down at him as if he was something the wagon had run over crushing but not killing. The sergeant, feeling the icy commitment of Arron's eyes, began to speak loud against the wind.

"Sir, it is with deepest regret that I, on behalf. . . ." The rage burst in Arron's eyes. He smashed the rifle down across the sergeant's shoulder crushing his collarbone. The soldier fell to the ground gasping.

Arron sprang to his feet beside the silent, absorbed Negro. "Bucky," he growled in a voice like a mine cave in, "get 'um off the Crows Foot, load this wagon and get 'um off the grass."

Smith looked up. "De guts Arron, you 'bout to get off with outen de guts."

Arron lowered the rifle at the make-believe soldiers as if their tacky uniforms were a natural target. "Law says trespass is a sin—how do you feel about it?" he said jabbing the stub saddle gun at them. "Load this wagon." He indicated the coffin with the black nosed weapon.

The men on the mailcart jumped to the ground. One of the others ran to the writhing sergeant and dragged him back across the track. Roy came from the rear. "He wants the coffin," he said.

"He can't do that," the undertaker whispered to a frightened woman beside him.

"Bucky," Arron said, his voice a cold extrusion of lumpy rage, "Get 'um off the land."

The men in uniform were lifting the coffin from the mailcart. They carried it over the tracks to the back of the wagon. They paused, looking to Buck for directions.

"Put it on the wagon," Buck hissed. The sound came out of him like some final deflation. He turned to the crowd, "Get the women to the cars," he said, realizing he had not yet spoken to Arron.

The undertaker led the way back to the parking lot, leaving only Buck, Roy, Harry and the soldiers. The chaplain with the help of the preacher supported the sergeant as he walked away, following the women, taking soft short steps.

The wagon trembled as they skidded the casket forward into it. Smith cursed the mule and raised the whip. They stuffed the new flag down between the low sideboard and the metal coffin.

Arron sat heavily on the spring seat. "Now Roy," he said, "you see these good folks to the gate." He turned to Buck. "Bucky, when I be wantin to see you, I'll come to town to do it. This is the Crows Foot." He gouged Smith with the rifle butt. "Move that mule, Smith."

242

Smith cracked the thin whip down on the mule's rump. With the same unfaltering rhythm, he lashed the mule seven measured blows before it stumbled awake and leaned into the harness. It was again as if the sound rather than the pain of the blows aroused it into motion.

The wagon wobbled and moved forward with a slow distended lurch. The single mule hitched cock-eyed to the double-tree pulled its load at an angular track. The narrow wheels left four distinct tracks.

Separated by the wind from Harry and Roy, Buck watched the slow moving wagon with the coffin and two men, one hunched and mechanically striking the mule, the other straight, immobile, holding the erected rifle, butt down, on the seat beside him. They seemed to diminish in size without moving away, their jerky angular movement not carrying them away but rather like something rotting at an accelerated rate, they dissolved in the distance and wind and dead grass.

Roy was the first to speak. He did not turn his face away from the spot where the wagon had dragged itself over the rise like an old dog with a broken spine.

"Crazy or not, the old bastard's got a kick or two left in him," he said finally, and turned back toward the depot. His eyes evaded Buck's and met Harry's. They exchanged something that was not quite a smile, something like a shared flicker of pride.

The sun was low in the west and the wind was dying with it. A brown darkness fell over the land, falling as if the dust in the air, abandoned by the wind, were night; settling, sifting down, thickening from tan to umber to black.

XXIII

THE men sitting in the cars with the green phosphorescent reflection of the dashlight on their chafed faces were feeling the tension. They felt cold sweat punch like needles up through their skin. The women, honed already by a frustrating sense of sacrilege, sat with the men vomiting their scorn.

They drove away, following the empty hearse which nosed through the billowing dust from the dead grass churned up by Roy's pickup which now led the silent caravan. It was dark and each man felt the oppression of what he knew they together were about to commit. The guilt of trespass was still on them, yet each knew something would rise to displace it. The women, ignorant of their commitment, harangued them, venting bitterness on their fumbling that was not yet impotence, spilling harassment on something that was not yet defeat.

In Roy's pickup the photographer asked, "Will they hang the Nee-grow?" He was already changing to night film and flash equipment.

"Shit," Roy said, without taking his eyes from the dim

trail in the grass. "It'll take every ball they got among 'um jest to drive back on this place."

"How will they do it? I certainly don't expect much in the way of leadership out of that fellow Harris."

"Mister you jest get your mind off nigger hanging and wait 'til something happens before you take a picture of it. And my advice is to leave off estimatin what's in a man 'til you see a few more. You seen one this afternoon and more'n likely you'll see one more tonight, like I say, if there's enough balls left among 'um to make up a good man."

The sagging perimeter fence of the Crows Foot came into view. Roy pulled off to the side and watched the cars file past. The men were hunched over the wheels. Buck's station wagon passed. In the dim light Roy could see Harry Eddens in the back seat; he was laughing at Mildred. Buck was silent, squinting at the road. As they passed, the chaplain turned his face toward Roy. He looked startled; a wilted, forlorn bewilderment hung from his eyes down over his cheeks and mouth.

For the first time today Roy thought of Elmira. Even the station house had evoked no thought of her. He sat watching the cars pass off the ranch, and a new potency opened like a night flower in his chest. I'll be the one watching this time, he thought, I'll watch the bastards, I won't laugh like Harry but I'll watch 'um feeling each other's sacks lookin for a ball.

He looked back toward the depot after the last car passed out of the gate, and then jammed the pickup in gear and joined the train of cars. The thin incision of light it had dragged across the land healed quickly in darkness, leaving no scar.

Four miles north the headquarters house was dark and would be until the coming moon raised it out of the night.

Arron sat on the wagon seat watching Smith struggle with the wide doors to the saddle and carriage shed. Hobbling and grunting, he got them open, they again were like props, thin and warped, buttressing the sagging low-roofed shed. Smith walked to the head of the exhausted mule. "Kick off the brake, Arron." Arron released the brake and Smith pulled on the dripping bit, feeling the hot wet breath of the beaten mule on his hand, breath that smelled already like blood. The trembling mule stumbled almost falling, its legs wobbled and jerked. Smith put a hand on its heaving side feeling the ribs moving and hot under the wet hair.

"You! Mule! Git up dere, ten mo' steps." The whole wagon began to tremble and slowly move into the shed.

When it was inside, Arron pulled up the lines and the mule began sinking to the ground as if he had pulled a plug deflating it. It crumbled down slowly but with un-mistakable finality, sinking across the wagon tongue like a heavy sack of hot mud, splintering it. The dry weather-beaten oak shattered with a sound like brittle limbs being blown from dead trees.

Smith knelt slowly, sinking with the quivering mule.

"Well, Arron, you done cost yo'self yo last mule." He shouted at the darkness, feeling the explosive throbs in the animal's throat.

"Get the lantern," Arron said, sitting still and upright on the wagon seat, holding the cold stock of the erected rifle. "Get the tools and lantern."

Smith slipped the bridle off the prostrate mule and left the shed, stopping only to drag shut the warped doors.

"I jest hope dat mule gets off his death spasms rite in dat Arron's lap, dat ain't no way to kill a mule," Smith said to no one as he approached the darkness of the hag-gard and hollow house.

Arron could see his light as he crossed the yard coming from the house with the lantern. As he came closer the rays of yellow light slid through the cracks of the wall and laced the wagon and casket with limber and moving poles of yellow light. As Smith dragged back the door the vertical strips of light sliced across Arron and the casket. Smith entered the low roofed shed and the shadows shrunk into the walls.

He hung the rusted lantern on a bare wire over the wagon and climbed down. Without looking at Arron he walked to the gasping mule. Again he knelt by its head, sinking into the shadow of the wagon putting down his hand to guide the brittle joint of his knee, feeling the thick pool of cooling liquid that had flowered from the animal's mouth where it lay in the powdered dust of the floor.

"Dey gonna come mule—dey gonna come anyhow, we done did what dey was to do and dey gonna come anyhow." He lifted the heavy head of the dying mule onto his lap and began to sway his body in the darkness, rocking slowly and moaning, feeling the warm draining mucus soak through the crotch of his worn absorbent pants, where it cooled.

With Smith out of sight, drowned in the shadows, Arron was alone. He listened to the muffled flapping of the clucking tongue of flame in the sooty lantern. It was hanging behind him over the coffin. He had not yet moved. His face was buried in the shadow of his grizzled head. His eyes were focused on the back wall of the shed where the dried dust-encrusted harness hung; a mass of rigging, the leather cracked and brittle, no longer supple. Also hanging on rawhide ropes from the low ceiling in front of him were the saddles, hanging by the pommels with their stirrups falling at limp angles. They looked like dead tom-turkeys hanging by the neck with their tails slightly fanned.

Under his line of vision where the moaning Negro sat cross-legged in the dust, the mule's body rumbled and shook. The wagon trembled with the quake, the mule's legs and neck distended suddenly as if with the concussion and a horizontal geyser of steaming liquid and gas erupted from it filling the air under and around the wagon with a hot stench. Smith's moan rose in the air with the smell as he felt the pain of the heavy head collapse again on his bony legs. The mule gasped in the throes of exhausted spasms.

The noise and odor of it moved Arron, though he did not look down. He put his hand behind him on the top of the coffin. Without looking back or even moving his head or the other hand which still held the rifle, he came to the full awareness of the coffin; of it and his purpose with it.

When his callused hand touched it, lay flat on top of it, he felt the heartbeat. The metal top was warm against his hand and he could feel under it a pounding heart. And he remembered something he had never known, something he had only a hint of in the words of Sarah when, the night of the fire, she had sent him to the wellhouse for the cloth, where the bones of the horse now lay bleached among broken fruit jars and rusted lids; something his night visions of twenty years had supplied him; something whispered by the blood on the landing under the dust where she had thrown herself on her great belly before the window of holocaust, screaming with constricted throat to him as he galloped the flaming earth, thinking of the cold wet cloth, on the horse-covered bones that lay naked and grinning on the wellhouse floor. Howling across the flames and bones to him in his old visions, "Oh God Arron it's my HEART MY HEART IS COMING OUT— push it back, Oh God Arron ram it back into me—Arron it's slipping out, My Heart! My God. My Heart is ripping out!"

Now he could feel that heart caught under his hand like a toad. He turned in the seat letting the rifle fall. He put his other hand on the domed top of the coffin, feeling with it, also, the soft warm pulse.

A hollow chill rippled inside him. He lifted his hands, then lowered them again. The warmth and throbbing were waiting. As he caressed the metal lid, he began to hear the steady sensual pulse. It felt like large bubbles of thick warm liquid bursting steadily in his ears. He removed his hands and chuckled with delight when the rhythm of softly bursting bubbles continued to perk sluggishly in his head.

He sat for a long time, listening to and feeling the pulse. His own heartbeats, explosive in themselves, came into unison with those of the coffin and began to build a burning pressure under his skin. He closed his eyes once and saw bone-white patterns like single snowflakes blasting into falling fragments.

The dying mule was quiet and Smith's oscillating moan became a part of the dark nervous shadows. Outside the moon was nudging out of the distant grass.

As it rose the cracks between the boards of the rotten walls began to show pale light. The privacy of darkness was evaporating. Arron felt the pulse fading with it. The throbbing was sinking back into the coffin like an exhausted spring. This fading away frightened him. His chest felt as though lumps of fat were being pumped through his heart. He climbed down from the wagon and began running his hands along the side of the iron box. When he got to the back of the wagon he saw the drawer of tools and junk sitting where Smith had left it on the tailgate of the wagon. The dull glint of a silver spoon caught his eye and he took it from the drawer. It was a large serving spoon. He stood for a moment, slapping the rounded bottom of it against the palm of his left hand, beating out the rhythm he still heard perking in his head.

Then, as if she were howling now to him instead of in the tearing throes of childbirth, he heard her voice, weak and almost buried in her agony. Standing in the discharge of a dying mule, with his hand on the coffin of a son he could recognize only as the spilled entrails of love, he heard that love dying. "God Arron—It's coming—it's coming out

Arron make it let go my heart! It's pulling—God Arron—
it's clutching—tearing out my heart!"

Then it became weak like the pulse and all he could
hear was the silver spoon slapping into the hard palm of
his hand. *I will return the guts,* he thought, *return the
heart gut to the grass—Smith knew I forgot the guts that I
put her in the grass in a horse robe without the heart-gut
and she has been silent to my hand.*

Now he was again driven as he had been for the damp
cloth. He clutched the silver spoon and scrambled up into
the wagon. He began feeling the edge of the coffin, searching for the screws as though he were feeling the buttons
of a bridal gown. His old hands were flushed with high
pressure blood, the fingers fumbled over themselves.

He found the flatheaded screws under the ledge of the
coffin lid and touched the handle of the silver spoon to
them gently, forcing it into the screw heads. He began
twisting them slowly loose. Working carefully with nothing
by which to measure time except the moving moon and a
mule death, he removed the screws, sometimes rattling
them around in his hand like salted nuts.

The sooty lantern hanging on a bare wire directly over
the coffin was burning low. The broad, orange tongue of
flame was getting sluggish and shortening; bits of moisture
carried up the wick sputtered and fractured its shape from
time to time. Smith had gone to sleep hunched over the
dead mule.

Arron removed the last screw. He put the warm spoon
in his mouth and dropped the screws in the pocket of his
shirt. He shifted to the center of the lid and, stooping over
it, grasped the ledge. He forced his long hoary fingernails
into the crack and after a deep breath jerked up, ripping
the nails off into the white quick of his fingers and throwing himself backwards off the wagon. He crashed through
the rotten wall landing on his back, with the shattered wall
planks under him on the hard ground outside the shed.

With the silver spoon pointing straight up from his mouth, he lay there stunned and blinking at the dark sky, his knees pulled up and his feet off the ground.

The noise woke Smith but he could not move. The weight of the mule's head, stiff in death, had pinched off the circulation in his legs. He cried out in the darkness of the wagon shadow.

"Arron, Arron you get dis mule offen me—Arron get here, you killed dis mule on me, now you get here and get it off—Arron!"

Outside on his back, the wind still knocked from him, Arron blinked faster and felt the burning vacuum in his chest. He could only hear his name and it was the same voice. A chunk of his mind crumbled off and splashed into the dark pool of his consciousness. It was as if he had just been slammed off the horse as it blasted itself through the low narrow door of the wellhouse. *The cloth,* he thought, *the cold wet cloth.* He was about to smell the smoke of the fire and feel the ache in his arms from swinging the wet gunny sacks when the chunk dissolved and the dark pool became quiet, except for his name. He still heard that voice calling "Arron." He sat up on the shattered boards under him and looked around. He saw the hole in the side of the shed where the boards had ripped off. The tall narrow opening in the wall framed the hanging lantern and the center part of the dull metal casket, and part of the rear wagon wheel.

"Arron—Arron Lee, you better get here."

Arron put his hand down to push himself up and felt the cold pain of his torn nails. His fingertips felt as if they were frozen. He got up, breathing hard now, with the spoon still in his mouth, and ran softly as if something had broken inside him, around to the door of the shed. He dragged it back and saw the wagon with its brooding load. He put his hand to his shirt pocket as if feeling for keys. He touched the screws and walked into the dim shed. As

251

he passed the dark hole in the wall he put a hand out and held onto the low wagon sideboard as if it were a banister and the tall door-shaped hole a black cavern into which he might be violently sucked. He passed it and made his way to where Smith sat pinned under the head and neck of the cooling mule.

"Whar you been wiff dat spoon?" Smith asked suspiciously, looking up at Arron who was standing over him, his coarse white hair tangled like fodder.

"You bedder get thet outen yo mouth quick an do somethin 'bout dis ole man thets talkin."

Arron plucked the spoon from his mouth, and tossed it through the hole his body had made in the wall. He bent over the mule and lifted its head up by the long furry ears, holding it while Smith dragged his lifeless legs from under it.

"While you got aholt of it you might as well say goodbye—I figger thet mule is about the last useful thin thet they is left on dis place, not countin me and *mine*," Smith said as he began rubbing his numb bony legs.

Arron let the long black ears slip through his hands. The open eye of the mule hit the powdered dust of the floor with a soft thud. Smith could move his legs now and was trying to stand up, pulling himself erect on a trace chain that hung from the wall.

The solid jolt of falling through the wall had jumbled Arron's thoughts and stunned the rising excitement he had felt as he began his violation of the casket. His mind was empty and repellent. The words that Smith was mumbling as he stood on wobbly legs hanging on the trace chain did not penetrate.

He was hungry for the spoon, a hunger like loneliness. Though he could not now think of what it was he was doing standing in the dim light over the dead mule watching Smith slapping the dust from his pants, the hunger turned his mind back into itself where it churned for a

moment in blank convolutions. Then as if the hunger had
been for a cigarette, he put his hand to the shirt pocket
where the tobacco sack would have been had he not forgotten to smoke one morning ten years ago. The sack had
fallen out unnoticed and that morning this same craving
sent his hand to an empty pocket. And the pocket had remained empty, he could not connect the craving with
tobacco, only with the pocket, the empty pocket. But now
that pocket was not empty, his idling, convoluting thoughts
caught like something mechanical jerked into gear by the
screws, the wad of individual, flatheaded screws that he had
removed as one might bite with his teeth through the
thread which held obstinate buttons.

"They's gonna be comin Arron—when thet sun comes
they's comin with it—I don't say what's in it ain't yours
an I don't say thet it is—but dis ole head knows dat de box
and de flag belongs to them." Arron could hear Smith but
the words were as glass, he saw through them without
noticing them. His purpose was again rising in him and
he said to Smith, "Get the pinch bar," and climbed up into
the wagon. His movements were slower this time. He approached the coffin as if it were something made unfamiliar
by long absence. He felt nothing as he touched the lid.

Smith came to the side of the wagon and handed him
a spring leaf from an old buggy seat. Arron took it and
removed the screws from his shirt pocket with the other
hand. He gave them to the baffled Negro as if they were
coin of payment.

Arron gouged the flat rounded end of the spring leaf
into the crack where three of the torn fingernails were still
wedged. Two of the thick yellow nails fell to the splintered
wagon bed. Arron stood over the coffin, his face destroyed
in darkness. Carefully he pulled, upward. A long hissing
sigh spewed into the coffin. He dropped the iron and forced
his bleeding fingers into the narrow crack. He pulled it up
slowly. There was no odor save that of fresh mule manure

and burning kerosene mixed with the mentholated smell of Smith which he could not have noticed.

As the domed top of the casket swung up it struck the overhanging lantern, casting a black shadow over its interior.

"Hold it," Arron said to Smith, who was staring into the blackness of the coffin. Smith climbed up on a spoke of the rear wheel and propped his arm against the half open lid. Feeling Smith take it, Arron dropped to his knees and thrust his hands and arms into the dark casket. It was as if he had plunged his hands into loose iron filings alive with electric impulses. He could again feel the heartbeat. That his hands were buried in the loose cloddy red clay cynically scooped up from a volcanic hill meant no more to him than the black greasy carbon of the spent napalm which shortened it. He could feel the heart-gut throbbing around his hands and wrist like small concussions under thick liquid.

"Get the bucket," he shouted at Smith, and rose slowly to his feet, pulling his hands reluctantly from the loose dirt. The itching glee rose sweet in his chest and throat when the sound of the pulse began again to perk in the sluggish pool of his mind. He lifted the lantern and pushed the raised lid back over its hinges where it stayed. The shadow of the lantern reservoir made a round dark spot, on the loose dirt, that moved with the swinging light. Arron put his hands back under the soil as if to warm them and waited, listening to the slow bursting bubbles.

Outside the moon was gone and night was dying of a blood disease, showing already a paling, anemic sky. The horizon to the east was beginning to rust where the watery sky touched it.

Smith hobbled across the yard to get the battered water bucket. The house, gnarled in shadows against the mouldering sky, looked as if night had drained from around it, leaving it shrouded without detail or relief in a surface scum of blackness.

He carried the large bucket toward the shed. The chill air made him contract into himself and move with a grotesque dragging hop.

So, dat boy done turned to dirt, he thought. Somethin for Arron to run through his fingers—all dis for a box of dirt—and them comin—comin on dis land—and they's comin, comin out here an stomp around sniffin and pissin ——. "Well it's dere box and dere flag," he said aloud as he hobbled through the door.

Arron took the can from him and dipped it into the long padded coffin. He filled the corroded can carefully as if the cloddy powder were some precious spice, packing it gently with the flat of his hand. Smith stood watching him, dribbling the screws from hand to hand.

When the bucket was full, Arron climbed down, lowering it to the ground by kneeling with it. Smith did not offer to help, feeling the privacy of the act. When the bucket finally rested in the dust, Arron climbed back into the wagon and squatted again beside the coffin where he had knelt while filling the bucket. He smoothed the remaining dirt with both hands like a child clears a dust slate in a grassless yard. The pulse was not in these remains as he knew it would not be. He climbed down for the final time. Kneeling again, he picked up the bucket. He held it against his chest, trying to button his levi jacket around it. Failing, he held it inside the coat and walked from the dim shed. Smith watched him carry it to the exact spot where the isolated clump of bermuda grass grew at the edge of the porch, that spot where the leaking water from that same can had rotted the flooring. He eased it down kneeling at the crumbling edge of the raw, weathered porch as if it were an altar.

The chicken darted from under the porch and Arron raised his head watching it trot, tottering from side to side toward the roofless barn. He got stiffly to his feet still holding the top edge of the can with one hand and turned back toward the shed, shouting to Smith.

"Get the horse!" Then he turned back to the high gallery and sank down again to his knees and put his arms around the rusty can.

Smith limped back into the shed. The lantern was dark above the open coffin. He took down one of the dead-turkey saddles and dragged it and the bridle out of the shed toward the corrals.

Looks to be one mornin thet ole smooth mouth doan gonna get his hot mash, he thought. Then he saw the hen trotting stiffly toward the barn like a man running with splints on his legs. "An one mornin thet hen doan have to wait for her breakfast to pass through an ole rotten-gutted hoss," he said aloud, dropping the saddle at the corral gate.

He caught the gaunt, archaic horse which had shuffled across the lot toward him. He saddled it and walked back toward the house. The horse, its heavy head hanging limp at the end of its bowed neck, followed the slack reins and in turn was followed by the hen, starting and stopping as it trotted with one-eyed suspicion and eagerness behind them.

A thin line of long-staple clouds low in the east were smoldering russet, about to ignite the sunrise. Smith led the horse to Arron and dropped the reins beside him.

"You better get gone Arron—They's comin wid dat sun —as sho as God made liddle green apples, they's comin wid dat sun." Arron did not move. "If you doan hear me, you jest keep on squattin dere huggin thet bucket." As he talked he reached into the bib pocket of his overalls and took out the little blue jar of ointment. He unscrewed the lid and dipped his finger into the jelly. Pausing for a moment with the clot of cold mentholated grease on his finger he said, "It doan take a big thought to guess what it is they got on dere head, and leavin you sittin here after what we done ain't even a liddle part of it." He turned toward the sunrise as if for heat and began smearing the cold ointment over the knots of grey scars that marked his shrunken face.

Then, as if he had just heard himself speak, he wiped his finger on the leg of the nasty overalls and put the jar back into the bib pocket, first removing the screws. "They gonna want somethin to bury," he said toward the rising sun as if it were a greeting; an acknowledgment of its arrival.

Without looking at Arron or thinking of him further, he started his dragging hobble toward the back door of the house. As if the mentholated fumes had cleared his head, he moved with purpose. He went in the kitchen door and returned with a long butcher knife. He was hunched forward under the burden of urgency as he jolted down the four wooden steps and moved toward the shed, watched only by the suspicious hen, with one eye then the other.

Inside the shed, he passed the open coffin without seeing it and went directly to the dead mule, hunkering down over its head. With the long sharp knife that had not yet rusted, he sliced at the base of the mule's ear as if it were a prime cut of beef. He severed both of the long black ears, holding them carefully out of the cold blood.

Leaving the knife, he stood up blowing the dust out of the thick black fur-like hair on the inside of the ears. Then leaving the ugly bald-headed animal, he took the ears to the coffin where he placed them side by side on the red oily dirt inside. They were beautiful, like any pair of perfectly matched animals caught in identical physical attitudes.

He removed the dead lantern from the wire over the casket and closed the lid. And with a dime from his pocket, a coin now faceless that had worn itself down to a thin silver wafer on the very cloth of the pocket from which he now took it, he began replacing the screws.

When they had been fumbled into place he put the warped dime back in the pocket and stood over the coffin.

257

His legs were shaky under him from the long squatting. He reached over the domed top and pulled the bright flag from between the casket and the sideboard of the wagon. He spread it over the top, trying to smooth out the wrinkles that creased the stiff new cloth. Under his hands it turned his mind to the white tablecloth.

He got down from the wagon bed and walked to the shed door. He looked at the house. Arron was gone, the porch empty, only the hen remained searching the bare ground where the horse had stood.

He then dragged both of the weather ravaged doors open wide. The wagon and cloth covered coffin were exposed, framed by the rotting shed. The stars on the new flag had about them a special whiteness in the cold morning shadows. He turned and saw the puzzled hen searching after the horse. He moved across the yellow sun-distorted yard. As he reached the front porch and stooped to crawl under the high gallery he said to the hen, "Doan you worry yo self ole gal, we gonna have egg and unshit oats purdy soon now, purdy soon now, on a white tablecloth."

XXIV

THE morning sky was hard and bright. In the aftermath of stillness it had the look of something honed and metallic, its blue polished by the grit the norther had blasted against it. The chill air, filtered by that same abrasive dust falling to earth after the collapse of the wind, was as pure and unnatural as distilled water. There had not yet been even the blemish of a bird's flight through it.

Smith did not have to see the short caravan of cars winding across the prairie to know they were coming. He sat at the head of the oak table in the chill dining room sopping up cold coagulated egg yellow from his plate with a stale bread heel. The old hen was pecking up the last few grains of oats from the white tablecloth at the other end of the long table.

He scraped the high-backed chair away from the table, pulled himself up and hobbled toward the kitchen holding his empty coffee cup. When he was gone the hen, in a sneaking guilty trot, ran the length of the table, stopping at his yellow-stained plate. It looked for a moment, then pecked hard at a grain of black pepper that was stuck in the scum of dried egg. The thin china plate shattered and the startled chicken jerked its head erect, indignant and astonished.

Smith appeared in the kitchen doorway and the insulted bird cocked her head at him with a fleeting look of betrayal, then flew from the table and hit the floor squawking and running.

Smith put the coffee cup on the table and with a limping, running hobble followed her into the hallway. He was by the tall guncase, where a dozen rifles were racked when he heard the cars pull up in front of the house. He took a shotgun from the case as an old woman would take a shawl from a peg, before going out into a chill night.

He went to a window and stooped over to see under the ragged window shade. The Sheriff's low prowl car was nosed into the yard, the others were back on the drive between the dead trees.

The Sheriff got out of the prowl car and stood half crouched beside it.

"Arron," he shouted, "Arron, we got a warrant."

It sounded like a question screamed at an echo.

"We got a warrant Arron—That's government property Arron—you took government property."

Smith was silent. The hen was scratching in the fireplace.

"You return what you took Arron—Arron we got a *warrant*." His voice was now coaxing and threatening as to a child who has locked himself in a toilet.

Smith watched through the cloudy window. The Sheriff turned back to the car and leaned over to talk through the window. He was talking to the skinny deputy and to Buck, who was in the back seat. A door slammed and Smith saw Roy's pickup parked behind the hearse.

The photographer ran up to the Sheriff's car, spoke to the lawmen, then to Buck, and darted off toward the barn holding the small black camera close to his chest. He stopped once and pointed it at the house. Smith's grip tightened on the stock of the shot gun.

Holding the gun with both hands, Smith moved to the broken window in the front hall, to that window Arron had smashed with a rifle barrel when they had come for Sarah. The floor and window sill were rotten where the years of rain and wind had blown through it. He squatted by it and watched. The photographer came running from the barn waving his arm to the Sheriff.

"It's out here," he shouted, "they've parked it out here."

The Sheriff looked at him, then stood full height beside his car. "Arron—you hear me?—We're taking the body—we got a warrant an we're takin it back to town—you hear me Arron, we're taking it back to town." He shouted it and was silent, waiting, knowing a rifle shot from a hundred different places could kill him.

Smith also waited, listening to the hen scratching around in the dead embers of the fireplace. You ain't gettin back on dat tablecloth whiff dem dirty feet, he thought, as he listened.

The Sheriff waved for the photographer to take cover and plucked the black revolver from his belt. Smith saw it and listened.

"Arron you come on out where I can see—we got a warrant—that means we ain't trespassin—now you show yourself." He crouched lower as he shouted. "We ain't wantin trouble with you—but you done wrong Arron, an we gotta take Ronnie to town—Arron, the judge said to bring it back to town." Again the morning stillness sought its own level.

The Sheriff turned his head to the deputy, then pointed the snub weapon up in the air and fired. The concussion and noise of the shot echoed hollowly against the crumbling buildings.

Smith was startled by the shot, even though he had expected it. The chicken, black with soot, ran flying up the stairs. Smith cocked both barrels of the shotgun, braced its butt down against the rotten floor, pointed it like a mortar out the broken window and fired both barrels. The concussion shattered the jagged remains of the windowpane and the butt of the gun dug into the floor.

Before the smoke and echo had died he was howling a thin asthmatic scream out the window.

"Royeee—Royeee—Royee Turner, you get up here."

The Sheriff had fallen flat on the ground beside the car and those inside were crouched on the floorboards. He crawled to the front tire and edged his head around it and shouted toward the window. He had not recognized Smith's voice.

"Arron you lay aside that gun!"

"Arron ain't here," came the howling thin answer, "he gone—you send dat Roy up here to me."

"Smith? Smith, this is the Sheriff. You put down that gun. Nobody wants to get shot."

"If'en doan nobody want to get shot why you shoot off dat pistol?—now you send dat Roy up here."

The Sheriff got up to a squatting position beside the fender. He turned and waved at Roy, who had gotten out of his pickup and was standing behind one of the dead trees. He waved again and Roy started toward the prowl car, half running, and shouting at Smith.

"Put down that gun—ain't nobody after you, old man." He squatted beside the Sheriff. "That old son of a bitch is as crazy as Arron," he said, breathing hard.

"I don't think so. I scared him when I fired that shot."

"Well if you don't think so, help yourself to walkin up there," Roy said, shifting on his haunches.

"Roy, we got to be in town by eleven and we can't go without the body, now I'll walk with you and we'll keep him talking while the rest of 'um load it."

"If it's bodies you want the best way I know of gettin two or three is to walk up to that window and let that inbred old bastard talk to you down the sights of that double barrel."

The Sheriff turned away from him and looked back toward the window. "Smith, I'm standin up, now put away that gun."

Slowly he got to his feet. His legs were numb and his knees stiff from squatting so long. Buck and the deputy straightened up in the seat of the car.

"Where's Roy?" the voice came lower and calmer from the window.

"He's right here," the Sheriff answered.

"Well tell him to get up here."

The Sheriff looked down at Roy.

"Well, goddammit," Roy said getting up, "it's a comfort to know he won't have to choose a target with that damn meat grinder."

Smith saw Roy and shouted, "Roy, you come on up and get my list."

"Well I'll be dipped in shit," Roy said.

"Get his what?"

"His list, I didn't get his grocery list Saturday."

"Ask him where Arron is," the Sheriff said.

"Smith, where's Arron at?"

"He gone, now come on and git dis fo he gits back."

Roy looked at the puzzled Sheriff and then started walking toward the house.

"You doan need to be comin in de house," Smith said as Roy started to step up on the rotten porch. "Where you is'll do fine." Roy stopped.

"We didn't bring the Sheriff and the undertaker out here just to get your grocery list, old man."

"I knows what you come after, I knowed you was comin 'fore you knowed it yo'self. Now shut yo mouth a minute an listen. De mule is dead so you gonna haff to tote de grub up here to de house come Saturday—an dey's somethin else besides what we allus gets. I wants a hundred pound sack of good layin mash—I got me a hen and I aims to feed her. Now you tell de High Sheriff and de undertaker and whatever else you got out dere to get what dey is after and git offen de place. It's a'standin in the shed. In case dey wants somethin else from us, you can give testimony to de fack dat dis ole man is still young 'nuff to load a shot gun. Now git!"

Smith turned away from the window and into the hollow heart of the dim house to begin looking for the soot-blackened hen. He left the double-barreled shotgun propped against the window sill. Leaving it to the wind and rain which had already corroded the sill and floor, leaving it to reflect the prairie lightning until the rain would rust it from black to orange and fill its twin barrels like rain gauges.

Roy turned and walked back to the Sheriff.

"Arron's gone. He said to take the casket and git."

"Well that's what we came for. Let's get with it."

"It's in the saddle shed."

Roy felt as he always did when he came to the Crows Foot; empty. He was now no longer afraid of Arron yet something like fear hung about him as he watched them back the shiny hearse up to the doorway of the collapsing shed.

He felt a new sadness, something connected with the brief pride he had felt watching Arron smash the funeral party. He wished that Harry was with him. Harry had shared that moment and now it too was gone. He wished for Harry to come and to explain; to stand with him; to show him how to mourn a flicker of pride that now lay stillborn before him.

But Harry was not there. He was in town listening to the agonies of a new madness, trying to calm the chaplain who only yesterday saw the face of God.

So Roy stood alone surrounded by the rotting buildings, watching these shiny well-dressed scavengers picking something bright and useless from the bones and feathers of Crows Foot history.

He watched them struggle with the box which reminded him somehow of a telephone booth lying on its side. He had not thought about Elmira, yet his rage, which had died with her, was quickened when he saw how easily her funeral had been postponed, how easily she had been dismissed. Even her death could not reach its culmination. The rage he could not turn back into himself when his own impotence had occluded a measure of finality for her, now vented itself against these tinkering bastards.

He had smiled when Arron smashed the soldier's collarbone. As Harry had smiled when they had stood in the back of the church basement last night while the indignant Baptists swore prayers at Buck for submitting them to the aborted funeral. He had smiled as those cold-eyed women forced the Sheriff to seek the writ, and sent Buck with him this morning to execute it. Only the trembling Air Force chaplain had spoken against it and the eyes of the men were soft with agreement until the women began praying out loud. Women seldom pray aloud in public. They had begun praying their mean-necked, narrow, female-prayers, jabbing their own thin frigid rage at God, indignant and outraged that He and these soft-eyed men had frustrated even this culmination of themselves.

He wondered again about Harry, remembering his face, the way a different kind of smile had come to it when Buck had pulled him aside after the meeting in the church.

"Harry, you got to talk to the chaplain—he don't know what he's doing," Buck whispered, hugging Harry close to him. "He still thinks God is talking to him—he ain't been to bed since Saturday. You got to talk to him—keep him away from the graveyard—you heard how he just now talked —give him a pill, we got to get him calmed down."

"Buck they don't make pills for that, talking to God ain't a sickness."

"Harry don't play, I ain't got time. He may be Moses himself but we can't risk it, now ain't the time. Try to get him some clothes. I'll buy 'um. Get him calmed down and into some decent clothes." Buck dropped his arm from around Harry's shoulder and hurried off to join the group of growling women. It was then that Roy had seen the strange smile come to Harry's face; it was something below the surface, something glowing beneath the deep unmoved wrinkles.

The casket was loaded now and the hearse followed the Sheriff's car down the double row of dead trees. The other cars pulled in behind the hearse. Roy watched them go. Yep, he thought, just a goddamned circus. He turned to the old red pickup. Just a goddamn three-ring circus.

As he stepped up on the running board he heard the photographer call. "Hey, Turner, wait," and saw him come running in a slow jog from the direction of the wellhouse. He jolted into a walk about ten yards from the pickup.

"Man, don't leave me in this bone yard," he said climbing into the cab. "You know I just saw a complete—man, I mean complete, horse skeleton back there in that wellhouse." He looked down at the camera bag in his lap. "I didn't even shoot it," he said almost to himself.

Roy started the motor and drove slowly down the drive under the jagged arbor of dead branches. They were silent as they rode away from the headquarters house.

When they were about a quarter of a mile away Roy stopped the pickup.

"What do you get for one of them pictures?" he asked, turning to the photographer.

"What do you mean, what do I get? I get money."

"Listen son of a bitch, I asked you a question," Roy said. The rage was quiet and dark in his voice.

"Well it depends on the size."

"I want it for my billfold. You think that ten dollar bill you owe me would cover it?"

"I think it would," the photographer said, seeing now the darkness around Roy's eyes.

"Well, we're coming to an old windmill up here a piece and I want you to take it," he said, putting the pickup roughly into motion.

Roy stopped about a hundred yards from the windmill which stood before them gaunt, and useless. The fan was wrecked and the shrunken weathered timbers of the tower looked as fragile as bleached bone. Behind it the open grass extended dead and infinite.

The picture was taken and Roy did not speak again until they reached town. He drove the pickup into the curb in front of the hotel.

"Get yourself another ride to the graveyard," he said as the front tire bounced against the low curb. "Leave the picture at the drugstore with Harry." He got out and slammed the glassless door. The door did not catch but he did not see it swing back partially open. He walked straight through the empty cafe and up the stairs to his room where he pulled the shades. The room looked queer and small to him. He was seldom in it at midmorning. He walked to the closet and then to the iron bed carrying the low-quarter two-tone shoes. He sat heavily on the edge of the bed and slowly removed his boots. Then he slipped his damp feet into the shoes and sat, feeling the clammy sweat on his feet cool in the queer dead air of the shaded midmorning room.

The photographer caught a ride to the cemetery with Harvy Ellins, the barber. They rode in uncomfortable silence, as if under a flag of truce. The barber spoke from time to time when he could no longer resist the compulsion to look at the beard.

As the car slowed to turn into the cemetery, the photographer said, "I'll just drop off here," and opened the door. Harvy stopped under the metal arch and the photographer got out. "Thank you for the ride out, I'll catch Mr. Harris back in," he said closing the door. The barber leaned across the seat and said, "You're much obliged and if you miss Buck feel free to ride back."

"I'll sure do that," the photographer said, straightening up so the barber could not see his face.

There were groups of people scattered all over the graveyard, all with their heads down looking at the markers. They spoke without raising their heads to look at each other. Only the undertaker and his assistant held themselves erect; they looked like guides among a scattered crowd of groping blind.

A grey canvas tent, with a flat top and three sides open, was standing over the grave site. The flag-draped casket had already been set on the low four-posted lowering device over the open grave. The back and only wall of the tent dropped between the grave and the mound of dirt outside. There were about a dozen metal folding chairs set in two rows under the canvas awning. Two uniformed boy scouts and another boy in glasses and knickers with a black trumpet case were standing beside the new flagpole.

Under the awning the mortician straightened the row of metal chairs which stood wobbly and uneven on the lumpy grass, and then motioned to several of the people standing near to be seated.

The Baptist preacher, holding a large black Bible as if it were glued to his left lapel, sat down. Buck and Mildred Harris sat next to him. The chaplain, dressed in a civilian suit, stared blankly through the mortician without seeing him. In back of the chairs, the sergeant, whose arm was in a broad white sling, and the chaplain hovered close to Harry. The druggist looked like a tired old doctor standing between two of the walking wounded. With a quick, apprehensive shake of his head Harry indicated that he and his charges would stand.

Several old people filed in and took seats, the rest gathered around the empty metal chairs. When the crowd had assembled and was silent, still with bowed heads, the undertaker nodded solemnly to the minister. He got up and the Bible melted away from his chest.

"Brethren and sisters, we are gathered here to witness the end of the flesh. It is not my aim to preach on this boy's grave, no mortal words can reach him or comfort him. I can not bear witness to the condition of his soul when he was taken from us, I can only pray that there on that field of battle he came to know our Savior, Jesus Christ. His roots were Christian, the blood he spilled yonder on foreign soil came to him from that which was united with Christ, and although I can not tell how he husbanded that blood, my prayers are that it found its way back to the fold. That our pride we now feel in his heroic physical death, having laid down his life for his country, will be multiplied ten-fold when we meet him at the right side of the Father's throne standing tall—a sentry in the army of the Lord." He folded the Bible back against his chest and sat down. A low mumble of "Amen" rose from the bowed crowd. The undertaker nodded to Buck. He got up slowly and pulled his coat down in front like a short apron and looked for a long moment with bowed head at the bright flag that draped the coffin. Then he turned to face the crowd. He glanced quickly over their heads, trying to locate the photographer.

Only now at the grave had he begun to feel the rise of something like victory. Now the heir would return to God and the land escheat to the state. He knew, standing with his back to the flag and the grave, that they were now at this moment burying the Crows Foot. Arron will die crazy and the vacant land will escheat, he thought, as he took a deep breath and cleared his throat, fighting the quiet urge to smile at the flood of emotion his thoughts had evoked.

"Friends, as the Reverend says, we are here to witness the burial of a body. But I say we are seeing something more, we are here to honor a boy brung up on this land, who gave his life that we might stand out here and bury him or anyone else by the Holy Book and under the red, white, and blue of the flag you see covering his coffin.

"I am proud to stand beside it and know that what this boy did and the thousands of others like him, makes it possible for us who remain to enjoy the life we have. And if it takes this kind of sacrifice, I am proud to be a part of a town that can supply its share of brave men. Amen."

He sat down quickly on the metal chair. It rocked on the uneven grass over against Mildred's and pinched a bite of her ungirdled fat that had bulged over the edge of her chair. She jerked away from him, her startled cry was muffled in the amens and humble grunts of approval that came from the standing crowd. The red-eyed look of shocked indignation she gave him extinguished itself as the imaginary tears she had been nurturing were made real by the sharp pain. She sobbed softly, turning away from him as the proper mortician gravely hooked his head toward the chaplain.

The chaplain, who was already standing, did not acknowledge the recognition. He had been looking directly at the timid undertaker, and as he walked from the back of the crowd his eyes did not move from the point where they had impaled the embalmer. The cheap suit he now wore fitted him as if he were made badly for it. Its newness dominated the shape of his body. He looked old and used in the new clothes.

He walked to the casket and with his back to them put his hands down flat on the flag. He stiffened his arms and lowered his head as though he were trying to press the coffin into the ground. The suit coat was tight across his back and his spread legs made a taut arch from the baggy crotch of the pants. A new and profound silence came into the air. Mildred sobbed and a light breeze flapped a corner of the awning with a sound like an old dog lapping milk.

After a long silent moment his voice began. It was muffled and downcast. The words fell from his mouth as if echoing back from the dark emptiness of the grave below.

"I stand before Thee O God with my hands pressed down hard against the remains of valor. Loosen my tongue Lord against this absence of love which we now hide with dirt; with trumpet and flag and dirt. Forgive us the ease with which we hate the living and love the flag-draped dead. Guide us O God. Reveal our sins as we now commit them. Let those who loved Ronald A. Parker mourn him. And those gathered here to love death and the flag see what they have done."

His body tensed and he opened his eyes. He had clenched a wadded fist full of the flag in each hand. The wads were wet with his sweat. He arched his head back and opened his mouth, breathing heavily through it with a sound like a cloud of bats leaving a cave.

The bowed heads of the listeners were raised by the sound of it. They watched and listened to the grotesque private act happening before them.

Then with a violent twist, he snatched the flag from the casket and wheeled to face them, his neck arched back, his eyes clenched in wet agony over his empty mouth.

"There it is," he howled, "look at it!"

He lowered his head and looked at them with drowning inflamed eyes. "How can we so freely give to death that which we withhold from life? Oh God, how safe it is to love the dead. I stand to tell you, death dies with man and I for one will no longer be its disciple."

He dropped the flag like a cape and dragged it behind him as he slowly walked from under the awning out toward Harry and the open grass.

The boy with the trumpet at the flag pole saw the flag removed and had started playing the Taps. The two boy scouts slowly raised another flag on the new silver pole. They raised it to the top and had lowered it to half-mast before there was a movement under the awning and then it was only the astonished undertaker who covertly stepped on the brake release which set the coffin into its final motion.

Their eyes did not follow it down.

And Arron to the north, kneeling beside the grave of Sarah, enclosed in four hundred square miles of dead grass which itself was the shape of her grave, felt the heat of the sun lodged now at the dead center of morning.

The ancient horse drooled its reins from its lowered head into the grass at the foot of the narrow place where she lay.

Arron was gently removing double handfuls of the russet, umber dirt from the can and smoothing it into the grass on top of the slightly hollowed place, as if he were smoothing fresh sheets. The soil throbbed against his hands and the clumps of grass became soft and hot under them. He emptied the corroded bucket into a small soft pile just below the center of the grave, and as he began rubbing it smooth the throbbing in his head quickened. He closed his eyes and redreamed a dream, not his own but one told him by his father, yet it was his body he saw and not that of Tom Parker.

There were six black mules hitched in three spans to his arms, lashed to silver rings that pierced his wrists. He lay naked on his stomach in the grass with a gold funnel stuck in the naked crack of his buttocks, his erected bull joint was embedded in the sod like a plow share. A snake whip cracked and the mules lunged forward, dragging him like a plow and a miniature column of buffalo and hunters came through the air like a long swarm of bees and began diving into the funnel as the long narrow furrow behind oozed and filled with blood.

Arron knew it was not his dream yet it came to him now as he ran his hands through the grass and loose soil. Then it was gone and the hot pulsing soil rose evenly under his hands, then his knees, then his chest and face were flat

272

against it. The small mound met his swollen crotch as the grass clump breast flattened under him. The dead grass pounded against him. "It's tearing out my heart Arron, it's ripping it out—ram it back Arron, Oh ram it back!" These words were ringing in him and he threw himself against the grass, smashing his body against it bruising and rupturing his plow share into the hard ground, finally clutching the grass on either side of the grave and jerking himself against it again and again until he burst within himself and the searing liquid erupted down shrunken and adhesioned vessels and out into his grimy underwear.

A paralyzed spasm jerked his body rigid. Grunting and moaning he fought the paralysis to grind his pelvis into the grass, pressing the sticky dampness into the flattened mound of dirt. Then with a final serpent-like twist his body contracted into an ugly crookedness. He ripped loose the grass and was still, face down against her.

He lay still against her for a long time. The sun dislodged from dead center and a slight breeze, already chill anticipating night, stirred the hanging blond grass roots of the bird's nest. He felt the chill and tucked his arms under him, putting one handful of torn grass to his wet face and the other under the damp cloth of his crotch.

The old horse now stood in its usual place up by the gnarled cottonwood tree where the yellow leaves were falling. It did not notice the shower of death nor was there a sign of impatience as it stood again in that lowly attitude of lonesome dignity.

Below, Arron's body lay sleeping in the shallow grass.